Ascendant

The lines of battle are drawn in
black and white

By Kimberly Grey

This is a work of fiction. Names, characters, places and incidents either are the product of the author's imagination or are used fictitiously. Any resemblance to actual persons, living or dead, events, or locales is entirely coincidental.

First edition June 2019

Content edit by Oren Ashkenazi with Mythcreants
Copy edit by Ariel Anderson with Mythcreants
Cover by Alex Scott
Alexscott57@gmail.com

ISBN: 978-1-7330440-0-4 (hardcover)
ISBN: 978-1-7330440-1-1 (paperback)
ISBN: 978-1-7330440-2-8 (ebook)

For more information about purchasing and permissions contact Kimberly Grey at
authorkimberlygrey@gmail.com
Www.authorkimberlygrey.com

To Sunflower and Rose
Bloom brightly no matter how fierce the storm

Chapter

1

Grace hates the dungeons. They're dark and cold and, worst of all, underground. Her wings bristle, and she tries not to imagine what would happen if the mountain collapsed on them. It has stood for centuries. It will not fall now.

She has been to the dungeons many times before. She should be used to it by now, but they remain oppressive and intimidating. Ahead of her, Father walks with the same easy pace as always, as though he has all the time in the world to get where he is going.

She all but jogs to keep up with him. She has to take two strides to match each one of his, even with his leisurely pace. The warden is waiting for them outside of the room, a thin woman with the pale skin and sleek wings of Mountain Clan. She offers Father a bow but ignores Grace.

Father waves away the gesture. "You have information."

"Yes," the warden replies. "This one was captured by a patrol several weeks ago." She gestures to the door behind her.

Grace feels her heart skip at the thought of what waits beyond it. She bites her tongue and focuses on Father's conversation. He will ask her about this later to be sure that she learned what she was supposed to. She isn't sure what, exactly, the lesson is meant to be this time, there are many things she might learn here.

"What did he know?" Father is asking.

"Nothing particularly useful," the warden says. "He was only a border guard, said a few things about troops moving to the east."

"They always speak of troop movements," Father says. He doesn't seem interested, but Grace's mind is racing.

"But——" Grace begins, and then cuts herself off, too late.

Father and the warden both turn to look at her.

Father's face is blank as she bites her lip. He doesn't like it when she interrupts. She is meant to be silent and learn, not interject her own thoughts, but this is important.

"Sorry," she says.

"What do you think is so important?" Father asks. His voice is neutral, but she knows she has disappointed him. She swallows hard and tries to speak without her voice trembling.

"A report came across your desk just this morning," she says. Father lets her read all of his reports so she can see the right way to write her own and judge the importance of others. "Allegiance is planning an attack on the eastern border in a few weeks' time."

The Black-Wings should have no way to know what Allegiance is planning, and no way to know they need to shore up their eastern defenses.

For one heart-stopping second, Father's face remains blank. Perhaps she misread the report, or maybe she should have waited until later to tell him about it.

Then he smiles.

It is like seeing the sun come out after the long, dark months of winter. "Very well done," he says, and he puts a warm hand on her shoulder. "Come, let's see what our guest has to say for himself."

See? she wants to say to him. *Look at how well I use your training. I can do whatever you need me to. I can live up to the title you have given me. I can be the Saboteur.*

Grace follows him eagerly, the warmth of his hand on her shoulder nearly enough to make her forget just what waits on the other side of the door. For a brief moment, she hesitates.

"Dear One?" Father asks.

"I'm fine," she says immediately. She only just managed to keep out of trouble for interrupting him. She cannot be weak on top of that. "I just tripped." It is a pitiful excuse, but Father lets it pass.

His hand returns to her shoulder. "The floors are a bit uneven in some areas," he says, then he guides her to stand before the prisoner.

There isn't a mark on the man, despite the fact that he is their enemy. They aren't the Black-Wings, that they need to resort to torture to get their information. A shudder threatens to run down her spine at the thought of the stories she has heard about what the Black-Wings do to their prisoners.

Even though he is chained, she shuffles a step closer to Father.

It makes her feel weak. She is meant to be a soldier; she should be able to stand in front of their enemies. She had thought she would be ready, but now that the sight is before her, she knows that she isn't.

If not for his wings, she could almost imagine that he was any normal man off of the street. There is nothing overtly monstrous about his face, nothing that would give away the evil that lies behind his eyes.

His face isn't what matters, though; his wings will always tell the truth that the rest of him conceals.

6

In the dim light, his feathers almost merge with the shadows. Her own wings bristle at the sight. He isn't the first Black-Wing she has encountered—she has been to the dungeon before—but still her feathers prickle with unease. The only white on his wings are the three wind feathers at his wing wrist. A reminder of what he could have been, just as the black of her own is a reminder of what she could be, if she allowed herself to fall as he has.

She doesn't know how the Black-Wings tricked everyone into believing they were good for so long. The Black-Wing's nature should have been clear to any who looked at them. She wonders if they had tricked even the humans—the First-Born—on earth, or if they had known what the Guardians were blind to.

She isn't really supposed to listen to tales, but sometimes she just happens to overhear them. Her favorites say that the humans, the First-Born were wiser than any Guardian. It is hard to believe beings like that could be tricked by anyone, even the Black-Wings.

She supposed that if the Black-Wings were good at one thing, it would be telling lies.

"Your information has been most helpful," Father says to the Black-Wing. "But my daughter has brought up an interesting question."

His hand squeezes her shoulder, and Grace leans into him. She is finally able to pry her eyes away from the Black-Wing to smile at him. He returns the smile with a proud look.

"She would like to know how it is your queen knows to bolster defenses on the eastern border. I must admit, I am curious as well."

The Black-Wing clenches his jaw and jerks his chin into the air in silent defiance.

"Well?" Father asks.

7

ASCENDANT

The Black-Wing maintains his stony silence.

The warden steps into the room. "I will see what I can find, Spymaster," she says, "but I fear we may have a traitor in the Citadel."

Father's lip curls. "And one high in the chain of command," he agrees. "A field commander at the very least. See what this one knows, and then ask the others."

"If they know nothing?"

"Ask again." Father nudges Grace out of the room ahead of him. She is glad not to have to expose her back to the Black-Wing.

Grace watches Father on the way up out of the dungeons. He doesn't *seem* angry now that he knows why she interrupted, but she did still speak when she was meant to be quiet.

"I'm sorry for interrupting."

"Dear One." He beckons her to his side. She swallows and obeys. Despite the temptation, she doesn't drag her feet—she knows better than that.

When she reaches him, he tilts her chin up so she is looking him in the eyes. His hand is somehow even warmer than the hearth in her room. "You did very well," he says. "I am *so* proud of you."

She tries to school her face into the same dignified mask he wears. "Thank you, Father." Her lips pull up into a smile regardless of her efforts. She tries to memorize him like this, happy and proud of her; she never wants to forget this moment. She wants to live in it forever. She wants time itself to stop so that she never has the chance to disappoint Father ever again.

"You are truly the best student I could ask for," Father says.

She dips her head humbly. "I owe it to your teaching, Father."

Father smiles approvingly and pats her shoulder. "Run along for now," he says. "You've earned a day off."

***

As nice as it is skip the sparring fields and the boring, repetitive work of learning forms, she doesn't actually know what to do with herself. Her days are meticulously scheduled with very little down time, especially during the summer, to make the best of the warmth and daylight.

She takes off, pushing hard against the air, and rises to the top of the White Mountain, where the palace is perched. She should take advantage of this rare opportunity and do something fun, something that has nothing to do with the Black-Wings and the war.

Instead, she angles her wings and glides down to the open double doors of the palace. Her landing is soft and easy—she barely has to bend her knees to absorb the impact. This is a place of quiet respect. It wouldn't do to disturb anyone else with a rough landing.

The Memorium is deserted when she steps in. Endless rows of tokens and weapons, all that is left of those who have fallen. She doesn't know anyone here, yet, but death is inevitable in war.

Perhaps, for someone, death looms closer than ever.

A traitor in the Citadel. Even in her mind, it seems impossible. How could anyone side with the Black-Wings? After all they'd done? Despite what they were?

But it isn't impossible; it's real, and she was the one to discover them. That should make her happy, the thought that she uncovered a traitor and likely saved unknowable lives by telling Father.

Instead, she just feels confused, and maybe a little bit scared.

ASCENDANT

She wanders through the maze of the Memorium. Her footsteps echo in the cavernous room. So many dead, brave soldiers, good people. And someone had betrayed them for the *Black-Wings*. For *Fallen*.

She shudders at the thought. The dark feathers of the Black-Wing prisoner flash behind her eyes, and she cannot help flaring her wind feathers, as though he is hovering over her. Of course, the air is still, aside from a light breeze that winds its way through the windows from the far side of the room.

A low humming disturbs her thoughts. She turns and finds that the Memorium is no longer empty. A man stands before an ornate sword hung on the wall at the back of the room.

As though he can feel her eyes on him, the man stops humming and turns to her. "Hello, youngling." The wrinkles around his eyes deepen as he smiles at her.

Grace dips her head. "Hello."

His smile fades. "Are you visiting someone?"

"No," she says, surprised, and then scrambles for something less rude. "I was just…thinking."

The man nods understandingly. "It is a good place for heavy thoughts."

"Are you visiting someone?" Grace asks, even though it is obvious that he is. She finds that she wants to talk to him. On some level, she thinks he is familiar, as though he has been hovering in the background of her life but has never spoken before.

The man gestures to the sword hung on the wall. "Someone I once knew," he says, voice warm, though his smile is sad. "Her name was Haven."

Grace's eyebrows fly to her hairline. "I didn't know she had a token here."

"Not many do. Justice prefers to do his mourning in other ways. I come by every once in a while to make sure that it is well kept."

Grace looks at the sword with new eyes. The blade is notched at the base, and there are a few scratches too deep to be buffed out. She wonders if history would be different if Haven had been carrying it the night she was murdered.

The man takes a cloth from his belt and pulls the sword down from the wall. "There's not many of us left who actually knew her," he muses as he turns the sword this way and that, looking for any new damage.

"What was she like?" Grace asks, half-afraid that the man will snap at her and drive her away, but too curious to restrain herself.

He doesn't get angry though. He smiles a sad, wistful smile and begins polishing the sword. "She was like the sun, warm and so bright you could barely stand to look at her. Some said that she lived life too fast." His smile falters. "I suppose, in the end, it's a good thing if she did."

"Were she and Justice really twins?" Grace can't help asking. The most common rumors said they were, but rumors weren't trustworthy.

"They were." The man nods. "I was never sure about all of that 'twins hearing each other's thoughts' business before I met them, but if you saw them on the battlefield, you couldn't doubt it."

And the Black-Wings killed her. Like they had killed so many others. Like the traitor would kill people. Grace swallows. In five hundred years of war, have they come any closer to defeating the Black-Wings than they were when Haven was killed? Or are they doomed to struggle against them forever?

"Do you want to hold it?" the man asks, gesturing with the sword as though to hand it to her.

"No, I...I couldn't." Grace backs away.

The man smiles. "She wouldn't mind."

Almost against her will, Grace finds her hands wrapping around the hilt of the sword. It is still warm from the man's skin, as though Haven had just set it down. On the blade, there is the imprint of one of her feathers, forever binding the weapon to her. Grace traces the edge of it, entranced.

Her eyes, reflected in the metal, stare back at her.

"If you could end the war," the man asks, his voice muted and far away, "would you?"

"Yes," Grace replies, almost absently. "Whatever it took."

The man might reply, but his voice is muffled and far away. Time seems to move both faster than normal, and slower.

A hand touches her shoulder. "Are you alright?" the man asks.

The world rushes back, snapping into place as though nothing had happened. "I must have gotten lost in thought," Grace says, but she can't remember thinking anything.

The man takes the sword from her and returns it to the wall. "Thank you for indulging an old man's desire to tell stories."

Grace dips her head. "Thank you for telling me."

The man smiles at her and opens his mouth, likely to say goodbye, but another voice calls out, "Grace." She turns and finds a Desert Clan messenger standing a short distance away. "Your father wishes to see you in the king's chambers. He's been looking for you."

Grace feels the blood rush from her face. How long has she been wandering around the Memorium? "I'm sorry, I've got to go," she says to the old man, and darts out of the room. She leaps into the sky the moment she clears the door.

Grace puts more power in the next stroke of her wings, pushing herself to the limits of her speed. But she is no descendant of Mountain Clan; she can only go so fast.

It's not fast enough! a panicky part of her mind says.

How long has Father been looking for her? Hours? Even minutes would be too long. And she is being summoned to the king's chambers. It would be bad enough if Father simply wanted to see her in his office, but making him wait in front of the king must be nearly unforgivable.

Not that the king is an impatient man; she met him once, when she was young. She had spent a lot of time in those days wandering the palace, seeing what places she could get into. Her sole visit to his office is a fond memory.

The king isn't the one who is going to be angry with her or, more accurately, disappointed in her. Father is.

She dips one wing and half folds her feathers, sweeping into a turning dive that brings her to the main balcony of the palace. She forgets to shed speed, and her boots skid across the smooth stone. She has to throw out her arms and flare her wings to keep from sliding into the doors.

The guards on either side of the doors don't react, but she knows there is no way they didn't see her clumsy landing. The day just keeps getting better.

Stupid, amateur mistake.

Grace takes a deep breath, folds her wings and settles her feathers. She dusts off her armor and closes her eyes. *Please let this go well,* she prays. *Please don't let him be too angry.*

13

ASCENDANT

She pushes open the doors and steps into the hall outside of the council chambers. The doors are shut tight, so she stands against the opposite wall and waits. She is still breathing hard from her flight, and her hands are shaking from adrenaline. She closes her eyes and breathes deeply; she must have herself back under control when she is called.

Appearing in the king's court wild eyed and disheveled would be almost as bad as being late. *Power comes from the appearance of strength.* One of Father's many valuable lessons.

By the time her breath evens out, the balcony doors open again. A flight walks through with a woman at their head, her dark skin and broad wings hallmarks of Desert Clan ancestry. They watch her curiously as they join her against the wall.

They don't line up and wait silently the way they are meant to. Instead, they stand facing one another in a clump, talking and nudging each other with easy smiles and quiet laughter.

Undisciplined, she can imagine Father saying with a scowl. She hasn't behaved so poorly since her flight feathers came in. *That is the difference between you and them,* part of her says. *Father made sure that you are the best, that you exemplify everything a warrior should be.*

She keeps her face carefully blank even as their conversation drifts to her ears. Perhaps they are here for the same reason she is. Any opportunity to use her training, the gifts Father has given her, is welcome. She will need these skills when he finally allows her into the field, a day that must be getting closer by the hour.

"Serenity says that Observants have been going around asking about suspicious behavior," one of them says. He is of Forest Clan, likely the flight's scout. "Sounds like there might be a traitor."

14

"I heard there'd been a fight down near the dungeons. A general or something found with suspicious letters," a Mountain Clan woman says.

"Chivalry, right? I heard that the guards confronted him but he escaped the city," the scout says.

The other Mountain Clan warrior says, "If he was a traitor, he got what he deserved." He scowls. His sleek wings bristle, wind feathers tilting sharply back. A medallion gleams on his armor. *Wind Weaver.* Whatever they have been called here for, it is serious. Wind Weavers aren't called out for just anything.

"Hush," their leader says, looking to the door. Grace realizes that it has opened.

"Come, Dear One," Father says. Grace steps smoothly away from the wall and follows him through the door.

The room beyond is a huge dome carved from white marble. At the center of the room, the ceiling is fifty feet above her head. A sturdy table has taken over the duties of the ornate throne that sits abandoned on its dais at the opposite side of the room.

Justice stands up as she approaches, and Grace crosses her wrists and bends at the waist. "My king." She bows deeply to him. She wonders just why she has been allowed into this meeting. Is it really about the traitor? Has he been caught already, as the flight outside said?

There are always rumors running around the Citadel. Father says it is because the soldiers don't have enough work to keep their minds busy, so they resort to making up tales. Grace thinks that his work is trying to figure out the truth of the latest rumors floating around the Citadel as much as it is trying to ferret out the Black-Wings' next move.

ASCENDANT

Her eyes dart to him. His face is impassive, and his wings give nothing away. Grace takes a deep breath and tries to keep from fidgeting beneath his stare. The moment seems to stretch forever, but it must only be a second.

"Welcome, little one," Justice says, and he gestures her to a chair beside Father. "I asked that you be allowed to sit in on this meeting. I understand you were the one to bring up the suspicion of a traitor?"

Grace can feel her wings lift with pride and tries to keep them under control. "I was, my king," she says with dignity. She glances to Father again, and there is a faint smile on his face. She feels her heart swell with pride.

"Then I owe you my gratitude," Justice says, drawing her eyes back to him. "You have done a great service to us all. We must always be watchful for the plots of the Black-Wings." The smile slips away from his face, and his lip curls into a bitter snarl. "They will forever seek to drag us into their darkness. You must watch for their evil in everything." As he stares into her eyes intently, she feels her wings prickle. She wishes he would look away; there is a dangerous spark in his eyes, like he is seeking treachery even in her.

Grace freezes for a moment. This isn't the kind man she remembers but someone else entirely. "I will, my king," she says, and bows to him again.

Thankfully, he seems to accept this, and again he motions her to the chair beside Father. "Of course you will," he says. The darkness is gone from his eyes, but she still cannot bring herself to meet his gaze again. "You're a loyal girl. Concord has raised you well."

Grace sinks into the chair beside Father and, on impulse, wraps her fingers around his hand beneath the table. His hand does not grip hers back, but he doesn't move it away.

16

Of course, sitting next to Father puts her across from the other person at the table: Allegiance, Justice's Air Commander and Grace's birth mother, her dame.

Allegiance is studiously reading the papers in front of her, as though she hadn't been aware of the conversation going on around her. As though she isn't aware of Grace at all. Grace crushes the part of her that remembers the cold, lonely days she spent at Allegiance's side while her dame was supposedly absorbed in paperwork.

Even now she imagines she can feel a phantom edge of Allegiance's resentment as she turns the page. Grace shoves aside the part of her that wonders what she did to earn it.

Grace inherited much of her appearance from Allegiance. They both have the same coppery skin and dark hair that marks them as Forest Clan. They even share the same short stature. The only physical trait she doesn't share with her dame is eye color: where Allegiance's are a light green, Grace's have always been the cloudy gray of her sire.

A quiet part of her wonders what else she inherited from Noble. If she got most of her looks from her dame, is her personality more akin to her sire's? She shuts that part of herself away as quickly as it popped up. It doesn't make any difference to wonder about such things. Noble died before she was born, and besides, she doesn't need her sire—she has her father.

Grace turns her eyes away from Allegiance and glances at him. He is looking at her as well, his icy blue eyes taking in every detail of her appearance. No doubt he is all too aware of the rush she'd arrived in, despite the care she had taken to make herself look presentable.

Their lack of blood relation is obvious. Father is a descendant of Mountain Clan, and it is apparent in his pale skin and hair, the sleek shape of his wings. Narrow and built for speed, while Grace's are rounded and made for maneuverability.

"Now then, Concord," Justice says, "you were outlining the known patrol routes?"

"Yes," Father says, leaning forward to trace his finger over the lines drawn on the map. "These are the previous routes from around two months ago, and these are the newer ones. As you can see, the Black-Wings are expanding their territory at an incredible rate…"

Grace's eyes drift away from the map. She already knows this—she was there when the Observants brought the news to Father. Her eyes slide over to Justice, whose expression is troubled as he listens to Father speak. The furrows of his brow only deepen the wrinkles on his face.

Centuries ago the Black-Wings had lived among the White-Wings, a creeping disease, corrupting and turning. Justice was the one to uncover their lies, to expose them as the Fallen Guardians they were. In retaliation, the Black-Wings began the war to kill any and all White-Wings, to see the fall of everything they stood for.

Grace is not supposed to listen to the tales the soldiers like to tell of the Burning. Father thinks they are too embellished and contain little of the truth. She knows that he is probably right, but she still likes to hear them.

If there is one thing in common among all of the stories, it is Justice and, of course, Haven. The first twins born since the days of the clans. They had tried to warn people about the treachery of the Black-Wings, and the Black-Wings murdered Haven for revenge.

18

From there, the war had spiraled out of control, too fast for anyone to stop. The Black-Wings murdered the queen, Clarity, when she wouldn't open a passage for them to earth, where they would no doubt have established themselves as gods over the humans, the First-Born.

It was Justice who pushed them out of the Citadel. He must have been younger then, because Grace can hardly imagine him taking to the field of battle now.

His hair is nearly as white as his wings, and unlike Father, he allows it to hang free instead of trapping it in a tail. It contrasts with the deep brown of his wrinkled skin.

He has to be at least eight hundred years old. Possibly even nine hundred, if anyone can live that long.

Father is a few centuries younger than Justice, but they've been working beside each other since before the Burning. Grace has heard guards say that he has been the Spymaster for as long as Justice has been king.

Allegiance is the second youngest, with her unlined face and bright eyes. At only a hundred and forty years old, Grace feels terribly young sitting with all of the gathered centuries of experience at the table.

"If your Observants could do their jobs *properly*," Allegiance says, pulling Grace from her thoughts, "then perhaps the traitor wouldn't have escaped." Allegiance's wings bristle and her wind feathers tilt back, she glares across the table at Father.

Grace glances to Father. He is silent, his face as unreadable as stone, but she can feel the tension in his body. She pulls her hand back to her own lap, hoping to avoid his attention. She swallows hard, her heart beating too fast.

ASCENDANT

When father replies, his voice is low and smooth, his voice low and smooth. His anger is like one of the northern sea serpents swimming beneath the ice. There is no way to know when or where it will appear until it explodes out of the tight control he keeps over it. "Perhaps, you would be kind enough to remember that security within the Citadel is *your* responsibility." His eyes are narrow slits, and the very air around him seems to crackle. "Perhaps you would like to explain how there came to be a traitor so high within the command of your *own* forces before you criticize me for the management of mine." His voice is a low hiss, and Grace finds herself leaning so far away from him that she nearly falls from her chair.

Her feathers press tight against her wings, and her jaw aches from how hard she is clenching her teeth. She cannot make her eyes move away from Father. His hands grip the edge of the table so tightly that his knuckles are almost as white as the stone of the mountain.

"Enough," Justice snaps, and Grace nearly gasps. She had all but forgotten that the was there. "This is exactly what the Black-Wings would want, us at each other's throats."

Father sits back, his face calm once again, as though the rage had never been there. "Of course." She could almost convince herself that she had imagined his anger. Allegiance is still glaring across the table though.

"Allegiance," Justice says, his voice low and almost as angry as Father's had been.

"My apologies," she says through clenched teeth.

20

Grace doesn't allow herself to relax. She knows that Father is still angry, and if she makes any slip now, she will be the one bear the brunt of his temper, not Allegiance.

"Regardless of who is to blame, the traitor has escaped the Citadel," Justice says. He sweeps his gaze over the table, daring someone to begin the argument anew. "A party must be sent to pursue him." He motions to the guard beside the door, who ushers in the flight from the hallway.

They don't seem to pick up on the lingering tension as they bow and fill the remaining seats. The Desert Clan woman who seems to be their leader sits at the end of the table across from Justice.

"No doubt, you will have heard the rumors of a traitor in the Citadel," Justice says.

"Yes, my king," the flight leader replies. "Though how anyone could betray our cause is beyond me."

Grace nods silent agreement. What could possess a person to turn their back on the White-Wings? What could the Black-Wings offer them but death and damnation?

There are only three laws that separate the White-Wings from the Black. Three simple laws that define the Fallen, that govern the righteous:

Do not willfully harm the innocent.

Do not knowingly aid the cause of the unjust.

Do not seek to overtake the mind of another.

Whoever the traitor is, they have broken the second law; there is no doubt about that. Grace wonders when their feathers will turn black. Have they been applying dye ever since they agreed to spy for the Black-Wings? Or is the change more gradual?

what would it take for someone to agree to serve the Black-Wings? To stand beside those who wear the sins of their forefathers on their feathers, to take the same taint into your own soul.

Justice nods solemnly. His eyes sweep over the table, the dark anger returning in his gaze. His eyes are searching, suspicious, as he says, "I do not know what sort of sick soul could willingly embrace the Black-Wings, but they cannot be allowed to live. Which is why we need you. You will take your flight into Black-Wing territory and find this traitor before they can reveal our secrets. Capture them if you are able, but kill them if it seems for a moment that they will escape you."

Though he is speaking to the flight leader when he says this, his eyes meet Grace's. She wants desperately to look away, but she fears that if she does, she will awaken something even worse than Father's anger.

"You will go with them," Justice says, and Grace cannot help but look behind herself as though someone else has appeared there.

"Me, my king?" she says. Her eyes dart to Father. She thinks that even he is surprised.

"You," Justice confirms.

"My king—" Father begins.

Allegiance speaks at nearly the same time. "This is a serious mission—"

Justice holds up a hand to stop them both. "You have claimed that she is the best you have ever trained," he says to Father. "She was the one to discover the traitor. She deserves the chance to see this through."

When he turns to her, a bright fire burns in his eyes, and she feels that in this moment, he is even more dangerous than Father. "I am giving you a chance to prove your loyalty, little one. To prove your worth to our cause. Are you not eager to take it?"

Grace swallows hard. She wants to glance to Father, wants him to say no. That she isn't ready for this, that she can't go. She is trapped in the king's gaze, though, and her mouth forms the words without her permission. "Of course, my king. It…It would be a great honor to prove myself in such a noble pursuit."

The fire in Justice's eyes dims, and he seems to grow older and wearier before her. "Good, good. I have no doubt that you will be successful." He even smiles at her in a charmed sort of way. As though she volunteered for this, as though she had any choice.

Distantly, she hears them discuss the mission. Her mission. Father's Observants are already scouring the forests and sending back information: where the traitor has gone, his description, what happened when he escaped. Outlining likely places he will attempt to cross into Black-Wing territory. They are only one group out of many being sent out.

She barely hears it, and none of it makes sense. She is going on a mission into Black-Wing territory to hunt down a traitor. She agreed to do it, right here, in front of Father, without his permission.

She glances to him, begging him with her eyes to understand. His jaw is clenched tight, and his hands are once more balled into fists, but when he meets her gaze, he nods. She nearly collapses with relief. At least he isn't angry with her.

"You leave in the morning," Justice says. "Be prepared, all of you."

This seems to be a dismissal because Father rises from his seat and offers Justice a stiff bow. "My king," he says, then he directs

Grace from the room with a hand on her shoulder. His grip is tight enough to bruise.

He isn't angry with me, she reminds herself. *I hope.*

He doesn't say a word as he guides her down the hallway. Grace tries to speak, but he tightens his grip on her shoulder in warning, so she keeps her mouth shut and her face impassive.

They do not speak until they are back in Father's apartments and the door is safely shut behind them.

"I'm sorry, Father," Grace blurts out immediately. "I didn't know what else to do. He was—"

Father holds up a hand to stop her. "I do not blame you, Dear One. I should have known better than to bring you before him." He sighs and pinches the bridge of his nose. "I thought he would be satisfied with you uncovering the traitor. You must understand, the king has faced many betrayals in his lifetime. You know what the Black-Wings did to his sister. It has made him...wary. He fears treachery from all sides.

"Has he always been like that?" she cannot help but ask. "I met him when I was younger, and he didn't seem so very..." She trails off. The only word she can think of is *paranoid*, but it seems disrespectful to apply that to the king. It is too close to saying *mad*.

"You weren't a threat when you were younger," Father says. "Now that you are older and well trained, you could present a problem if you were a traitor."

"Will I really be going?" she asks. Part of her is thrilled at the prospect, no matter how the opportunity came about. Here is the chance to prove to Father that she is a good student. That she can live up to the plans he has for her.

The rest of her knows that this will be dangerous. She will be going into Black-Wing territory. They won't be prisoners; they will be soldiers, trained to hate from birth.

It will be just like sparring, she tells herself. *You have the training. Now you only need to apply it.*

"I'm afraid you must," Father says. "If you don't, Justice will become convinced of your treachery, regardless of whether it is true or not."

She bites her lip. "Will you come with us?"

Father shakes his head. "I cannot. The king has charged you to prove yourself, and you cannot do that if I help you. You will have to undertake this mission by yourself."

Her heart sinks and fear churns in her belly. "Oh."

"Don't worry, Dear One," Father says as he takes her chin in his hand and makes her meet his eyes. "It is not the first mission I would have chosen for you, but you would have been going on your first soon. You have prepared for this all your life. You are a diligent student, and I have been impressed by your progress each and every day. I have no doubt that you will succeed."

She smiles up at him. "Thank you, Father."

"Always, Dear One. Now, you have much to prepare and little time to do so."

Chapter

2

The sun is setting when Haven leads him to the garden, shadows falling over them as soft as silk.

"Where are we going?" Endurance asks, confused, tired, hopeless.

"Not much farther," she says, taking his hands and pulling him after her. Her feet skip over cool grass, nearly dance steps. Her wings flutter, too happy to stay still.

A reluctant smile tugs at his lips, and he picks up his pace. His steps aren't nearly as graceful as hers, despite all her attempts to teach him to dance. They don't wander far from the path, only to a small grove of trees. The same grove where they had met what seems like a lifetime ago.

"What is this about?" he asks, taking note of their destination.

She is so happy her smile could light up the whole garden. She opens her mouth, ready to tell him the good news, ready to share her joy with him. "I—" the words cut off with a low, sickening thunk. She gasps, and her hand touches her abdomen instinctively. She feels something warm and wet, and something hard and sharp.

An arrow, her mind says. *You've been shot with an arrow.*

Then the pain blooms through her. Like fire, like ice.

Haven? Her brother's voice is frantic in her head, just as pained as hers.

Justice, I— She can't make herself say the words. It doesn't really matter; he knows just as well as she knows. He wails into the place where their minds meet, full of fury and denial.

Don't you do this to me! he cries. *You can't!*

They both know that she doesn't really have a choice. *I'm sorry,* she whispers to his mind.

In the physical world, Endurance holds pressure over the wound with shaking hands. He's saying something, but already it is hard to hear him. The sound is muffled and distant, as is the pain.

I love you, she thinks to the both of them, though only one hears her.

"*Haven, please.*" Justice's voice is desperate, pleading.

She imagines that Endurance's is the same. Her hand feels beyond heavy, but she still gathers her remaining energy to lift it to his face. He presses it between his cheek and his shoulder, unwilling to take pressure off of the wound. He must know as well as she does that it will do no good, but he has never been one to take helplessness well. Tears rain down his cheeks, and he keeps shaking his head. Around them, guards are swarming, too late.

She can hear her heartbeat slowing in her ears

"*Please, don't go,*" Justice begs one last time. She can feel him falling into the darkness alongside her.

I'm sorry. I love you, she replies, and then the darkness rises up, and she knows no more.

***

Grace wakes with the taste of blood and bile in her mouth. Her hands rip the blankets away and clench over her stomach. There is no arrow, no blood.

Of course there isn't. That was a dream. *A nightmare.*

She takes a deep breath and tries to calm the desperate thumping of her heart. She swallows down the bitter taste and she hugs her pillow tightly against her chest. *It was only a dream,* she tells herself firmly.

Her hands want to shake as she sets the pillow aside, but she folds them into fists instead. She shouldn't be worried about a dream. She should focus on her mission, the mission she will be leaving on in—her eyes flick to the window, and she nearly squeaks when she sees that the sun is already brightening the horizon.

The lock on her door clicks, breaking her from her thoughts, and Father enters. His mouth tightens and his brow lowers upon seeing her still in bed "Why are you not ready?" he asks, wind feathers dipping back.

"I was just…lost in thought," she says, hesitating over the near lie.

Father sighs. "I understand you are nervous, but you have duties to attend to."

"Yes, Father."

"You have five minutes," he says as he turns to leave, and the door clicks shut behind him.

She shoves all thoughts of the dream firmly out of her mind, unties her sleeping shift, and lets it fall to the floor, then steps across the cold stone to the chest that holds her clothes. She dresses quickly and quietly, first in the warm underclothes and then in her armor.

Last come the gauntlets from a drawer below the armor stand. She pulls them over her wrists like old friends. On each of her fingers she slips a delicate ring. With a flick of her wrist, the hidden catches release and the talons unfold, enveloping her fingers in deadly points.

This is one thing she knows she inherited from her sire. He had been a master of the ancient Forest Clan weapon, and from him, she had the muscle memory of a thousand years spent honing these talons. They are both throwbacks of a sort. Talons have, for the most part, fallen out of use. There are weapons that are easier to make, easier to learn, and with a longer reach besides.

It doesn't really matter, she sometimes tells herself. *He was only your sire, not your father; he was dead before you were born.* But a small part of her still loves having something of her sire for her own.

The actual weapon isn't Noble's but entirely hers; a part of her is within them. When the Black-Wings were exposed, they cursed the entirety of Caelam, stripping away all but the most basic powers from all Guardians, White-Wings and Black-Wings alike. But one of the few things that they were still capable of was creating the metal for weapons. It was a rare Guardian who was willing to delve below the ground to hunt for the metal ores that hid beneath the surface. Being cut off from the sky was just unnatural. But thankfully that wasn't the only way to get metal.

With time and care, the likeness of a weapon could be carved from a piece of wood, and when the Guardian who would wield it plucks one of their own feathers and combines them, it creates a material somewhere between wood and metal. Strong and light, buoyant, and nonconductive—which was a very good thing during storm season. Though weapons were the most common, many things could be made from the material.

Grace traces her finger along the outline of her feather on the surface of her gauntlet and thinks about the feather in Haven's sword. Maybe that was why she had such a dream, too much stress and too many reminders of a woman murdered by Black-Wings. Grace just hopes that she won't meet the same fate.

She shakes herself out of her thoughts—this is no time to be distracted. She has a mission. Grace scoops up the bag beside her door and checks through it one last time. She has everything she needs.

You can do this, she tells herself firmly. *Father trained you. Father trained you and now you have a chance to prove his efforts worthwhile.*

After this, who knows what the future holds? Father said he would have sent her out on her first mission soon anyway. Perhaps before the year is out, she will be slipping into Black-Wing territory on her own. Maybe she'll find the Black-Wings' secret city, or maybe she'll finally uncover the identity of the Black-Wing heir, the Ascendant.

She imagines bringing the Ascendant to Father, how proud he would be. All the lives she would save. The border guards wouldn't have to fear being kidnapped by the Ascendant anymore. She could put an end to the rumors of torture and experiments conducted in the heart of the Black-Wings' secret city.

Before her thoughts can get away from her, she realizes her five minutes are up. She takes a deep breath and meets Father in the main room.

He is standing beside a pack "Your rations." Grace takes it and slips it into her pack, trying not to think about how it is enough food to feed her for weeks. And it is all for her, plus whatever edible things they can find in the forest.

Father hands her another strip of dried meat, and she takes it automatically.

"You should eat before you go," he says.

"I think I'm too nervous to eat," Grace says, her stomach flutters in agreement.

"Eat, Dear One," Father says. "You will need the energy."

Despite the churning of her stomach, Grace obeys.

Once the meat is gone and her belly full, they fly up to the roof where her traveling companions are waiting. The Desert Clan woman who leads the flight bows to both of them.

"Spymaster, Saboteur," she greets them both.

Despite the circumstances, Grace allows herself a private smile. She is the Saboteur; she has a title to live up to. Father had chosen her, trained her, made her the warrior she is now. Surely she can track down a single traitor and bring him back to the Citadel.

Father nods solemn acknowledgment to the woman.

"Liberty. Your record speaks for itself. I know that you and your flight will serve well in this mission."

Liberty dips her head, but Grace is distracted from her reply by one of the flight moving to stand beside her.

It is one of the Mountain Clan warriors, not the Wind Weaver, the woman. "Don't worry, we'll keep you safe."

"I'm not untrained," Grace says.

She smiles tightly. "Even trained warriors need help. That's why we have flights."

Father turns back to Grace. "Remember, capture the traitor if you can. Kill if you cannot. Don't disappoint me, Dear One."

She smiles up at him, trying to pretend that she is more eager than afraid. "I won't, you'll see." She doesn't think that he believes her, but he doesn't say anything more to her.

"You all have your mission," he says to them all. "Go forth and fulfill it."

They bow and take off one by one, falling into a long-distance formation for the journey. When Grace looks back to him one more time, he is standing at the edge of the balcony, watching them fly

31

away. She wishes again that he could come with them, that she didn't have to undertake such a dangerous mission alone.

***

Grace quickly realizes just how *boring* traveling is. There is nothing to break the monotony of flying in a straight line and watching the person in front of her. They have to travel high in the air to avoid being spotted as they head out. Above the clouds, there is nothing to look at.

They fly in an open-ended triangle, staggered in the air so that the ones at the head of the formation break up the wind resistance for those behind. It is all very practical, but that doesn't help with the boredom.

At the head is Liberty, the flight leader. Her broad wings are perfect for long flights, a gift from her Desert Clan ancestors. In the middle flies a pair of Mountain Clan warriors. Speed is their gift, but their stamina is still better than Grace's.

Grace flaps a few times and then breaks into a glide, saving her energy as much as she can. The flight's scout flies beside her. Their Forest Clan blood gives them great maneuverability but takes from them the stamina required to fly further up in the formation.

A few hours into the flight, when even the scout is starting to lag, the Wind Weaver takes Liberty's place at the head. His wings move powerfully, and the air around them shapes to his will, cradling her and the others so they barely have to flap at all.

Grace tentatively stretches a hand out into the air. It tingles faintly against her skin, and she isn't sure if that is because of the cold or from the Wind Weaver.

Unfortunately, taking her focus off of her looming exhaustion gives her mind free rein to think of other things. There are too many things for her to worry about. Going into Black-Wing territory. Failing the mission and coming back to disappoint Father. Failing the mission and *not* coming back.

A sharp whistle interrupts her thoughts. *Going down.* It is the scout.

Acknowledged, Liberty whistles back, and the scout folds his wings and dips below the clouds.

A few moments later, he is back. *Adjust course six degrees east. Altitude three degrees down.* Liberty whistles acknowledgment, and their course shifts. They must be getting down from the mountain now.

Grace checks the position of the sun. If they continue at this pace, they'll make it to the edge of the trees before sundown. She would much rather spend the night there than try to find a warm place to camp on the mountain.

The scout dips beneath the clouds three more times before he comes back with more than course adjustments.

Trees below.

Finally, they are above the forest.

Circle down, Liberty whistles.

Acknowledged, Grace and the rest of the flight reply. Flight Language is simple and limited compared to proper Song, but it is useful. The wind whips away the quieter sounds of Song, but the piercing whistles carry easily.

The warrior ahead of Grace folds her wings and falls below the clouds. Grace follows. They trickle down like a light rain, scattering through the canopy of the forest. Grace and the scout slip easily through small gaps in the branches, twisting through branches that

ASCENDANT

would snag the larger wings of their companions. Liberty and the rest of the flight fan out and find clearings to drop through.

They meet up atop a fallen tree, wings spread for balance on the slanted trunk. Grace digs her talons into the bark. She could stick her entire hand into the gaps if she wished, some of her arm too. The entire flight could walk side-by-side down the trunk. Each leaf is as big as her head. What could possibly have felled the giant, Grace isn't sure.

The forest covers most of Caelam, and there are things deep within it that have not been seen since the time of the clans. This tree was probably there for those times, Grace thinks. Some of them in the deep forest have been around since Caelam was formed.

Liberty seems to be gathering her thoughts, and Grace glances at the other members of the flight to see their reactions. They are all looking back at her. Liberty clears her throat, and Grace meets her eyes. She shoves her nervousness down into the bottom of her mind. *Power comes from the appearance of strength,* she reminds herself.

"I don't believe we have had the chance to introduce ourselves," Liberty says. "This has all been rather...impromptu."

That's one word for it, Grace thinks as she nods silently.

"I am Liberty." She gestures to herself, then to the Mountain Clan man beside her. "This is Faith." The Wind Weaver dips his head. "This is Hope, and my scout is Amity." The Mountain Clan woman and the scout dip their heads in turn.

Grace nods greeting to all of them. "I'm Grace," she says because she doesn't know what else to say.

"Right," Liberty says. She seems just as unsure of where to go from here as Grace feels. "We have a lot of travel ahead of us, so I suppose we should get started." Liberty unfolds the map from a pouch on her belt and spreads it out across the trunk. Grace and the rest of the flight gather around it.

"From here on out," Liberty says, "it's going to be slow work. We have this section to look over." She traces a rough square of forest on the map, just at the edge of the Black-Wing border. "If we don't find anything here, we go deeper into Black-Wing territory."

From the looks of it, they have maybe another half a day's travel before they hit their target. Grace resists the urge to groan. Already she is developing a passionate hatred for travel. At least now they'll be beneath the canopy instead of above the clouds.

Liberty folds up the map and tucks it back into her belt. "Amity, if you would be so kind as to find us a place for tonight."

Amity bows and flutters off into the treetops.

"Faith, you find water."

He nods and heads off. Soon after him, Hope is assigned to find food, and she takes off in a different direction.

"That leaves us to find bedding and firewood," Liberty says.

Grace looks around the woods and says, "Wherever will we find some?" She says flippantly, then snaps her mouth shut. Father doesn't like it when she speaks in such a tone.

But Liberty smiles and actually laughs. "I'm sure you'll be able to do it."

The sound of her laughter is pleasant, but Grace still scolds herself. *What will you do, run off into the woods for a few days and come back half-feral?*

Father's voice whispers through her mind, *Discipline always, Dear One. There is no room for children in war.*

It is only a memory, but Grace cannot help but feel chastised, and she glides to the ground silently instead of continuing to joke with Liberty. *There is no room for children in war,* she reminds herself, echoing Father's words. She lands quietly and begins gathering firewood, breaking twigs off branches as wide as she is tall.

She brings her haul back to the fallen tree. In the shadow of the trunk, there is a pile of brush, most of it is old and dead, except for a few things at the top, but they are already wilting.

I hope that's not what we're sleeping on. Grace sets her firewood a good distance from the pile so they don't get mixed up. She wipes sweat from her brow. It is only the beginning of summer, but already it is hotter in the forest than it ever gets in the Citadel. Her armor and furs are sure to bake her tomorrow when they will have to keep traveling through the hottest parts of the day.

On her second trip back with wood, she catches Liberty, apparently making a new pile. Grace's brow furrows. As glad as she is that they won't be sleeping on dead leaves and twigs, it seems pointless to gather two piles. "What's that one for?" she asks, gesturing to the original pile.

"Which one?" Liberty asks, setting down an armful of moss. She catches sight of the pile Grace is pointing to, and her eyes widen. She grabs Grace around the shoulders and tugs her away from the pile as though it will leap up and attack them. "That's a nest," she whispers, "for a throwing lizard. I should have been keeping a better eye out. They're a native predator, very aggressive, especially when defending their nests. *Never* touch one."

They move their piles well away from the nest and gather in the opposite direction from it, working closely together, on Liberty's insistence.

When Faith and Hope return, Hope's bag is missing. Hopefully, she left it full of food wherever Amity has found to camp. With the five of them carrying firewood and bedding, they only need one trip to get the supplies to their camp.

Amity has found a low branch—perhaps a hundred feet off the ground—that has grown straight enough for them to sleep on it. Grace lands directly on the branch, but the others, with their wider wingspans, must land on the trunk itself and climb up.

"You couldn't have found a branch the rest of us could land on?" Liberty grumbles as she climbs.

"I didn't have a problem," Amity says innocently.

Liberty begins setting up as soon as she reaches the branch. Unpacking a tripod and hanging the fire pit, Amity starts shredding tinder and striking his flint. Faith grabs Hope's bag from where it had been left and pulls a bounty of fresh food from it. A few small creatures with dark fur and sharp claws, small enough to crawl through the cracks of the tree bark. Hope begins skinning and gutting one while Faith continues to pull things from the bag.

Mushrooms and leafy stalks, a few round yellowish fruits and a pouch full of berries. Grace doesn't let the longing show on her face. Plants cannot grow in the frigid temperatures of the Citadel, and with the Black-Wings controlling most of the fertile ground along the river, crops are limited. The land is mostly used to grow food for the animals hidden in the snowy tundra behind the mountain. Fruits and vegetables, even spices and seasonings, are only grown in small patches. The dried meat rations that are common fare throughout the Citadel taste like old smoke.

Hope hands the meat over to Faith and begins on another tree crawler. Faith pulls leaves from one of the stalks and begins shredding them and rubbing them into the meat. Hope puts a few berries into the empty cavity where the animal's internal organs had been and wraps the whole thing in one of the leaves from the tree. Amity's fire is blazing, and it accepts the bundle with a cheery hiss. By the time Faith sets a second bundle in the fire, a delicious smell is rising from the first.

Hope gives Faith another, and his hand takes a detour as it returns to the meat, dipping into the bag of berries. Hope smacks it away.

"I need those," she scolds.

Faith reaches for the bag again.

"No." Hope moves it out of his reach, closer to Liberty.

He pouts. "But I like them, and *you* like me. So if you're really a friend…"

Hope remains unmoved. "Then I won't let you spoil your dinner."

"But *Mother*," Faith says sarcastically.

Hope levels a glare at him.

"If she lets you eat them now, then you won't get dessert," Liberty chides, the only one of them keeping a straight face at this point. Then Liberty leans around the fire pit and snags a handful for herself. "Besides, I like the red berries more than you."

Hope swats at Liberty's hand as well but misses. Grace isn't sure if it is on purpose or not. Either way, Liberty escapes with her prize and offers her hand to Grace.

"Want some?"

The temptation is there, to joke along with them, to say, *But then I'll ruin my dinner.* But that would be childish. She only smiles gratefully and says, "Thank you."

There is no room for children in war.

She rewards herself by taking half the berries. They have been partially squished by their rough handling, but that just means she has an excuse to lick the juice from her fingers. The few berries that weren't crushed explode in her mouth, popping between her teeth.

She nearly spits them out when the juice floods her mouth. It is too much. Sweet and tangy and sour all at once. She forces them down anyway. They are too good to waste, even though her wings ruffle with the overwhelming sensation. Liberty eats her half of the ill-gotten gains more sedately, popping one in her mouth at a time.

Above them, there is a low rumble, followed by a high-pitched cheep. Grace's head whips up, wind feathers fanning wide, trying to read the air currents. There is something in the shadows above them. By the light of the fire, she can see two pairs of eyes shining back at them.

Grace flicks her wrist, unsheathing her talons. The others have looked up as well, but they are calm. She hesitates. "What are those?"

Hope looks over to her. "Oh, they're just forest cats. They probably smelled the meat. They're wild but pretty friendly. Here." She holds out a pile of entrails to Grace. "They'll take it from your hand if you hold still. Their whiskers tickle." Her eyes sparkle with mischief.

Grace extends her hand, and the bloody pile is dropped in her palm. She holds her hand up to the glowing eyes, and they tilt. Another cheep, then a lanky body lands beside her.

In the light of the fire, Grace can see the patterns on the cat's fur. The coat is warm brown, like the bark of the trees, lighter on the belly and speckled with golden spots. Grace slowly lowers her hand and offers it to the cat. Hope is right—the whiskers do tickle.

Liberty mimics the cheeping sound to the other cat and offers it her own palm. It drops to the branch and has no problem climbing over Amity to reach her, perching on his shoulders as it eats. Liberty reaches out her other hand, gently touching a dark band on the cat's leg. Grace returns her attention to her own guest.

It licks her palm, cleaning off the blood and the last of the berry juice. Its long tail—twice as long as the body itself—waves slowly in the air. Grace slowly raises her other hand and touches the tip of one tufted ear. The cat lifts one lip at her, and Grace quickly puts her hand back down, trying not to take it personally.

"These guys *are* friendly," Amity notes, reaching his hand back to pet Liberty's cat. It hisses at him, and just like that the pair is gone, up into the safety of the dark and the branches. "Or not," he says sheepishly. "I guess they just like Liberty."

Liberty leans back, sticking one hand into a pouch on her belt and depositing something there. The rest of the berries maybe. "They are very good judges of character."

They toss the rest of the entrails to the ground—apparently, Hope had been saving them in case of guests—and use sticks to carefully pull the wrapped meat out of the fire. It is flavorful and moist, worlds better than the dried rations in her bag. They will eat those if they have to, but for now, she pulls more meat from the bones of the tree crawler and enjoys the flavors.

The bones and other refuse are tossed off of the branch as well, and then they get ready for bed. The leaves that Liberty gathered have been arranged into a comfortable nest against the trunk of the tree. Liberty and her flight curl up together without hesitation, blanketed by each other's wings and warmed by the body heat of their companions. Grace hesitates.

She is used to sleeping alone. Father is far from physically affectionate, and his duties often require him to work late into the night. Grace has always slept alone.

"I'll take first watch," she says and moves to sit beside the banked fire. She curls her wings around herself, hands absently rubbing up and down her arms. Her eyes keep going back to the nest and the flight curled contentedly in it. She viciously jerks her head away and scans their surroundings, searching for any signs of Black-Wings.

The others hesitate for a moment, apparently unsure of leaving her to watch their backs on her own. Grace fights the urge to scowl—she can manage this much at least.

After a few hours, Hope comes to relieve her, and Grace settles on the edge of the group. It is surprisingly easy to fall asleep, despite the strange sounds of the forest.

***

Haven sighs and rubs her temples, knowing it won't do any good. Her current headache isn't nearly so easy to get rid of. *The Court chose him*, she says in her mind, fighting to keep her tone even. Not that there's much point—Justice knows her mood as well as she knows his.

But the Trinity didn't. He has no right to remain king. If you weren't so blind to his every fault, you would acknowledge that, Justice replies. His anger scrapes against hers, and she grits her teeth. They've had this argument at least once a day ever since the ceremony, and neither of them is willing to budge.

Who then? If not him, then who should be king? Her question, at least, makes him quiet for a long moment. There is no leaving

41

the place in their minds where they speak, their very souls are connected. But he is quiet enough that she thinks he is ignoring her.

We could, Justice says. *You could. Everyone loves you, they would listen to you.*

I don't want to be queen. She makes a cutting motion through the air as though she could destroy the very notion.

Endurance gives her an odd look, distracted from writing in his journal by her gestures. This is why she hates to have these conversations during the day. She waves him away and leaves the room.

Why not? Justice asks. He never lets anything go. He knows exactly how much it annoys her, but it never stops him. *You would be a good queen, and Endurance could still have enough of a position to soothe his ego.*

She growls, shutting the doors of her room with a touch more force than is strictly necessary. *Why would I want to be queen?* she demands. *After...After everything that's happened, I can barely stand to look at that throne, much less sit on it.*

That does make him stop. Their argument is forgotten momentarily in favor of a soul-deep hug as they both fight back the image of their queen, their friend, fallen at the feet of her own throne. Reverence standing over her. Haven and Justice wracked with the shared agony of their wounds, only Endurance to guard them.

Can we just drop it? she asks. Sensing his argument, she amends, *At least for now.*

For now, he agrees.

***

Grace wakes with her nails biting into her palms, frustrated and somehow more tired than when she'd fallen asleep. Faith sits by the fire, feeding it a pile of small twigs. She is curled against Hope's side, blanketed by Liberty's wing.

Grace sits up and stretches her wings, resettling her feathers. It is easier to put the strangeness of the dream out of her mind with so many other things to focus on, and she does so gladly.

They eat the leftovers of last night's feast, the meat warmed again over the fire. Grace snags one of the yellow fruits and takes a *small* bite. Never let it be said that she doesn't learn.

The flavor washes across her tongue, tart and bitter, but not entirely unpleasant. Once they have eaten their fill, Liberty checks the map again, sending Amity above the treetops to make sure of their position.

Liberty traces a path over the paper. "This is the quickest route we can take that will keep us out of the open. We should be entering Black-Wing territory by seventh hour or so. We'll stop then and disguise ourselves."

Their feathers will stick out like snow in summer when they are in Black-Wing territory, directing any patrols in the area right to them. That can easily be solved by coating their feathers in a black powder. There is no helping the fact that their wind feathers aren't the right color, but it is the best they can do.

Hopefully, they won't get close enough to any Black-Wings for them to tell. In their bags is stolen Black-Wing armor, lighter than their own due to the higher temperatures of the forest.

With their path decided, they set out. Grace and Amity can fly easily in the thick vegetation, but the rest of the flight have larger wingspans, and they must walk. Thankfully, they don't have to go all the way down to the forest floor.

The trees are so old and have grown so close together that, for the most part, they can walk easily from one branch to another, only having to climb occasionally. In the places where the trees are farther apart, there are ancient remnants of Forest Clan to help them across, bridges woven from living branches and vines millennia ago.

They travel along these for most of the day. Grace shoulders part of Amity's scouting duties, finding the easiest path for the others while he keeps an eye out for any Black-Wings on the wrong side of the border.

Toward evening, Liberty whistles for them to return. Grace dives once more, landing on a wide branch. Liberty, Faith, and Hope are already there taking off their armor piece by piece. Grace unbuckles her own armor and stows it in the hollow of the tree. One of Father's Observants will be by at some point to pick it up.

Once they are in only their woolen clothes, Liberty pulls out the powder. They take turns helping each other coat their feathers, slowly covering up the white with inky black. Grace shudders at the "Black-Wing" flight that surrounds her. The dark feathers are unnatural, a reflection of the soul beneath them.

The first Black-Wings earned their dark feathers when they betrayed the Trinity, long ago, and now their descendants carried their shame, with only their white wind feathers to remind them of what they once had. It seemed wrong to purposefully cover their own pure feathers, but it was necessary.

The powder itches. It has to be applied to both the top of the feathers and the underside, leaving tiny grains to rub against the skin on her wings. Grace ruffles her feathers, trying to get some of the extra dust to come out. When she flattens them again, they are just as itchy. Great.

With their wings disguised, they don the Black-Wing armor. It is almost a relief to wear after the stifling heat of White-Wing armor. Almost. It is still off-putting, being in the enemy's armor. Grace pulls at the stiff collar of the dark-green shirt, which rises about halfway up her neck and feels unnatural. Every time she lowers her chin, it brushes the fabric and tickles. The pants are loose as well, which is very odd after the sleekness of White-Wing uniforms. Thankfully, her boots can remain the same.

When they take to the air again, there is still a good two and a half hours of travel they can do before tenth hour when the light will begin to fade. Beneath the cover of the trees, sunlight fades faster, leaving sunset at about ten-half instead of twelfth hour. Grace and Amity continue patrolling the area around the rest of the flight as they walk.

At ninth hour, Grace and Amity begin looking for likely places to camp: wide, flat branches with good cover over them so they won't be spotted from the air and the smoke from their fire will be broken up in the leaves. They whistle to Liberty when they find a suitable place, and the rest of the flight climb up to them.

They are higher up than last night, a comfortable five hundred feet or so above the ground. This time, when Liberty hands out camp duties, Grace asks to accompany Hope on her foraging mission.

Hope is happy enough to let her tag along and seems to take delight in pointing out the various edibles of the forest. Hope allows their conversation to wander from topic to topic. She only interrupts to point out plants to Grace and tells them their uses.

After awhile, Hope touches her wrist. "I wanted to ask…" She hesitates, and Grace nods to encourage her. "Are you…happy? With your father?"

Grace blinks at her. "Of course I am. Why wouldn't I be?"

Hope bites her lip. "I've heard about the Saboteur Program and it seems like you didn't really get much of a childhood. Always training and such, and now you're on a mission, in Black-Wing territory."

"There is no room for children in war," Grace says. "Nobody gets much of a childhood these days."

Hope doesn't look convinced, but she doesn't argue.

Grace swallows, feeling oddly nervous. "I do wish that my first mission had been something less…dire, but the king knows what is best."

"I guess so," Hope mutters, but her tone says something different.

"Father says that he is just wary of betrayal," Grace says. She isn't sure which of them she is trying to convince. "He can't be right all the time, but he does his best."

"I wonder what else he's been wrong about," Hope whispers, so low that Grace isn't sure if she heard it or if it was a trick of her mind. She debates asking what Hope means, but she is distracted by a dull red splotch on a nearby leaf.

There is a clear trail of broken branches and trampled grass through the undergrowth. Trapped in the branches of a low bush is a white feather. "Hope," Grace gestures to the path.

Technically, any wounded soldier could have left such a trail. But the likelihood of two White-Wings in this specific area who are wounded are low.

Hope pats her on the shoulder with a tight smile. "Looks like you've found the first signs of our traitor," she says. Her voice isn't quite as happy as Grace thinks it should be, but they still have a dangerous mission ahead of them.

They follow the trail to its beginning. Hope's eyes study the broken branches and crushed leaves. From amid the wreckage, she pulls a handful of white feathers.

There is no doubting now, they're on the traitor's trail.

Hope leaves Grace in the clearing and goes to fetch the rest of the flight. Liberty regards the bloodied foliage with a blank face. "It is too late to search tonight," she says eventually. "We'll pick up the trail in the morning. Good find." She nods to Hope and Grace.

They return to camp and eat quietly. The relaxed atmosphere from the night before is nowhere to be found. All of Liberty's flight is on edge. Their eyes watch the flickering shadows cast by the fire, their hands often straying to their weapons.

It is a long time before any of them are ready to sleep.

Chapter

3

It is dark when her eyes open again. Grace stares into the night for a moment, finding herself surprised and relieved that she didn't have another of the strange dreams from Haven's eyes.

Warm breath spreads across her cheek, and Grace tenses.

"It's only me," Liberty whispers.

"What's goin' on?" Grace asks, relaxing and rubbing her eyes.

"Nothing. It's your watch."

"Oh." She yawns, sitting up.

Hope murmurs and shifts a wing in her sleep, but doesn't wake up. Grace picks her way out of the pile and sits beside the fire. She sweeps her gaze over the landscape, leaning over to check below them. Nothing.

Satisfied, Grace listens to the forest around her. There are tiny chirps and buzzes in the air, from what she isn't sure. Occasionally something scrapes or scratches on bark—tree limbs rubbing together or maybe animals going about their business.

In the quiet, her thoughts are harder to ignore. The tiny, wordless doubts that seem so far away in the light of day and the company of others.

As much as she has tried to convince herself that this mission is the best thing she could hope for, a true test of her training, she knows she isn't ready for it. She wishes Father could be with them. She misses his steady confidence at her side.

Her eyes stray to the tangle of limbs and wings just out of arm's reach. She feels something stirring within her, something soft and small, a longing for something she dares not name.

She wonders what it would be like to have wing-mates, to have a flight. People to fly and fight beside. People she could trust to have her back no matter what.

Like a family.

She shuts the thought away. She has a family. It may be small, but it is hers. She has Father and his patience, his kindness. Her eyes drift over to the others. The feeling stirs again, soft and warm and glowing in her heart. It seems so precious, so fragile. So wrong.

You must be strong, she tells herself. *They would only weaken you, like roots creeping through stone. Father is the only one you need. He loves you. Isn't that enough?*

She jerks her eyes away from Liberty's flight. They have each other, and she has Father. Once this mission is over, they will continue to do their duties, and she will continue her training. That is all this is, a test of her training. A test of her love for Father.

Deep down, a quiet anxiety moves like a glacier into her awareness. What if she fails? What if she doesn't kill the traitor, or capture them. What will Father do? She imagines his face drawn tight with disappointment, his eyes cold and hard like they get when she hasn't done a form correctly or put together his hints.

His voice will be sharp when he says, "I told you not to disappoint me." Anger will cloud the air around him until he seems ten times his normal size. There will be condemnation in his every word and action, and then, when she is almost ready to throw herself on the ground and beg for his forgiveness, he will sigh and shrink, and his eyes will fill with that terrible, terrible sadness.

He will shake his head and stare quietly for a moment, wonder just how he could raise such a worthless *failure*. He will say, "This is my fault. I thought you were ready. I thought you knew enough to do this for me. But I was wrong."

Grace cannot stand the thought of it. It sends something desperate lancing through her heart. Her muscles tense with the desire to rush back to the Citadel, to beg him for his forgiveness, to tell him, "No, it's *my* fault. I am the one responsible." *Not you, never you.*

"Grace?"

She whips around, apologies crowding around her lips before she realizes that it is not Father, only Liberty. Grace blinks away the image of Father's eyes, caught somewhere between rage and sorrow.

"What?" Her voice is strange, thready and weak.

Liberty's brow furrows. "Are you alright?"

Grace forces herself to hold her breath, then lets it out, draws in a deep lungful of air. "I'm fine."

Picking her way out of the nest, Liberty comes to sit beside Grace. "You sure?"

Grace opens her mouth, almost tells Liberty about her fears, about the horror of Father's anger. "I..." She breaths deeply again. "I'm..." She can't do it. "I'm just worried about the mission."

Liberty extends a wing over her. "I'm worried too," she says quietly. "But we must have faith that everything will go according to plan. That we'll all get out alright."

They sit quietly together, even though it isn't Liberty's watch, and Grace can't help the gratitude that wells up within her. "Do you have anyone waiting for you?" she asks quietly.

The pensive expression on Liberty's face softens into a faint smile. "Yes. I've pledged myself to someone. This is supposed to be my final mission before we can fulfill our vows." She pulls a small medallion from her armor, toying with it. In the low light Grace can see a faint etching she doesn't recognize—crossed wings, she thinks. An odd token for a pledged couple, but she supposes if it makes them happy then there is no real reason it shouldn't be.

"Congratulations."

Liberty gives her a grateful smile. "What about you?"

"Only Father."

Liberty tucks the medallion away. "Haven't you got friends or anything?"

Grace looks away. "I don't have time for friends, I have to train." She tries to say it with pride, to imbue the words with the duty she feels. *Should* feel. But they come out small and lonely.

Just like you, something in her hisses spitefully.

Liberty doesn't say anything, only scoots a little closer.

Somehow, that is better than anything she could have said.

***

The rain starts in the early hours of the morning. Everyone is still on edge and now there is an air of urgency to their movements as they pack up the camp. The rain will wash away the trail if it goes on for too long, and they would have to start all over.

They return once more to the place where the traitor landed—crashed, more like—and follow the trail from there. They spread out, still within sight of one another, but far enough apart that no hint of the traitor's passing will escape them.

It is tedious work, and though most of the rain is caught by the leaves above their heads, a good portion of it still falls to the ground.

51

Before an hour has gone by, Grace is nearly soaked through, and the dye on her wings is getting patchy. There is no way to replace it now; it would only rinse off faster. They will simply have to hope that they do not encounter any Black-Wing patrols.

They search through thickets and treacherous mud pits, losing the trail several times and backtracking in the hopes of picking it up again. Thankfully, the traitor is wounded and has left many signs of his passing.

By midday the rain has grown heavier, and distant flashes of lightning appear above them. Grace pulls her boot out of a deep puddle and slips immediately into the next one.

Hope stops to haul her out, but both of them freeze when Faith motions sharply. He holds his hand low, fingers clenched into a fist as he crouches against a tree trunk.

Stay low, stay together.

He glances to them and makes another sign: *Enemy.*

Grace stiffens and feels as though even the blood in her veins has frozen. Hope curses under her breath and signs back, *How many? Positions?*

Faith slowly peeks around the tree and then pulls back. *Six. Ahead, and to the left.*

Liberty appears beside them so quickly and silently that Grace flinches. Her eyes are hard and her teeth are clenched. Amity is just behind her, creeping up to join Faith watching the Black-Wings.

Amity moves past Faith, keeping low to the ground, only moving when the wind shakes the foliage to cover him. Grace quickly loses sight of him, and she holds her breath, hoping that he will return.

A minute later he does.

Objective, he signs grimly, *center position.*

They have found the traitor, but he is in the middle of a Black-Wing patrol. Her heart pounds against her ribs.

Point position, Amity signs, *Wind Weaver.*

Grace thinks her heart stops altogether. Having a Wind Weaver on their side is a great advantage, but getting caught between two of them in a fight could spell disaster.

Hold position, Liberty signs immediately. She creeps forward to join Faith and Amity. They watch silently for a moment, and then she signals Hope and Grace forward. Grace feels as though the rustle of every leaf she touches is as loud as thunder. Somehow, though, the Black-Wings are still oblivious when she peeks around the tree to see them.

They are gathered in loose formation around the traitor. His white feathers stick out like a beacon as a Black-Wing healer winds a bandage around his side. They are speaking in low tones, too far away for Grace to hear even without the rain and thunder.

Grace squints at the traitor's wings. Oddly enough, she feels somewhat disappointed. She had thought that his wings would turn black when he switched sides. Maybe it is a more gradual change.

The leader of the Black-Wing force is easy to pick out. He stands beside the healer and watches the forest around them as though he is waiting for something. Another patrol? His hair is blood red, cut close to his skull and plastered down by the rain.

On his armor is a round medallion, and though she is too far away to see what is engraved on it, she knows that it is a pattern of swirling lines. The mark of a Wind Weaver.

She feels her skin crawl as she turns away from the Black-Wings to see what Liberty's orders are. It feels wrong on every level to turn her back on them, even if they don't know she's there.

Strike now, Amity insists. He touches the quiver of arrows at his side and then his chest before pointing to the traitor. *I could take out the traitor first.*

No, Liberty signs, with a firm shake of her head for emphasis.

"This is our only chance," Faith whispers. "They could vanish into their city the moment we look away."

Liberty only shakes her head again.

Amity starts to sign a response, but gives up and instead hisses, "War is dangerous. This is our mission. We have to do it."

Liberty looks at him for a long, quiet moment. Indecision flashes across her face, then acceptance, and finally determination. "It isn't my mission," she replies.

And then she springs away from them. Grace twists to follow her automatically, half rising before her mind catches up. Liberty didn't order them to attack; she just leaped for the Black-Wings. Was she sacrificing herself? Was this some sort of strategy that Grace doesn't know about?

Liberty lands among the Black-Wings and doesn't draw her blade. Instead, she shouts, "To arms!" and turns to face the rest of her flight. The Black-Wings draw their blades, but they don't raise them against Liberty. "They're in the brush over there," Liberty says, and as if they're following her orders, the Black-Wings charge.

No. Not *as if* they are following her orders. Liberty is ordering the Black-Wings. Liberty *is* a Black-Wing. Liberty has betrayed them.

For a split second, Grace is frozen, staring at Liberty where she stands unharmed beside the Black-Wing Wind Weaver. Between her flight and the healer. Then her eyes slip to the Black-Wing patrol that is charging through the underbrush, weapons drawn.

"Liberty, get Chivalry out of here," the Wind Weaver barks, gesturing to the traitor.

"Move!" Faith barks, hauling Grace to her feet and all but throwing her behind him as he draws his sword. Grace trips but catches herself. She whirls to face the Black-Wings and flicks her wrist. Her talons unsheathe, and her wings flare instinctively.

The Black-Wings don't pause. The first one catches Faith's sword against his own. The second meets Hope's. Amity leaps before the third and fourth soldiers, blades flashing in the low light. Grace stands before the fifth.

His drawn blade glows with blood lust and malice as she stares at it. She has never sparred with real weapons. Wooden ones, yes, blunted ones, many times. Never real sharpened blades though.

This is nothing like sparring.

She meets the soldier's eyes. They are mostly hidden in the shadows of his helmet and the darkness of the forest around them, but she can see them glint when lightning flashes.

She steps backward onto a root, and her right wing brushes against a vine. This isn't the level training floor, with bright lights and open spaces. She isn't fighting a White-Wing soldier who will stop if she makes a mistake. She will have more to worry about than Father's disapproval if she slips up here.

This is nothing like training.

The soldier pauses just out of striking range. "Surrender," he says. His voice is low and stern. He isn't afraid of her at all—why would he be?

"Never," Grace replies. It doesn't sound strong and determined like she means for it to. Her voice cracks and wavers, and honestly she isn't sure if he can understand her at all.

He must, though, because he tilts his head in acknowledgment, and the next second he is upon her. She nearly gets tangled in the vine when he lunges forward. She deflects the blow with her gauntlets. Dips beneath the vine and ducks out of range of another blow.

She can't keep doing this. She has to attack at some point, or he'll corner her somewhere and then it will all be over. She ducks another blow.

The air around them tingles with power. Not the gentle tickle against her skin like when Faith was making the flight here easier. This is like a thousand needles stabbing into her skin. The underbrush sways, and a few of the smaller trees groan as the wind whips around them. Faith and the Black-Wing Wind Weaver have found each other.

A swaying branch nearly smacks her in the face, and she has to keep her wings tucked tight against her body to keep the wind from tearing at them. The Black-Wing staggers as the winds gust harder, but he isn't giving ground.

She needs to do something.

He is so much stronger than her though. One strike would be enough to take her down if he catches her. She dances back, and only a shift in the air over her wind feathers warns her that she is about to run up against a tree. She tries to angle away from it, but the Black-Wing feints. She can feel the tree looming over her, and she braces herself on it when her foot slips into a mud puddle.

Her talons dig into the bark. The Black-Wing stands before her, his stance relaxed. He knows he has her cornered. "Surrender," he says again, over the roaring of the wind.

"No," Grace shouts back.

"You have nowhere to go."

Then she realizes he is Desert Clan. His wings are too long and broad to fly here. It is true *he* has nowhere to go. If possible, her heart beats faster at the thought. At best it's insane; realistically it's just short of suicidal. But it's her only option.

She whips around and uses her talons to pull herself up the tree. She plants both of her feet against the trunk and pushes off with all her might.

Her wings snap out, scooping the air around her as she flips over his head. For one shining moment, she rises above the Black-Wing, above the battlefield. The air is abruptly still, as if the whole world is holding its breath.

Then the wind turns against her.

Woven into a great net, it smashes her back to the earth. Her breath flies out of her lungs, and she lies gasping on the forest floor. Above her, the red-haired Wind Weaver appears.

"Take her," he orders. The air around them is still, but for a weak breeze. Faith lost.

Grace scrambles to get up, but her head is spinning, and she seems to be moving slower than the rest of the world. The Black-Wing barely has to touch her to get her back on the ground.

He grabs both of her wrists in one hand. She tugs weakly against his hold but can't get her body to cooperate. She needs to get away. Needs to move. There is only one reason to bother with taking her from the battlefield.

They want to take her to the Ascendant. Her mind can't seem to operate her hands and feet, but it has no problem with flashing an image of the Ascendant before her: ghostly pale skin, burning red eyes, wings blacker than a starless night.

She comes for you after the battle is over, her mind whispers. *She finds the ones that haven't died yet, the ones that are too weak to fight back. Then she takes them. She takes them, and she twists them until not even their own families recognize them.*

Her heart lodges in her throat. She can't breathe around it. She kicks at the Black-Wing, but he barely notices. Fear curls icy talons into every inch of her. She isn't going to die. Her fate is going to be so, so much worse

Then Amity bursts into the clearing. His blade is a silver flash of death as he lashes out at the Black-Wing. The soldier deflects it and retrieves his sword to answer. Their battle quickly leads them out of the clearing.

The Wind Weaver turns to Grace.

She doesn't give him the chance to try and capture her himself. She's still dizzy, but she gets to her feet.

Liberty bounds into the clearing, her wings high. "Glory!" she shouts, a tinge of desperation in her tone. "Chivalry is dead."

The Wind Weaver curses. "Fall back."

"Not without you," Liberty snaps.

"That's an order."

"You're not my commander."

Grace darts past them while they are distracted. Through the wall of brush, she finds Amity and the Black-Wing. Amity's dagger glints from the ground where it's been buried to the hilt.

Amity is barely standing, holding one arm against his stomach and breathing in heavy, uneven gasps. The Black-Wing stands before him, blade in hand.

He does not give Amity the chance to surrender. He says nothing as he steps forward. Says nothing when his blade slides into Amity's flesh. Says nothing when Amity's body falls to the ground, a fountain of blood rising from beneath his armor.

Grace opens her mouth to scream, but nothing comes out. She feels as though she is a thousand miles away from her body, as though she is simply watching this. Or hearing about it in a tale from the safety of a shadowed corner. It can't be real. Amity can't actually be dead.

But it is real. He was killed right in front of her. That is his body lying on the forest floor. His blood mixing with the rainwater and mud.

This is nothing like training.

She wants to go home. She doesn't want to be here, in the real world, on a real battlefield. She thought she did, but she was wrong. She never wants to be on a battlefield again.

The Black-Wing turns to face her. His helmet was knocked off in the fight, and she can see his eyes now. They're brown. The sword in his hand is stained with red.

He takes a step toward her. Shifts his grip on the pommel.

A shudder runs down her spine. She wants to fly away, but she can't. Not with the Wind Weaver just through the brush, waiting to strike her down again. She will either die here or be taken back to the Black-Wing's city and given to the Ascendant.

The Black-Wing takes another step forward. His lips move, but she cannot hear what he says over the roaring in her ears.

No. *No.* She isn't going to die. Not without a fight.

She shifts her feet. Takes a stance drilled into her muscles by a hundred thousand repetitions. Her talons glitter on her fingers, winking in the light.

The Black-Wing pauses.

She doesn't hesitate. From first position, she shifts into a lunging strike. Her opponent evades. Raises his sword. Says something.

Words don't matter. All that matters is the battle. She can almost hear Father's voice: *Very good, Dear One. Don't let yourself get distracted.*

She shifts into third position. A low crouch, ready to spring up from below. Leaps directly into her next attack. Don't think, just act. Strike, defend. There is nothing else but these two things. Hurt and avoid hurt.

Her opponent answers with a block and kick that catches her in the chest. She lands in a puddle on the forest floor. It is warm against her skin. So warm that it burns into her. It isn't rainwater—

No. No. She can't think about that. Her opponent is still standing before her. She isn't finished yet.

She gets back up. Her chest aches. The world seems muffled around her. Has the rain stopped? Too many things are moving around. Branches shifting, the wind whistling though them. Bright spots of flowers.

Her opponent is still. He holds his sword away from himself. The blood hasn't been washed away.

Sloppy.

Always clean your weapon, Father admonishes. She shifts back into first position. Launches herself again. He blocks. She darts away. He catches her next blow on the blade of his sword. It bites into her palms where they aren't protected by the gauntlets. She can barely feel it. It all seems too far away and too close at the same time.

She strikes again. Misses as he sidesteps.

She is so tired. Her muscles are screaming, begging for her to stop. Sit down, let them rest. Even her heart seems tired of beating. She can't stop though. She can't fail. She can't lose.

Her opponent—the Black-Wing. She can't lose sight of that. This is a Black-Wing, not just a sparring match—throws her to the ground and holds her by one shoulder.

He pins her right wrist beneath one foot. Her left hand is free. Her arm moves without her telling it to. It rises and swings.

Her talons shine in the light.

She watches as they glide through the air, as they meet with the flesh of the Black-Wing. As they bite through skin and muscle and bone. Blood splashes over her fingers, over her face.

The Black-Wing falls to the side, fingers grasping at his throat as though he could stop the blood. She can smell it in the air, thick and heavy.

Another wave of blood washes over her hand, like the push and pull of a sea wave. Then one more. Then it stops.

She stares down at the Black-Wing, waiting for him to get up. Waiting for Father to step forward and judge her form, her speed, her reflexes. But this is not sparring. The Black-Wings killed Amity, and now she has killed one of them.

It should feel good, shouldn't it? It should feel like she has done the right thing. She has heard the other soldiers speak of avenging the deaths of their comrades. They brag about the battles they have fought. They are proud of the lives they have taken.

So why does she feel like throwing up? Like screaming and screaming and never stopping. She wants to run away, to hide somewhere in the forest where no one will ever find her again. She wants to turn back time. She doesn't want this to be real.

ASCENDANT

Someone is shouting. When she looks up, one of the other Black-Wings is staring right at her. No, not at her, at the…the body beneath her. Her knees waver, and she nearly falls

.

Chapter

4

The world is distant, the sounds muffled, the colors flat. Her mind is full of a strange buzzing that creeps up into a ringing through her ears. There is no thought, no emotion. She is only an empty vessel, to be filled with orders.

A mission. She has a mission. She has to find the traitor.

No. The traitor is dead.

The *first* traitor is dead.

Liberty. Where is Liberty? Grace's eyes dart over the shadows. *There.*

The redhead is pulling Liberty after him, falling back behind two more Black-Wings. Grace looks to Hope. She is doing well, but she is outnumbered. More Black-Wings are joining the battle, falling from the sky.

Liberty is getting away—she's nearly out of sight. Grace steps toward Hope; she will die if Grace leaves her. Or worse, the Ascendant will come for her.

Hope glances to her, and their eyes meet. "Grace!"

Grace takes another step toward her.

Pain lances through head, like someone is poking the backs of her eyes with red-hot needles. She turns to Liberty's retreating form.

Father's voice reverberates within Grace's mind: *Capture the traitor if you can, kill them if you can't.* It bounces off the inside of her skull, the words overlapping until they are senseless noise, pounding to the beat of her heart. *Don't disappoint me, Dear One.*

There is a ringing in her ears, and before she even realizes it, Grace's feet are carrying her into the trees after Liberty. Father's orders echo in her mind. *Kill. Capture.*

"Will the others be alright?" Liberty asks. For a split second, Grace thinks that she is talking about her flight. Then she realizes that she can't be. Liberty betrayed them. Betrayed the White-Wings.

She is talking about the Black-Wings.

Grace slips into the shadow of a large plant and watches as she draws closer.

"They'll be fine," the Wind Weaver—hadn't she called him Glory?—says as he takes her hand and tugs her away.

"What about the girl?" Liberty asks. Grace thinks that she should be afraid, but everything seems so far away.

"She can't hide forever," Glory replies.

Grace isn't hiding though. She has a mission to complete.

Capture.

She has no chance of capturing Liberty. Not while she's outnumbered by the Black-Wings and outclassed by the Wind Weaver.

Kill her, Dear One Father's voice seems to murmur.

Grace obeys.

Grace leaps over the brush pile and knocks the sword out of Liberty's hand. Liberty's eyes meet hers, wide with fear. Grace doesn't feel anything.

Glory's sword sails past her head as Grace ducks, the thrill of battle singing through her veins. This is what she was born for: to hunt, to kill, to do Father's bidding. She had allowed herself to lose sight of that, charmed by the soft thing that crept through her heart, but there is no place for it here. This is battle, hard and sharp, with no room for softness in it, or in her.

Grace blocks another blow with a gauntlet and shoves Glory's sword aside. Before she can take advantage of the opening, her wind feathers detect the motion of another body behind her. Liberty. Grace abandons Glory—he is only a distraction. This traitor is her target.

Kill, Dear One, Father's voice murmurs.

Her stomach lurches at the thought, and she is assaulted by the memory of that last terrible rush of warm blood from the Black-Wing's throat. She hesitates, wanting to pull back.

The ringing returns, loud enough to drown out the roar of blood in her ears. *Kill her,* Father's voice orders. Her heart pounds. Her teeth grit together so tightly her jaw aches. Liberty and Glory drive her back toward the brush pile, trying to tangle her feet.

Grace springs ten feet into the air, but doesn't unfurl her wings, allows gravity to throw her back down, right onto Liberty. Her talons bite into flesh. As warm blood spills over her hands, Liberty makes a high-pitched, choked sound.

The ringing cuts off so abruptly Grace is left reeling. Her talons are buried in Liberty's throat. As death takes her, Grace watches her eyes glaze over and tries to make herself let go, but her fingers won't obey.

ASCENDANT

She tries to look away. Glory is still there, and she has to keep fighting, has to defend herself—he will kill her if she doesn't. She can't think.

She can't breathe.

She can't stop staring.

She can't—

A low hiss rises from behind her. Her wind feathers catch the rhythmic motion of air that indicates breathing. From the amount of air it's moving, whatever is behind her is big. Grace never gets the chance to turn around and look at it.

Something hits her back, just under her wing. For half a second, she thinks that the other Black-Wings have found them and for some inexplicable reason are now throwing rocks, of all things. Then the pain sinks in, burning through her body. Like someone has peeled the skin away from her bones and shoved hot coals into her bloodstream.

She leaps for the sky with no thought. It is instinct: rise up from the pain, from the threat, find safety in the sky. It is a mistake.

Dimly, she is aware of screaming, of falling. The pain of impact with the forest floor is nothing compared to the torture of her back. She writhes on the ground, trying to reach it, trying to get away from it. Her wings flap desperately.

Then there is nothing.

She is somewhere beyond pain. Her skin burns, her veins melt. She opens her mouth to scream, and that hurts too. Hands pin her down, points of concentrated agony. Voices ring above her, deafening and unintelligible. They force her mouth open, pour something down her throat, hold her mouth closed until she swallows. The burning in her body fades, like a flame with water poured at its root. The world blurs back into semifocus.

Greenish-blue eyes look into hers, the dark skin around them creased with worry. "Rest. You won't want to be awake for this."

KIMBERLY GREY

She slips back into the darkness, where there isn't any pain.

Chapter

5

In the dark, it is peaceful. Then the screaming starts.

Screams of pain, of horror, of wordless fury. They echo around her. Light flares, and standing before her is someone with long pale hair. They face away from her, and there isn't enough light to see any more of them.

"Hello?" Grace calls. Her voice seems too quiet next to the screams. "Where are we? What's happening?"

The person doesn't turn, but their shoulders start to shake. She can't tell if it's with laughter or sobs—the sound is drowned out by the screams. They grow louder, press closer.

"Please!" Grace's voice cracks. "I don't understand!"

The light shifts, and she can see that their wings are black. So black they almost blend with the shadows. The Ascendant looks over her shoulder, her blood-red eyes glowing.

Grace steps back and hits the ground. Lands in the puddle of Amity's blood. It isn't the Black-Wing soldier standing over her this time. It's the Ascendant. Her mouth moves, forms words, but the screaming is so loud.

The Ascendant stares down at her, eyes burning, her hands dripping with blood. Her hair hangs down her back, pale as a cloud but straight as a blade. She speaks again and then turns away.

Grace gets up before she realizes what she's doing. She puts a hand on the Ascendant's shoulder. The Ascendant turns, and suddenly she is male and much taller. He towers over her, stares her down with disappointment clear in his eyes.

They shine with icy rage, cold and blue. Not red.

"You failed," Father snarls.

The screaming stops. Cut off so quickly that it echoes in her ears. Light spills across the room, and a man stands in the doorway. "Father," she dares to whisper, "I'm sorry. I'm so sorry. Please, I'll do better. I can fix it!"

But how does she fix this? She failed. She tries to sit up, but her muscles scream in protest, and she nearly joins them. Her breath catches on a sob, and she squeezes her eyes shut. A shadow falls over her, and she flinches.

"It's alright," a voice says. She doesn't recognize it, but it definitely isn't Father. "He isn't here." The man continues, "You're safe, I promise. Go back to sleep."

Grace dares to open her eyes, but she can't see his face. She opens her mouth to ask a question, but her voice only comes out as a hoarse rasp.

"Hush," he says. "It will be alright. Just go back to sleep."

Everything fades away.

***

She wakes alone in a dark room.

She lies on her side in some sort of medical cot, uncomfortable but convenient for healers. The room around her is nearly in complete shadow, but a thin sliver of light shines from beneath the door.

She doesn't remember how she got here, but she must be in the healing houses. Did something go wrong in training? She had slipped once on some ice and nearly broken her skull. Had it happened again?

No, it must be something else. Then, only her head had hurt; this time, *everything* hurts. A low pulsing ache makes her want to curl up in a miserable little ball until it all goes away.

She tries to run a hand through her hair, but her wrist jerks back before it is even halfway to her face. Something encircles her wrists, tight and unyielding, metallic when she taps a nail against it.

This is no healer's house in the Citadel, and she was in no training accident. She was captured—she remembers now. Her heart flutters against her ribs. It is trapped, just like she is.

Attacked, from behind—how typical of Black-Wings.

She cannot allow herself to think, because once she thinks, she will panic. She will imagine how disappointed Father will be. Or she will dream up a thousand tortures the Black-Wings could put her through. No, Grace cannot afford to be distracted by fear. She must act, not react. Escape and return to the Citadel.

She feels the manacles that keep her chained. They are anchored to the wall at the head of the bed, instead of a bed rail, which makes getting out of them much harder. Grace feels along the metal around her wrists. The cuffs are wide, perhaps three inches across, and thick, too thick to even think about breaking them.

They are held shut by some inner mechanism, the only access to which is a small keyhole. They are too tight on her wrists to try breaking a thumb to get out. They won't even slide forward or backward. They barely rotate. Another dead end.

Grace feels down the chain, following it to its anchor point on the wall. The chain is threaded through a hole in the wall, out of her reach. She has nothing.

No. No, there has to be something! Grace feels along the individual links of the chain. She'd once watched one be made; each link was actually just a stick of metal curved around to interlock with another curved piece and then welded shut. She feels along the welds—maybe there is a weak one? What does a weak weld feel like?

There has to be a way out, she tells herself. Her heartbeat pounds in her ears, like footsteps. No. She freezes, holding her breath. That isn't her heartbeat. Someone is coming.

Don't think, just do, she tells herself and drops the chain, lies back down, and closes her eyes. She forces her body to relax and her breathing to slow. The footsteps get louder, coming closer.

They stop.

Grace forces her breath to be even and deep, no matter how much her body fights to make it quick and shallow. *Inhale...two...three...four...Exhale...six...seven...eight...*

The lock makes a dull thunk, and the hinges creak when the door is forced open.

In...Out...

It is torture to leave herself vulnerable knowing that an enemy is approaching. Light from the hallway spills across her face, and she fights to keep from twisting her head away. It is bright, too bright.

In...Out...Don't move, don't tense up. Just breathe.

She forces away the tension that creeps into her shoulders, makes her feathers lie flat. She can hear the Black-Wing breathing from beside the door. Do they know that she is awake? Are they waiting for her to give herself away? Are they sneaking across the room while she lies here, willingly vulnerable? Her inhale is too deep, too fast; she slows her exhale.

"I know you're awake."

Grace can't help but flinch at the voice, then she curses herself and gives up. Her eyes open carefully, giving her time to adjust to the light. She will do herself no favors by being blinded. She glares at the Black-Wing and realizes that she knows him. He is the one with the blue-green eyes and the gentle voice, the one who lured her to sleep. Her lips twitch with the desire to scowl at him.

He steps farther into the room, and she glares but has no choice but to lie still and allow it. The longer she is awake, the more her injuries become apparent.

The pain is mild if she lies still, but when she moves, it flares up like a punishment. Perhaps the Black-Wings gave it to their prisoners to discourage escape attempts?

"Where am I?" she asks, even though she already knows.

"The Refuge," the Black-Wing replies. At her blank look, he clarifies, "It's the name of the city."

Grace hadn't considered just what the Black-Wings called their city. There were many names for it in the Citadel, most of which she was not allowed to repeat.

The Black-Wing takes a seat on the stool beside her head. She hadn't even noticed it until then. *Foolish. Always know your surroundings,* Father's voice scolds.

Father. He won't just be disappointed—he will be furious when she escapes. She wonders how he will punish her for this. Is there a punishment that could earn forgiveness for this many mistakes?

A memory threatens to rise from the back of her mind. Screams all around her, Father's voice hissing, *You failed.*

Grace casts her mind away from the thought, shoving the memory back where it came from. What Father will or will not do isn't the problem. What this Black-Wing will do is. She stares up at him, waiting for him to make a move, to attack or draw a weapon.

He isn't even looking at her. His gaze is directed to the door he came in, *waiting.* Before long footsteps echo down the hallway—more than one person. At least three.

The first person through the door is the red-haired guard. *Glory,* Liberty had called him. Grace's feathers bristle at the sight of him, but he doesn't react. His eyes sweep over her, checking for weapons.

I wish, she thinks sourly.

Behind him enters another Black-Wing in the same armor, but without the Wind Weaver's seal. A Queen's Guard—which means Glory is one too—and then a third. The pair take up positions on either side of the door, and behind them, Grace sees a woman who must be Queen Charity herself.

Charity sweeps into the room and the very air seems to crackle with her presence. Her wings flare and feathers bristle, and her eyes gaze down at Grace. Anger pools darkly in her eyes, like a current beneath calm waters, just waiting for her to make a wrong move, to come just a little bit too close so that it can drag her under.

The healer stands and steps away from Grace's bedside as Charity comes closer, Glory on her heels. He is still impassive, even in the face of his queen's temper. It is probably easier when it isn't aimed at you.

"So." Charity's voice is calm, but there is still tension underneath. Like water speeding up before the rapids. "You are

73

Concord's student. I would have thought the Spymaster would keep you on a tighter leash. He has always been such a perfectionist."

Grace has to think fast. She cannot escape, not yet. She is injured, poisoned. Her only weapon is her mind. *You have been trained for this,* she tells herself. *You know what to do.*

Charity's words provide the perfect solution. When people look at her, they don't see the danger; they only see the vulnerability. *Power comes from the appearance of strength,* Father had said. Right now, power isn't what she needs—what she needs is safety. She has no way of protecting herself, so she must not appear to be a threat

Grace clenches her jaw, too tight, and jerks her chin into the air. She pours emotion into her eyes. Anger, uncertainty, fear. She is an unprepared child, faced with the monster under their bed, but trying to put up a brave front. *See what I want you to see.*

"Unchain me, and see just how good I am!" she challenges, and allows her eyes to meet Charity's for a brief moment before they dart away. *I'm scared. I'm not sure I could really do anything. I'm putting up a brave face, but really I'm terrified.*

She has to keep from smiling when Charity's feathers ripple dismissively. She's falling for it. Charity takes a step forward, and Grace scoots a tiny bit back, then bites the inside of her lips like she is scolding herself.

Charity sniffs disdainfully. "Concord should have kept you in the Citadel. Unfortunately for you, he didn't. I assume you have already deduced the truth of your situation, but allow me to make it clear. You are a prisoner of war." Her face is placid, like the surface of the sea on a windless day, without even the anger lurking underneath. "Glory will be in charge of your case. He will ask

74

questions of you, and you *will answer them*. You shall be returned to health under the care of Healer Honor and then transferred to a more permanent room. If you cooperate, it may well be a comfortable room. If you resist, it will not be."

The Ascendant. Grace can't keep herself from shuddering. The Black-Wing soldier had been so insistent on taking her alive. *What does she want with me?* she almost asks. She can't bear to hear the answer, though, and instead she rasps, "I won't tell you anything. You can't make me."

They could though. Who knew what the Black-Wings were willing to do to get at the information she had? Grace's breathing comes a bit faster at the thought. *It's just part of the act,* she tells herself.

Does the Ascendant get prisoners too? Or does that take the fun out of it? Does she only want people that she goes out and picks herself?

It won't come to that, she tells herself. *I won't let it. I can do this.*

"We will see," Charity says. Her face is distant again, eyes narrowed with disapproval and disgust. Then she sweeps back out of the room, as quickly as she had come in. Glory and her guards follow after, and Grace is left alone.

No, not entirely alone. The healer is still with her. *Honor,* Charity had said his name was. He is a large man, almost as tall as Father, perhaps an inch shorter. His skin is the same deep brown as Charity's, and his wings are inky black. Her eyes dart away from the sight of his feathers, and she has to grit her teeth to keep a shudder from running down her spine. His curly hair is kept short, much shorter than anyone in the Citadel. Just another reminder that she is so very far from home. Grace eyes him warily, like she expects him to begin torturing her here and now. He sighs.

"I'm sorry, the queen can be…intense. Please, will you allow me to examine you? I will not harm you." His voice is gentle and soft.

Thank the Trinity, Grace thinks fervently. Even if Charity hadn't been convinced by her act, clearly the healer had been. She just needs to keep him on her side. She looks down and away, playing up her uncertainty. She glances at him, bites her lip, fidgets with her fingers, looks back down.

"I only want to make sure you aren't suffering any long-term effects from the throwing lizard," he says calmly.

Grace's head pops up, brow wrinkled. "Throwing lizard?"

He tilts his head, considering. "I suppose you wouldn't know about them. They are rather common here, but not so in the Citadel. They are a native predator, very large, very aggressive. Especially during nesting season. You stepped into one's nest."

Liberty had warned her about them. She quickly shuts away any thoughts of Liberty and how she betrayed them. How Grace killed her. She needs to focus on the here and now.

"You mean that brush pile was—"

"A nest, yes. The mother shot you in the back with one of her spines. That is where they get their name." His voice falls into a lecturing tone, and he seems as though he has forgotten exactly whom he is talking to. "They hunt by flinging the spines on their tails into their prey. Each spine has a very powerful venom, as I'm sure you noticed. Thankfully, it usually isn't potent enough to kill. But you are young, and there may still be side effects. So if I may?"

He motions toward her, and Grace nods hesitantly. His hands are gentle as he guides her to sit on the edge of the bed, her chained wrists in her lap. Grace hunches down on herself, partially to keep up the act, but partially because any motion is painful.

"Now, are you experiencing any pain?" he asks, voice crisp and businesslike.

"My muscles ache," Grace tells him truthfully.

Honor nods understandingly. "It is common after a dose the size you got."

He checks her eyes, covering first one, then the other, and watching as they react to the light. Then he snaps his fingers beside each ear and blows gently on her wind feathers, waiting for the reflexive twitch as they try and locate the source of the airflow.

He moves around her, directing with gentle touches and words. Grace relaxes into the familiar routine. She has been examined by healers back in the Citadel the same way. If she closes her eyes, she can almost believe that she is back home. That Father will be waiting for her back in their rooms.

Father. Her eyes squeeze shut. She doesn't want to think about how angry he will be.

"Would you like a painkiller?" Honor's voice interrupts her thoughts.

Grace scrambles for a moment. Should she accept it? No, she doesn't trust him that much yet. Doesn't trust him at all. "No," She says quietly, not meeting his eyes.

He accepts this with a nod and taps her left wing. "Extend please?"

Grace shifts to sit sideways, unfolds the wing gingerly, and stares. The black dye clings in sparse patches, which only adds to the terrible state of her feathers. The ones that remain are ragged, and half of them are broken all the way down to the skin. What's worse, though, are the ones that are missing.

77

ASCENDANT

Five out of six of her primary feathers, the ones mainly used for flying, are gone. There are gaps in her secondaries as well, and patches of coverts. Frantically, she unfolds her other wing, hoping against hope that it will be in better condition.

It isn't.

Only four of her primaries are missing from this wing, but it looks worse because the gap is between the one on the leading edge and the one right before her secondaries. There are more broken feathers on this wing, some snapped nearly in half, seemingly hanging on by sheer willpower.

She can't help but look to Honor, as though he will tell her that she is hallucinating and her wings are just fine. From the look on his face, this isn't a likely outcome. "You thrashed around a lot," he says gently. "It did a lot of damage. I've been working through, but there's still a lot to be done. They'll grow back though. The damage is only to the feathers themselves."

So she won't get Sky Hunger at least.

Assuming she lives long enough. Assuming the Ascendant doesn't come for her and do things worse than damaged feathers and Sky Hunger to her. Grace shudders.

Honor's hand hovers over her shoulder as though he wants to comfort her, but thankfully he decides against it. Instead, he works on her left wing in silence, pulling the worst of the damaged feathers and pressing a rag against the spots of blood that rise up.

Grace is glad for his silence. She doesn't think she could pay attention to what he was saying while her thoughts are spinning so wildly out of control. She won't be able to escape like this, even if she could get out of the cell, out of the city, and outrun any Black-Wings.

It would be nearly impossible to get up to the ancient bridges left behind by Forest Clan without flying. Even if she did risk climbing, even the lowest bridges were a hundred feet off the ground. One slip could lead to broken bones or worse.

"Alright, that's all I'll do for now," Honor says. "Too much at once will do more harm than good. We'll give you a couple of days before we continue, alright?"

He steps back and wipes a wet rag over his hands, trying to get rid of the dye. Grace shakes out her wings and then folds them back against her body, watching Honor out of the corner of her eye.

There is a somewhat-new process in the Citadel for damaged wings. It involves inserting thin rods halfway into the shaft of a shed feather and the other half into the shaft of the damaged feather. It is difficult, though, and it doesn't usually hold up to anything more than gentle flying. Grace wonders if the Black-Wings do something similar and if she could talk Honor into doing it for her.

They would have to use Black-Wing feathers, though, even if she could convince him to all but hand over the keys to the cell. Dye is one thing, but could she really put *actual* black feathers onto her wings? Even to escape?

Her mind shies away from the idea. What if the Black-Wing feathers infected her somehow? No. She will have to wait for her own feathers to grow back and hope that she survives long enough.

Silence fills the room with Honor gone. There are no footsteps in the hallway, no voices echoing down. *What now?* Is she to be interrogated? Will Glory return to drag her off to some dark cell underground?

Will the Ascendant come?

ASCENDANT

Grace tries to control her breathing. Her eyes won't leave the door.

The thought makes her shudder. She probably will. There are no solid reports of the Ascendant, but the rumors are all equally terrible. Most agree that the Ascendant is female, that she is of Mountain Clan, and that her hair is pure white, her eyes blood red. They say she is mad, that she likes to watch things suffer, that she visits the sites of battles to watch any left alive die a lingering death.

The worst rumors say that she takes the wounded back into the Black-Wing city—the Refuge, apparently—with her. That she tortures them until they forget their own names, that she twists them into her own servants.

She wonders if even Charity fears her own heir.

Grace shakes her head as though the thoughts are physical things that can be cast away. Father will come for her, or she will escape. If they do give her to the Ascendant, Grace will break free and kill her. That will make Father proud. Maybe proud enough that he won't be angry with her for getting captured in the first place.

She huffs self-deprecatingly. That *is* a feeble hope. She has messed up too many times for him to forgive her for getting one thing right. One of these mistakes, he may have forgiven. For allowing herself to act so childishly during the trip, possibly even for not figuring out that Liberty was a traitor. Getting captured is unforgivable though. He has taught her better than this. She deserves his anger. She will be *happy* to have him angry with her if she can only get back to the Citadel.

She sighs and kicks her feet, watching them move through the air. Now that she has a plan and isn't panicking, she realizes that being captured is actually pretty boring. There is nothing to do in the room. She isn't sure the chain is long enough for her to get off the bed. If the Black-Wings are smart, it isn't, but that means that she can't even walk around. It's quiet too. Aside from her heels bouncing, there is no sound.

Grace sighs again, a bit louder. Mind-numbing terror is better than mind-numbing boredom, she thinks.

She rolls to her side, spreading one wing over herself like a blanket. She straightens the feathers nearest to her. Part of her still refuses to comprehend the absolute carnage of her wings. How could she have done that much damage to *herself*?

She had only just begun her training in the healing houses when all of this happened. Father wanted her to at least be able to perform field medicine so that she could keep people stable enough for the real healers to get to them. One of the very first lessons she'd gotten was to secure the patient's wings.

She had assumed that it was to protect *her* from the patient if they decided to fight. A wing strike could do serious damage, and a soldier with wing blades could tear a healer to ribbons. She hadn't considered that she was protecting the patient from their own thrashing.

She had actually enjoyed the lessons in healing. More than those focused on combat and strategy. The healers were generally calm and patient with her, and Father had been content to let one of his Observants oversee the lesson instead of staying himself.

When she had messed up, the healers had simply corrected her with steady voices and hands and made her do it over again. Quietly, she wishes Father were that patient in their lessons together.

She makes herself stop thinking about that before she starts worrying about what Father will do. She has more immediate concerns. She should come up with some sort of escape plan, even if she can't carry it out yet.

She's safe enough for now. Safe as she can be in a city of Black-Wings with the Ascendant lurking somewhere in it. She can afford to be patient, to gather information and make a detailed plan instead of doing something impulsive and hoping for the best.

First things first. She can't get out by making sad faces at the guards. She will need to get her hands on a weapon. The guards hadn't carried weapons with them when they came in, even though they were letting their queen into a room with her.

They weren't going to be sloppy enough to carry a weapon into her cell then, so she would have to improvise one and steal something later.

She looks at the chain around her wrists. Could she use this? If she gets it unhooked from the wall, there are a few possibilities. She can tie a knot in the end, or several knots and use it as a sort of improvised flail. She can use it as a garrote, if she can get behind someone. If it is off her wrists as well, she can ball it up and throw it into someone's chest. Grace frowns. That isn't the best idea, though it would probably work if she has the element of surprise on her side. But it will mean that she has lost the chain. If she has other options, then it won't matter. She isn't really the best with long-distance weapons, but she doesn't know how long it will be until she can steal something better.

So throwing it is out.

She thinks the flail will be her best shot. Assuming she can get the chain off the wall. Assuming she can get out of the cell. Assuming the Ascendant doesn't come for her before her wings are sky-worthy again.

No. She has to remain hopeful. She *will* escape, she will get back to Father, and this whole thing can be behind her. Everything can go back to the way it was. Grace lies back on the bed and allows her eyes to slip closed. She needs to be well rested no matter what the future holds.

***

There is a knock on the door. Her eyes open and narrow. Father never knocks—why would he, when he has the key to open the door? So why are the Black-Wings knocking? Don't they have a key as well? She certainly can't open the door for them.

"Grace?" Honor's voice comes, muffled through the door. "May I come in?"

She sits up and stares. Why is he asking? He can open the door no matter what she says, so there is no point to this. Is he trying to put her in her place? What will he do if she says no?

She makes him sit in silence for a few seconds, waiting for him to force the door open. He doesn't. As far as she knows, he stands patiently outside, waiting for her permission. She doesn't really want to see him—she doesn't want to see *any* Black-Wing, ever.

That isn't an option, though, and this will give her an opportunity to continue to cultivate him as an ally. She makes her voice soft and hesitant when she calls, "Alright."

When Honor steps into her cell, he has an uncertain sort of smile on his face, as though he is unsure of his welcome. His wings shift uneasily, feathers lifting and relaxing. He has a book tucked under one arm. Grace carefully doesn't look directly at it. She tries to read the spine out of her peripheral vision, but Honor keeps shifting.

"I thought you might be bored," he says, holding up the book as evidence.

Grace puts her persona in place. She is half-trained and captured. Terrified, but bored out of her mind. She shrugs as though she couldn't care, but gives the book a longing glance as she turns away.

Honor steps toward the stool he'd occupied earlier. *Got him.* He takes a seat, almost slouching, wings low and close to his body, wind feathers turned back, still uncertain.

She glances at him and bites her lip, pulling her wings in around herself. "What book is that?"

He brightens considerably and sits up in the stool, wings folding comfortably against his back. "It is a collection of old legends," he says as he opens it, flipping through to the contents.

Grace tilts her head. She has never read any Black-Wing legends—she didn't realize they had any. It could be interesting, and useful; Father said that there was much you could learn from a person by what they did in their free time. Old songs and stories have to fall into that category, she thought.

"There's 'The Origin,' 'The First Song,' oh, and 'The Legend of Sanctum.' That one is my favorite," Honor tells her, running his finger down the page. He looks up to her, silently asking for her opinion.

She is tempted to ask about "The Origin." What do Black-Wings think of their creation? Do they glorify their ancestors' sins? She still needs to solidify her place with Honor though. "I haven't heard the one about Sanctum before."

It's even the truth. Father has never been a great lover of the old songs and legends. They distract from the present, deluding fledglings and fools into thinking that they are in one of the stories, that they are the heroes. She has heard snatches, though not of Sanctum, but she has heard it mentioned.

Honor smiles and flips to the page. He doesn't hand her the book, and she doesn't expect him to. Books are rare and precious, not something you hand to an enemy. He clears his throat and begins in a quiet, steady voice.

In the days after the death of Abel, we were a people adrift. Leaderless and in a new land, we wandered for many months, seeking a place that we might call home. The White Mountains were too cold, the forest too deep, and the desert too dry. Many began to despair and cry out that we were being punished, that the Trinity had banished us to this place to wander for eternity. Others rebuked them, saying, "We have been spared the Flood, and you cry of outrage. We have been given a home, and you cry of injustice. Will you ask to be spared food as well? Will you be offended to be offered drink?"

Among those rebuked was a woman named Tranquility and her three children. She took these words to heart and left those who complained. She prayed to the Trinity for a sanctuary, for the sake of her children and for their children.

The Trinity answered her, "Have I not spared you from the Flood?"

Tranquility replied, "You have, but now we have no home, and my children are tired."

The Trinity said, "Have I not given you a land of your own?"

And Tranquility said, "You have, but this land is harsh, and my children are frightened."

ASCENDANT

The Trinity asked, "Are you not tired? Are you not frightened?"

Tranquility answered, "I am always tired, for I stay awake at night to watch my children sleep. I am always frightened, for my children are mischievous and I fear they will come to harm."

The Trinity smiled upon her and said, " For the love of your children, I will answer your request. For by loving them, you have loved me. Go into the desert, fly as far as your wings will take you, and there you shall find a place where your children may rest and play without worry."

Tranquility thanked him and did has he bade. At the very end of the desert, she found another great range of mountains, and beyond them was a green land. It was gentle and looked kindly upon those within it.

She returned to those wandering and said, "Come with me, for we now have a home."

They replied, "Why should we listen to you? You are not our leader."

But Tranquility said, "We have been given this land for the love of my children, and you shall all be my children in this land." And with that oath, she was turned into the first of the golden-winged Heralds.

For many centuries, there was joy in the land behind the mountains. Tranquility was a wise and kind Queen, and she loved her people as her children, as she had sworn. They created a great city at the roots of the mountains and named it Sanctum, for it was their sanctuary from the harshness of the rest of the land.

But Tranquility grew old and died, and her children began to ask among themselves, "Who among us should come after her?"

Compassion, who was oldest, declared, "It should be me. I am the greatest fighter!"

Credence, who came next, said, "It should be me! I am the most learned!"

Courage, who was youngest, argued, "It should be me! While you were learning and fighting, it was I who sat beside Mother."

And so the siblings argued, and the more they argued, the more the land turned hard against them. The people began to fight as well, for there were those who supported each of Tranquility's children.

A great war broke out in Sanctum, and its streets ran like rivers with blood, but still, none could agree on who would rule. For a century they fought, and still no victor emerged. When one sibling raised a sword against another, the ground would shift, or the wind would blow, and the strike would miss. The animals grew fierce and attacked those they had once lived alongside. The trees shifted their branches and broke the wings of those who flew through them.

Finally, Courage called his siblings together and cried, "See what our greed has wrought. Our mother was given this land for her love of us, and what have we done with it? We have fed the animals with the corpses of our people, we have watered the trees with their blood, and we have cast aside our love for one another. We have sickened this land against us and forever tarnished what was meant to be our sanctuary, for how can our people be safe here now?"

And the three siblings were wracked with shame. "What can we do now?" cried Credence.

"There is no safety for us here!" mourned Compassion.

They laid their quarrel aside and disappeared for many days, thinking and praying together. Finally, they returned to their people and said, "We have destroyed this land, destroyed this city, and we are no longer welcome in either. We must leave at once, before we are destroyed with them."

And the people followed Tranquility's children out of Sanctum and into the wild lands that they had not dared set foot in. They parted from one another. Those who had supported Compassion fled to the icy realm of the White Mountains, and they became Mountain Clan. Those who supported Credence withdrew to the darkness of the forest and became Forest Clan. And those who supported Courage stayed in the desert, guarding the way back to Sanctum so that none could return to claim the crown for their own. And they became Desert Clan. And so the land of Caelam was returned to peace.

Honor shuts the book, fingers trailing lovingly over the cover. He looks calm, at peace. Grace tries not to feel the same way. She wishes that she had heard the tale before, so that it is not tainted by the memory of where she is.

She does her best to commit it to memory anyway. She won't hear it again once she escapes, but she likes it. There is something appealing about the idea of Sanctum. Something that touches her heart. Perhaps it is the idea that peace is possible. Perhaps it is the thought that if one just loved and prayed hard enough, the Trinity would come down from on high and bless you with everything you could ask for.

It is a pretty tale, but tales are not reality. No one is going to help her. She has to get out on her own.

Chapter

6

There is no sunlight in the Black-Wing cells. In the Citadel, she always woke before first hour, when the sun rose from behind the horizon, but in the Refuge she cannot tell if the sun rises at all. She doesn't know how long she has been prisoner, but it feels like a long time—weeks, perhaps even months.

The only way to tell is by the progress of the wound from the throwing lizard and the state of her wings. The wound heals quickly, but her wings are another story. It takes Honor at least two weeks to pull the worst of her feathers since he refuses to do them all at once and they have to wait a few days in between.

She has lost nearly half of the secondaries on her right wing and several patches of coverts. There are still a few with cracked shafts, but they are healthy enough that Honor decides not to pull them and give her body even more work to do. If they get worse she'll have to pull them, but for now she's keeping as many feathers as she can. Until her wings are sky-worthy again, she is trapped in the Refuge

Honor doesn't work on her wings every day, but he visits nonetheless. Sometimes with the book, but sometimes he brings games to pass the time. She is glad for the company. Even if she didn't need him to keep her safe, the cell is disturbingly silent without him.

There is nothing she hates quite as much as the silence of the empty cell. It presses too close, reminds her of the failures she has made in the past and the punishment for them. Father rarely raised his hand against her—he didn't want to hurt her, only to make her better. To teach her what was right.

Sometimes she needed a firmer lesson than a simple lecture. It did her no real harm to be locked in the quiet and the dark, but she hates and fears it all the same.

The Black-Wing cells aren't quite the same. They're warmer, for one, and Honor brought her a candle that she can keep lit after the lantern has been snuffed for the night. It doesn't last longer than an hour, and if she decides to blow it out, then she has no way to relight it, but it is still there.

She stares at the blackened wick of the candle. It should be morning. Honor is usually here by now, but today he isn't. The guards came by and lit the lantern nearly an hour ago. Honor usually arrives about an hour after that, dragging his feet and rubbing his eyes.

Maybe he just slept in.

Maybe there's something else going on.

She waits for what feels like another hour before there are footsteps in the hall. Grace sits up abruptly. What if it's the Ascendant?

It's been weeks with no sign of the pale-haired, red-eyed ghost of the battlefield. Grace has let herself get complacent, allowed herself to forget the very real threat that lurks in the hallways.

Maybe Charity has been keeping her heir away from Grace, at least until she answers their questions, but everyone knows that not even Charity can control her heir entirely. She does what she pleases and everyone else suffers for it.

The key turns in the lock, and the door swings open. Grace holds her breath, her heart in her throat. She is so ready for the image of pale skin and red eyes that she almost misses Honor coming into the room.

In his hands he carries a tray of meat and fruit. Not a knife or shackles. His skin is a warm brown and his eyes a reassuring blue green. She sighs and can't resist pressing a hand to her chest as though that will slow her heart down.

The air seems warmer with the both of them here. The cell isn't cold—she knows this logically—but in the dread of the silence, it always seems frigid.

"Morning," he says with a smile, carrying the food over. "Are you alright?"

"I'm alright. Did you sleep well?" Grace asks, scooting back to the head of the bed as he sits down at the foot, setting the tray between them.

"As well as one can sleep sitting at a table all night." At Grace's odd look, he elaborates, "I had an idea, and I spent a good portion of the night researching."

That must be why he is so late today.

"What sort of idea?" Grace asks, putting a handful of berries in her mouth. The flavor is less overwhelming now than when she first tried them.

"Nothing terribly important." Honor shrugs and takes a slice of meat for himself. "But it was an interesting thought. Which reminds me, how old are you?"

"One hundred and forty," Grace answers honestly. Why?"

He waves the question away. "Part of what I'm researching."

"What about you?"

Honor seems almost surprised. "Two hundred and thirty."

Grace looks at him, she'd thought he was older than that from his demeanor. She would have put him at least at two hundred and fifty but now that she is looking, she can see he is only a few decades into adulthood. He has only just finished his apprenticeship. Odd, then, that he was trusted with her care.

"Did you find what you were looking for?" she asks.

He frowns. "No, I did not. Perhaps I simply wasn't looking in the correct books." He gazes into an empty corner of the room, eyes far away. His lips move as though he is speaking to himself. The silence presses against her.

Grace throws a berry at him, and it bounces off of his cheek and down into his lap. He starts and gives her a reproachful look. "I was thinking."

"And now you're not." Grace shrugs.

"Hmph." He goes back to eating. "What about you, how did you sleep?"

Grace shrugs again and avoids his eyes. "I didn't really sleep all that much. I may have caught a bit before first hour though."

"You need to sleep more. You have only just recovered." Honor reaches out to feel her forehead.

Grace allows him to feel. If she doesn't, he'll be worried about it all morning, and he'll be too distracted to read. "I think I've slept enough. And I feel fine."

Honor huffs again but settles back into his place. "Very well, but if you begin to feel sick again, do tell me."

"I will."

ASCENDANT

They finish the rest of breakfast in companionable quiet, nothing like the cold silence that suffocates her when he is gone. *He is the enemy,* she reminds herself. *When you escape, he will try to stop you. He is healing you so that you can withstand torture.* She makes herself look at his black feathers, as black as his soul. He is Fallen, and she is not.

Even so, her eyes stray to his wind feathers. Are three white feathers enough to save his soul? She wonders. A quieter part of her whispers, *Are three black ones enough to damn yours?* Her own wind feathers pull down against her wings, and she closes her eyes.

Such a thought is ridiculous. It isn't the color of their feathers that damns the Black-Wings, and besides, the three white feathers are a reminder to them, of what they lost, just as her black wind feathers are a reminder of what she could be, if she allowed herself to fall.

"Are you alright?" Honor asks, head tilted.

"Just a thought," Grace assures him. He nods, apparently satisfied, and clears the tray off of the bed. The book is still sitting on the stool where they left it last time, marked with one of Grace's shed feathers.

Honor opens the book, tucking her feather behind his ear to keep track of it. Grace bites back a laugh at the sight. As though there aren't enough of her feathers around to mark each and every page. "Any requests?"

"Would you read Sanctum again?" she asks.

"You still haven't gotten tired of it?"

"I don't think I ever will," Grace says.

He laughs, but dutifully begins the tale. She wonders what the outcasts of Sanctum thought when they first spread through Caelam. Were they afraid? To be so far from home, in dangerous territory, with no shelter to call their own?

They had each other though. Through it all, they had the people around them to keep each other safe, to lift those who fell, to heal those who were hurt.

They're both in the mood for another story, so Honor flips through the pages, looking for another one. Even Grace can't hear Sanctum twice in a row.

"Oh, here's the one about the first twins," Honor says, perking up.

Her heart skips a beat.

Grace leans forward. "Was that Mercy and Honesty or Gratitude and Harmony?" There is a hint of tension in her voice, but she hopes he will mistake it for excitement.

"Mercy and Honesty," Honor says. "You're better than me. I still get them mixed up."

Grace smiles, but she can't bring herself to feel too proud over it. Her mind is too preoccupied. "Do you think they could actually talk to each other in their minds?" she asks. Her voice sounds casual, even to her, but her heart is thumping loudly in her ears.

She hasn't had another of the strange dreams since she arrived in the Refuge, the ones where she lives as Haven. The ones where she hears Justice in her mind. Perhaps they were only brought on by the stress of her mission—she gets strange dreams all the time.

Perhaps, though, a quiet part of her says, *they were something more, something important.*

Twins are rare, and special. According to the legends, they were meant to be omens of great change. They always came in identical male and female pairs. One to represent the good things that the future might hold, one to represent the bad.

They were always said to have powers beyond that of any normal Guardian, only matched by Heralds. That tiny part of her wonders if there was something to those tales. It's stupid, and she should write it off immediately. Even if twins *were* that powerful, they couldn't overcome death itself. Haven is dead, and Justice would have no reason to send her such dreams even if he were capable of it.

"I don't know," Honor says. "In the stories they always seem to work so well together that you'd *think* they could hear each other's thoughts, but they've also been together since before birth. That might have something to do with it."

Grace hums. It isn't the answer she wanted to hear, but it isn't as though Honor has any more information than her. Perhaps he even has less.

They put the question aside to actually enjoy the story. Grace listens carefully to every word as though it might hold the answer to the quiet question looming in her mind, but of course it doesn't.

Honor has hardly finished the tale when footsteps echo through the hall outside. There are at least four people coming, Grace thinks. Which is odd—patrols are usually just two soldiers.

The patrol stops right outside of the door to her cell, and a fist pounds against it. "Healer Honor, step away from the prisoner." Glory's voice comes through the door, flat and emotionless as always.

Honor's eyes narrow, and he leaves Grace to open the door a crack. "Glory, what do you need?"

Glory doesn't answer, instead pushing Honor gently to the side and opening the door the rest of the way. His seemingly ever-present guards stride into the room and take up positions on either side of the door. They are staring at Grace with cold determination. When Grace stands, the rattle of her chain seems unnaturally loud, as though it is laughing at her. Reminding her that there is only one reason for Glory to come now, reminding her that she is trapped and unable to stop him from doing it.

Glory steers Honor into the hallway outside of the cell. They have a conversation in low voices, and Grace can barely hear them.

"…have told you that I need time." Honor's voice is the closest to anger she has ever heard.

"The decision is no longer in your hands," Glory replies. "The queen has ordered—"

"*I* am her healer, and…" Honor's voice dips below her hearing, but she can tell from his tone that now he truly is angry. Grace is surprised at the emotion in his voice. He has always been quiet and patient for as long as she has known him.

Glory's escorts shift their weight, watching her carefully. Grace jerks her wings higher, her feathers, ragged as they are, bristling and her wind feathers flaring wide.

"This is for your own safety, Honor. You have forgotten just what she is." Glory doesn't react to Honor's anger; his voice remains emotionless.

"No, I think *you* have forgotten. All of you."

Glory is silent for a moment. "The queen has indulged your research, but I cannot do the same. People are dying. Concord is tearing apart the whole of Caelam looking for her, and he *will* find her—of that I have no doubt. We must make use of her while she is here."

"This isn't right," Honor says quietly. He's buckling to pressure. Even after weeks of friendship.

Work. Weeks of work. He isn't really her friend.

"It is necessary," Glory says, and Honor doesn't reply.

This is happening. Grace swallows. Her muscles are tense, ready to fight, ready to run, but where can she go? She is chained to the wall and outnumbered, unarmed, and her muscles are weak from fatigue and recent sickness. *I don't want this.* But she doesn't have a choice.

No. She has a plan. She won't like it, but she has planned for this since the first day that she awoke in Black-Wing custody. *You can do this,* she tells herself. *Hope has been going through this just as you have, and she hasn't had Honor on her side.*

But she hasn't seen or heard of the others from the flight since she awoke. *It makes sense,* she tells herself. *You have been kept in your cell constantly.* She is alive. She has to be. Even if Hope isn't being held prisoner, Glory said that Father was looking for her, and that had to mean something. She must have escaped and gotten back to the Citadel.

When Glory and Honor step back into the room, Grace doesn't make any effort to hide her fear; she needs it. She stares at them with wide eyes, wrinkles her brow, and partially opens her mouth. *I trusted you,* she thinks, accusing Honor with her eyes.

He shuts his eyes and turns away, taking a deep breath.

She may still be able to get out of this. If the Trinity is on her side.

"Honor?" she asks, like she doesn't want to believe that he would allow Glory to interrogate her. Like she is just waiting for him to step in, to stop Glory's escorts from approaching her. Like she doesn't believe that he will betray her.

But why wouldn't he have? He is her enemy, a Black-Wing. Who knows if he is even capable of goodness, no matter how well he pretends?

It is only an act, she tells herself. *A mask to put on and take off. He hasn't betrayed you because he never had your trust in the first place. It was all fake.*

It doesn't feel fake, part of her protests. Grace shoves that part of herself far, far away.

One of Glory's guards wraps an arm around her shoulders, pressing her against his chest so she can't unfurl her wings. The other roughly yanks her wrists forward, pulling a second pair of manacles from his belt.

Grace shoots a glance at Honor, who is still standing just inside the door. He watches the Black-Wings restraining her with a pained expression. *Just another little push.*

"Honor, please!" She lets her voice crack, struggles feebly against the Black-Wing. Her heart skips a beat when he tightens his grip; she can't do anything against him. Her only hope is Honor. "Don't let them do this! *Please!*"

"Stop," Honor commands, stepping forward.

The relief that floods her veins isn't an act. The guards pause and look to Glory. Grace follows their gaze. There is a tiny wrinkle on Glory's brow, a slight tightening around his mouth, as his eyes narrow.

What is he thinking? Her eyes dart to his wings, but his feathers are still and lie flat.

Honor approaches her slowly, wings held slack and hands open. "Grace, it's alright. They won't hurt you, I promise." His voice is quiet, gentle, reassuring.

"Why would I believe that?" Grace asks.

"I'll come with you. I won't let you come to any harm," he promises. Grace tells herself the feeling rising in her chest is victory, not gratitude.

"*Healer* Honor," Glory snaps. "You have other duties to attend to." There is a touch of disapproval in his tone.

"My duty is to my patient," Honor replies, turning to face the Queen's Guard. Glory says nothing, but his chin dips slightly. Honor turns back to her. "Will you trust me?"

Grace looks away from him, bites her lip and rustles her feathers, squeezes her eyes shut and nods. She tells herself it is part of the act. It doesn't really matter if Honor is there with her or not— he is a Black-Wing as much as Glory is. He isn't really her friend

"Thank you," he says sincerely, meeting her eyes when she looks back to him. He takes the manacles from the guard and gently fastens them around her wrists. They release her from the wall, and Honor guides her to the door with a hand on her arm. Glory walks ahead of them with the two guards at her back, but Grace doesn't feel afraid.

Grace keeps her body small and withdrawn through the long corridors, shoulders rounded and wings curled in around herself. She keeps her eyes on the floor, counting her steps. Fifty from her cell to the first corner, turn right, twenty to another locked door, thirty-three to another corner, turn right again. Her wind feathers flare wide, feeling the motion of the air around her.

The guards lead her halfway down the corridor to a closed door. The interrogation room. Grace doesn't have to force her feathers to bristle upward or her breathing to come faster. She takes a half step closer to Honor, so that his wing brushes hers. He looks over to her, pity in his eyes, and flares a wing over her shoulders as though she is a fledgling.

Glory pushes open the door, stepping into the room without a backward glance. Honor gently presses her forward, and Grace allows herself to be guided into the room. The pair of guards take up posts just inside the door, unobtrusive but able to come to Glory's aid should he call them.

Grace expects the room to be like the ones in the stories from the Citadel. Dim lights and walls covered in all manner of sharp instruments, bloodstains on the floor, shackles gleaming and gaping like hungry mouths. Instead, she finds a simple table with three chairs around it. Glory takes a seat at the far side, leaving Grace to keep her back to the door guards. Honor scoots the third chair to its own side, between Grace and Glory.

Grace sits gingerly, keeping her hands in her lap, but there are no manacles on the chair's arms, no clamps to spread her wings. The walls are blank—no empty hooks to hold knives and other instruments, only flat stone. Besides the table and chairs, the room is empty. The floor is nearly spotless, aside from a few scuffs from the chairs.

Grace looks around again, as though the room will transform into a *real* interrogation room if she blinks at it enough. Of course, it doesn't. Maybe the real rooms are the Ascendant's territory. Yes, that must be it. They wouldn't bring her there, not if Charity is hoping to get whatever answers she wants willingly.

Glory's hands are folded neatly on the table before him. A small stack of paper sits on his left, and a quill and inkwell on his right. "Let us begin," he says, taking up the quill. It is a black feather, likely one of his own, with a metal nib affixed to the end. Aside from her chains, it is the only metal in the room.

He doesn't mean to simply *question* her, does he? Grace's wind feathers flare, searching for the motion in the air that means the guards are moving, drawing their weapons, coming closer. Nothing. There is only the rhythmic brush of their breath. Far away, and steady, not like they're getting ready to rush her.

They aren't even going to threaten her?

"What is your name?" Glory asks. His voice, as always, is flat and emotionless. He isn't even looking at her, merely waiting with quill hovering over paper for her answer.

Grace almost wants to keep quiet. See what he will do if she proves uncooperative, but this will be the easiest question to answer. She will need her strength for later, when it matters that she keep her mouth shut.

"Grace."

Scritch, scritch goes the quill against paper.

"Biological parents?"

"Dame, Allegiance. Sire, Noble."

"Other kin?"

"None blood related."

"Adoptive relations?"

"Father."

The quill pauses. "Name?"

You know who he is, she wants to shout. The room is silent without the scratching of Glory's writing, and the quiet creeps around her shoulders, putting her on edge. This can't be it. There has to be a real interrogator somewhere. Maybe they will come in when she refuses to answer questions. They will have to bring all of their tools with them if so. That must be inconvenient; maybe they have a little cart to wheel around. She perks her ears, trying to catch the squeak of a wheel.

"Name," Glory prods again.

"Concord," she makes herself say. *You will need your strength later.*

The scratching resumes. "What is your place in the White-Wing army?"

She takes a breath, sneaks a glance at Honor. He is watching quietly, idly straightening feathers. He must feel her eyes on him, because he looks up and nods encouragingly.

"I am the first of a new class of White-Wing special operations, designated Saboteur." Now is when things get dangerous. They will want to know about what Father has told her, secrets and intelligence that she cannot allow to fall into Black-Wing hands.

The scratch of Glory's quill seems to run over her spine, sending chills through her body. Her feathers prickle up again, and she strains her ears, listening for footsteps outside of the room. The guards by the door still haven't moved. Grace watches her knuckles go white as she clenches her fists.

"Tell me of your training," Glory commands.

She snaps her head up. She hadn't planned for this, and she has no half-truths, no well-rehearsed lies to throw them off. Why would they want to know about this, when she has had access to all sorts of other, more relevant information?

"When did your training begin?" The question is harmless enough. She can't think of anything that they could gain from knowing how old she was when she started training. She opens her mouth to answer, but nothing comes out. She tries again, and a tiny strangled sound makes it out.

There is a high ringing in her ears. Like someone struck a bell and somehow shoved it into her skull.

Her thoughts slow, like she is trying to run through waist-high snow, and her head pounds. She rubs a hand up her face and squeezes her eyes shut. She knows the answer; she has to tell them or they will think she is resisting.

But she can't.

She has to tell Glory what he wants to know.

But she *can't*.

She tries to push past the pain, to put the ringing at the back of her mind, but it only grows louder. Her jaw works uselessly. Somewhere, Father's voice murmurs, *You must never tell anyone of your training. Do you understand, Dear One?*

A low groan that wants to be a word, be a number, makes it past her lips.

A slow pulsing pain rises from the base of her skull and slowly fills up the space behind her eyes. A high-pitched whining echoes through the room. She shuts her eyes tightly and tries to think. The world drifts into vague shadows, and she feels disconnected from her body, as though she might float away from it. At the same time, she feels too heavy, like she has been tangled in a weighted net and tossed into water, watching the last shreds of daylight fade away as she sinks to the bottom, unable to swim free.

It would be easier for her to just obey. He doesn't like to hurt her, but she must listen to him. He is her father; he loves her, and he shows that by teaching her. She must prove her love by obeying him. Doesn't she love him?

"Grace?" Honor asks.

Her eyes open, and she turns to him. He watches her with open concern, his wings neatly behind himself, giving her his full attention. She glances at Glory, who is watching as well. The quill lies forgotten across the page, but his face is impassive as always.

She lowers her hands from her face, and her skin stings when she squeezes her eyes shut again. "What?" she asks. Her voice comes out strange, hoarse and small. Her breath is too fast. She cannot make it slow down.

Glory picks up the quill again. "Let's focus on something else," he suggests. "Tell me about your latest mission."

Honor looks as though he would like to protest, but Glory glances at him and flicks his wind feathers. Glory's eyes meet hers for the first time. "How did you learn of the traitor?"

She shakes her head, trying to get rid of the phantom weight around her thoughts. As soon as she stops resisting them, the pain and the ringing begin to fade away.

"There was a prisoner. In the cells. He said something about the eastern border. But he couldn't have known about the attack— the report had only just come through. I interrupted, and Father was angry." She shudders.

She is gasping now—she needs to get control of herself. She is talking too much. She has to be quiet. Her thoughts are too light, like dreams. They float out of her mouth. Get caught up in memories and take those with them. The ringing is quieter though.

She stares down at the table, tracing the patterns in the wood with her eyes. She needs to think about something else.

"And after that," Glory says.

She doesn't look up at him, just keeps tracing the patterns. That one looks like a mountain. She imagines it is the Merciless Mountains, and behind them is Sanctum. They had prayed to the Trinity in Sanctum, and their prayers had been answered. Why didn't he come for her? Why didn't he end *this* war?

"What happened after that?" Glory asks again.

"I was summoned to the palace. I was going to be late. Father was there, and so was Justice. He was angry…so angry…because of his sister. The Black-Wings killed her. Father said so. I wasn't supposed to be there. Justice made me come."

"Did Concord know Liberty was a traitor?" Glory interrupts her.

She is still talking too much. She shakes her head, trying to clear it, but it doesn't work. "No," Grace says. "None of us knew. She betrayed us though. She betrayed us, and I killed her." Her eyes burn with tears, even though she shouldn't cry over a traitor. Liberty was on her way to becoming a Black-Wing. Would her wings have actually changed color?

"I killed her," Grace says again. The image of Liberty's face, so open when she looked at Glory, her hands so gentle when she touched him. She had mentioned being having a partner. Was it Glory? Had they been in love? Was that what love looked like?

Like gentle hands and open faces. Not Father's stony mask, his harsh words.

The quill scratches against the bottom of the page, and Glory blows across the paper, drying the ink before setting it aside. She watches his hands, but she can't make herself look any further than that. If she looks, she will have to see his face, his wings, the blank expression he wears. Like the one Father has when he is angry.

They sit in silence for a long moment. As Grace stares at the patterns in the table, she feels Glory's and Honor's eyes on her. She doesn't look up. Perhaps hours later, perhaps only minutes, Glory clears his throat.

"I think we're done for now," he says tonelessly.

"Wait," Grace says.

Glory pauses.

"Please, I've cooperated. Tell me what happened to Hope."

He is silent for a long moment, and she thinks he won't answer, then: "I'm sure you'll be pleased to know she escaped and promptly informed Concord of your whereabouts."

It should be a relief, to know that Father is coming for her. Part of her is surprised that Glory would tell her, but part of her suspects that he is lying. Why give her hope? Unless he knows with absolute certainty that Father will not find her, which may be true, since the Refuge has managed to hide from him for so many centuries.

A small part of her mind hopes that Glory is right, that Father will never find her, that she can hide from him forever. He is going to be so *angry*. And what about Hope—had he punished her for not returning with Grace? Perhaps she had survived the Black-Wings, but could she survive him? A shudder runs down her spine, and her mind cannot let go of the thought of his rage.

"Grace?" It is Honor.

She cannot make herself meet his eyes. "I would like to go back to my cell now." Her voice is too quiet, and if the room were not nearly silent, she isn't sure either of them would have heard her.

"I think we can manage that," he says.

Grace nods her thanks and gets up. Her mind keeps circling back to how angry Father will be when she returns. If she returns.

Another shudder makes her feathers fluff upward as though she can physically ward off the cold of Father's anger that she can always feel, no matter how far away he is.

She forgets to count her steps on the way back to her cell, and she seems to get there far too quickly. Honor gently fastens the shackles back around her wrists, chaining her to the wall once again.

"Are you alright?" he asks.

"Fine," she answers automatically. Sometimes, it feels wrong that she should be so afraid of Father; she loves him, and he loves her. That is why he must be so harsh—*strict*, not cruel, just strict— with her training, to make sure that she can survive on the battlefield. Because the world *is* cruel, because the Black-Wings are cruel.

"Do you think you could handle a visitor?" Honor's voice once again pulls her from her thoughts. She looks up at him and then blinks. At some point, while she was lost in thought, a forest cat appeared in Honor's arms. She blinks again because it is a ridiculous image.

The cat is still there. Her brow furrows.

A smile touches Honor's lips. "His name is Solace. He's mine, but he makes good company, in case you didn't want to be alone." He lowers the cat to the floor, and it sends him an offended look over its shoulder, as though it can't believe that it has to walk on its own feet. "I've been training him to carry messages. He's very good at finding people, though he doesn't really like to. Mostly he just wanders off for a nap."

Solace crosses the short distance between them and eyes her speculatively, then launches himself onto the bed beside her. Hesitantly, Grace touches a spot on top of his head that is almost sword shaped. Solace chirps and presses his head into her hand, closing his eyes contentedly.

"He likes you," Honor says, laughter in his voice.

"Thank you," she says to him, because she really doesn't want to be alone.

Honor dips his head in acknowledgment. "I'll see you later," he says, and closes the door behind himself. The lock clicks quietly.

Chapter

7

"What does it mean?"

Haven is beginning to fear that question. She considers never going outside again if it means she never has to answer it again.

On a purely logical level, she understands. These are chaotic times, and the stability everyone was hoping for still hasn't come. In fact, things are even more uncertain now. This woman, and all the other people who have come to her with the same question, are simply seeking reassurance from the only sources they believe they can trust.

On an emotional level, however, she wants to tear her hair out and scream that she doesn't know either. That she is just as lost as everyone else. But she can't, because she is a twin and she is married to Endurance and she is one of the only certain things these people have left.

She opens her mouth to give another empty platitude when Valor rounds the corner. She nearly sags with relief as the woman turns to Valor. "My lady," she says, dipping her head respectfully

Valor gives the woman a perfunctory nod in return, her face a stony mask. There was a time when she would have offered something more, a smile, a kind word or a gentle touch. Now all she says is, "Do you need something?" Her tone isn't quite cold, but it is far from warm.

Haven feels a pang in her chest. Of all of them, Valor was closest to Clarity, beyond even her guard. The death of their queen affected all of Caelam, but it shattered Valor.

"My lady, what are we meant to make of this?" the woman asks, not too put off by Valor's tone, though Haven is. Perhaps it isn't as obvious to those who don't know her. "Is Endurance not our king? Is the court seeking a new Ascendant?"

"Of course he is your king," Valor snaps. "The court has chosen him, and we stand by our decision." She glares at Haven as though she is the one who put such a thought in the woman's head. "There are simply other factors at play."

She moves as if to walk away, but the woman reaches out and catches her by the arm. "What factors? Does the court know what happened? Do you have a plan?"

Haven can see Valor grinding her teeth, but her voice is civil when she answers, "There are many possibilities, and we are preparing for them all. It may be that there are more Fallen in the city. If you'll excuse me, I must be on my way." She snatches her arm from the woman's grip and stalks away.

Panic spikes in Haven's gut, and she darts forward before the woman can leave or take Valor's words too close to heart. "I'm sure there are many possibilities," she says, "and I'm sure the court is looking into all of them. Please, don't worry too much. Things will right themselves before too long, as they always do. The Trinity has a plan for us all."

111

The fearful light in the woman's eyes dims a bit, and she smiles at Haven. "I imagine you feel that more than most," she says.

Haven forces her face into an easy smile. "I do."

There is still a hint of worry in the woman's face when she leaves though. They part ways, and Haven finds herself darting after Valor, a spark of annoyance burning in her chest. She manages to catch up with her before she descends into the courthouse, and puts a hand on her shoulder. "Valor!"

Valor turns to her, glare on full display. "I have things to do, Haven." She jerks her shoulder away, and Haven feels a pang of hurt, just as quickly smothered by another wave of annoyance.

"Valor, stop." She winces at the shocked hurt in her own tone. Now isn't the time to deal with their fractured, fading friendship. There are more important matters at hand. Valor stops, acting as though she is doing Haven a great favor.

"Did you mean that," she asks, "what you said about the Fallen?"

Valor is grinding her teeth again, her wind feathers pinned back. "They need someone to blame while keeping their loyalty to the king secure," she says, as though she is talking about how to train forest cats. "Allowing them to believe that there is another Fallen in the city will unite them."

Haven resists the urge to stumble back as though she has been punched in the gut, though it feels like she has. "You can't just lie to them!" she hisses.

"I will do what is necessary to keep our people together," Valor snaps in return. "There is every chance it is true. I only presented it as a possibility, not fact. Do not accuse me of exaggerating, Haven. We all know what the truth was the last time."

This time, Haven does flinch back, and Valor takes the opportunity to jerk the door of the courthouse open. Her apprentice is waiting for her there. "My lady," he murmurs, his head low and voice sullen as always, his blue eyes flash in the light.

"Come," Valor snaps. "We don't have all day."

They slip down into the courthouse, leaving Haven gaping in the hallway.

Haven? Justice asks. She can feel his confused concern. *Is everything alright?*

I...yes, she replies. *I don't know. I was talking with Valor.*

Oh, Justice replies. She feels his understanding brush against her hurt, soothing it a fraction.

She shares with him the memory of what happened with the woman, and Valor's response to her own questions. Justice is quiet for a long moment, but she can feel his indecision on the matter.

You can't possibly agree with her! She allows him to feel her reproof.

Technically, she didn't lie.

But that was the only solid answer she gave! People will take it as truth. You know how things get twisted when people talk.

She feels his resigned frustration. *I know,* he thinks to her, *but it isn't as though we can start countering what the court says. People are looking to us as much as to them for security.*

That doesn't make it acceptable to lie to them, she replies. She knows he can feel just how much she resents that he is right, but he offers only wordless sympathy in return.

We don't know what the truth is, he tells her. *Anything we say could be a lie. At least this one keeps people together. They will trust the court to find any Fallen.*

It doesn't make her feel any better, but it isn't as though he has any more answers than her.

***

113

Grace wakes with Haven's phantom annoyance and despair lingering in the back of her mind. Or perhaps it is her own emotions. She had thought the dreams were gone, that they were only a figment of her own mind, that they had stopped.

Now, it seems, they are back. She sits up and rests her head in her hands. Solace makes a muffled complaint, but she ignores him. Now there isn't anything for her to distract herself with to avoid thinking about the dreams.

Are they a sign from the Trinity? Some hint about her current situation? Some lesson or warning? Or were they really only dreams? Strange, inexplicable dreams filled with people she's never heard about, never met. Dreams that seem to confirm rumors and stories she has heard all her life.

The death of Clarity at the hands of the Fallen, the Black-Wings before Justice had ripped away their disguise. The mental bond that Haven and Justice have as twins. Should she believe that the dreams are true because they confirm these stories or doubt them because of it?

She wants to pace; she wants *answers*. She wishes that she had these dreams before the mission began, so she could ask Father about them. Surely he would know?

Why would he? It isn't as though he is an expert at dreams. The only one who could confirm that the dreams were real or not would be Justice himself. She shudders at the thought of facing him again. Surely if only *discovering* a traitor was enough to make him suspect her of her own treachery, then coming to him with impossible information would be far, far worse.

That's assuming the dreams are real, that they mean anything.

She growls and rakes a hand through her hair. This is impossible. There are no answers for her to find. She can only chase her own thoughts around in circles.

A knock at the door breaks her from her thoughts. Grace resists the urge to sigh and tosses the blankets aside. Solace watches her with half-lidded eyes, his feline face disapproving, as though it is *her* fault that people are knocking.

Grace breathes deeply and wishes for her room back in the Citadel. It is always cold, a persistent chill that nipped at her no matter what time of year, but it is home, where she is safe and Father is never far.

Someone raps their knuckles against the door again, and Grace pushes the longing aside—it will do her no good. She doesn't think it is Honor; his knock is different, more casual and less crisp.

"Come in," she says before they can knock again. It's not like she can really keep them out, anyhow.

The door opens, and Glory steps through, regarding Grace with his trademark neutral expression. The effect is somewhat lessened when Solace springs from the bed and leaps to his shoulder. The cat's long tail hangs down over Glory's pristine uniform, and she can already see a few hairs sticking to the dark fabric.

"The queen requests that you join her for breakfast," Glory says shortly.

Grace feels her heart leap into her throat. Had she been too free with her answers? Does Charity suspect some sort of trick? If she does, what does she plan to do about it? There is only one way to find out. "I suppose we shouldn't keep her waiting then."

Glory's guards advance cautiously, and Grace regards them the same way. Without Honor here to keep the peace this time, either party can decide to attack. They pause just out of arm's reach, and one of them puts a hand to his waist, as though he is searching for a weapon. It isn't there; they have been cautious about allowing her near possible tools or opportunities.

This is going to take forever. Grace hesitates, but in the end she is going to see the queen one way or another, and she would rather not start out with bruises. She holds her hands out away from her body.

Taking the peace offering as it is, the Black-Wing guards fasten the second pair of manacles around her wrists and unlock the first set, freeing her from the wall. Once again, they lead her down the hallway to a second locked door. This time, she is directed to the left.

The trip this time is shorter, and the room they bring her to is larger.

Like the interrogation room the day before, it is empty except for a sturdy table. The table is bigger, with room to seat six instead of four. There are only two chairs, and Charity sits at the head of the table, regarding Grace calmly. Grace doesn't meet Charity's eyes, but keeps her body small and only sneaks glances at the queen.

"Welcome," Charity says. She seems calm, like the surface of a lake, but there are cracks in her mask. Her hair isn't quite perfect, and there are faint shadows under her eyes.

She looks tired.

What could make *Charity* so tired that she shows it even this much to Grace? If she was so tired, why would she call Grace to her? Grace had assumed that Charity was suspicious about her easy answers, but now another possibility looms in her mind.

She answered their questions. All of them.

She has given away her only safeguard.

They wouldn't give her to the Ascendant while she still had information, but now Grace has given that up. Carelessly, thoughtlessly, stupidly.

What if Charity looks so tired because the Ascendant has been pushing to get her hands on Grace? Even if the Black-Wings don't trust her answers, Charity can only keep her heir in line for so long before the Ascendant does as she wishes, regardless of orders.

If the Ascendant just takes her, Charity will look weak. But now Grace that has given up her information, Charity is free to give her to the Ascendant and save face.

Grace's heart pounds as her thoughts swirl in panicked circles, like animals in a stampede. She has to escape, but her feathers have only just started growing back in. It will be days more before even the primaries, the first to grow in, are ready to fly on.

Her only defense is the persona. If she looks pathetic and vulnerable enough, maybe Charity won't hand her over. Even a Black-Wing wouldn't doom a *child* to the Ascendant's torment, right?

But there is no room for children in war.

"Have a seat," Charity invites her, motioning to the only other chair at the opposite end of the table. Grace sits, glancing up from her plate to look at Charity again. She meets the queen's eyes *accidentally* and quickly breaks the stare. Charity twitches an eyebrow but doesn't comment.

Food is laid out on the table: a fruit bowl and a plate of meat, smaller bowls of nuts beside each place, with another empty bowl beside them for the shells. It is more food than two people would eat for breakfast in the Citadel. This food would have been divided as much as possible so that everyone could have a chance to eat, if not to be full. But the Black-Wings aren't nearly so desperate for food—they won the majority of the croplands in a battle not long before Grace was born, and they have the bounty of the forest to fall back on.

Charity takes one of the pieces of fruit from the bowl. Grace glances at the bowl of nuts, but her stomach churns with nerves, and she doesn't want to throw up in the middle of a meal with the Black-Wing queen. It might help maintain her persona, but some things are just too much. To keep up appearances, Grace takes a piece of fruit for herself but only nibbles at it.

Charity cuts her fruit into pieces and takes a delicate bite, swallowing before she says, "I have not lived as long as I have by being trusting, and certainly not by trusting White-Wings."

Grace doesn't answer, only stares at the yellow fruit in her hand. She may have ruined herself; if the queen is willing to question the easy answers Grace gave her yesterday, will she question the persona Grace has adopted? Is all of this a pretense to try and get Grace to drop the mask?

Without the mask, Charity may just hand her over to the Ascendant. She may still hand her over with it, but hopefully she'll at least feel guilty then.

No. The mask will protect her. Even a Black-Wing wouldn't be that cruel.

In her mind Grace repeats, *You are scared, you have been captured by the enemy, and you don't have any way to escape. You aren't well trained enough to get out of this. You are so, so scared.*

Grace's wind feathers flare, taking in the position of the guards. They are flanking her seat, and Glory has taken up a similar position beside Charity. They aren't tensed to attack, but she keeps a part of her mind watching them with all the attention she can spare.

"It is not an easy position you have put me into," Charity says, forcing Grace to meet her eyes. "I did not accept the crown to keep a child as a prisoner of war."

There is no room for children in war.

"You could just let me go," Grace says without any real hope that it will work. She glances away from Charity, lifts the fruit to her mouth, but doesn't take a bite. She doesn't think she could keep it down even if she were hungry.

The queen snorts delicately, taking up another slice of her own fruit. "You and I both know that isn't an option. However, it isn't your *only* option."

Grace frowns. Surely Charity doesn't expect her to turn traitor, does she?

Charity nods, though, confirming the thought. "You would hardly be the only white-feathered Guardian among our ranks."

"You want me to betray the king. Like Liberty did."

"Liberty's situation was far different to yours," Charity says, waving the thought away. "She was never truly loyal to your king."

Impossible. It has to be. There can't be white-feathered Guardians who are members of the Black-Wings. There is a *reason* they're called Black-Wings,

Charity watches her with an evaluating expression. "You didn't think that their wings would change color, did you?"

"No."

Charity raises a disbelieving eyebrow. "Regardless, your situation would be different from Liberty's, but you wouldn't be the first. Honor has proved as much."

Grace tilts her head.

"He didn't mention it?" Charity asks. "I will tell you then: Honor has been scouring the archives for the past week because of you, looking for some sort of precedent for your situation. He found it too. Not truly an equal scenario, but close enough that the others accepted it, along with some other evidence. Nearly four hundred years ago, a White-Wing child was found wandering in the forest, younger than you, if memory serves, and not nearly so well trained, but still the enemy. He was taken in and listed as a prisoner of war. Justice refused to negotiate for his release, and we couldn't simply send him back out into the wilds."

Grace doesn't mean to speak, but the words slip past her lips: "What did you do to him?"

Charity looks at her, one eyebrow arched. "*To* him? Nothing. Regardless of the lies you have been spoon-fed all your life, we are not monsters. We took care of him, fed him, washed him, educated him, and he decided to join us."

He defected? Grace nearly shouts. At the same time, a different part of her asks, *Justice let them have him?*

Why would Justice have abandoned a child to the Black-Wings? What had they asked for? Had they hoped to force the White-Wings to surrender? Yes, that must have been it. Justice could not have sacrificed all of the Citadel for the life of one boy.

More likely, he wouldn't have trusted that the boy wasn't a spy. The dark fire in Justice's eyes when he proclaimed that she would go on this mission flashes through her mind.

"I see from your face that you do not intend to follow his path," Charity remarks dryly. "Which leaves the question of why you were so eager to hand information to your enemies."

120

Grace nibbles at the fruit again to buy time. She needs to come up with something that Charity will accept and that will maintain her persona. If she says that the information she handed over is not all that sensitive, they will suspect she knows more and be rougher in their seeking of it. Another half-truth then—it seems her life is made up of them these days.

"I know you have less pleasant ways of gaining the secrets I hold," Grace says quietly, not meeting Charity's eyes. Silence stretches between them for a long moment, when Grace glances at the queen out of the corner of her eye, Charity is studying her with an unreadable expression.

"You are correct." Charity nods. Somehow she looks even more tired than she did at the beginning of the meal. "But even if I were willing to use such methods, I doubt my son would allow me to."

"Son?" Grace whispers. At first, she thinks that she has misheard. The Black-Wing Ascendant is a woman. A woman with skin paler than any descendant of Mountain Clan and eyes red as hellfire.

Charity's face is carefully blank—she knows she has made a mistake.

Charity cannot afford any information about her heir getting to Father's ears, and Grace is already a prisoner. Slowly, Grace shifts in her seat, her wind feathers flaring as wide as they can go, monitoring the guards behind her chair. They haven't moved yet, but it will only take a single word or gesture from the queen to change that.

Grace's fingers carefully wrap around her fork. They weren't foolish enough to give her a knife, but a fork could stab into cooked

121

meat, couldn't it? Even if it failed, she could smash her plate and hopefully find a shard large and sharp enough to use as a weapon.

"Return her to her cell." Charity's voice is quiet but strained, and she gets up from the table before the guards have even started moving. Glory follows close at her heels. Grace allows herself to be guided up from her chair, leaving behind the barely eaten fruit as she is escorted by the silent guards.

Their hands grip her arms with near-bruising force. They know their queen has made a mistake just as well as Grace does. Their footsteps echo through the hallways, too loud in the tense silence. They leave her in her cell without a word—not that she has heard them speak before—and Grace sits on her bed, chained to the wall once more with only her thoughts to occupy her.

Why would Charity's Ascendant—her son—have cared if Grace was tortured? She—no, *he*—had a reputation for far worse things than torture. The countless tales flash through Grace's mind.

Dark magic, demons summoned from hell itself. Twisting bodies and minds beyond all recognition. Not done by the pale-haired, red-eyed girl everyone believed, but by some unknown man.

Is it Glory? War orphans are always taken in. Had Glory simply been lucky enough to be chosen by the queen? Had the rumors simply changed his pale eyes to red and his red hair to white? But the Ascendant would have wanted to watch Grace suffer. Glory had all but gone out of his way to avoid her.

But there was one person who hadn't.

The only other option slips into the back of her mind, looming over her like a great shadow.

There has been one person at her side at every available moment. One man who has been there since the beginning.

An idea that I spent the night researching, he had said. *Nothing terribly important.*

Then he had asked her, oh, so casually, just how old she was. She had thought it odd that he was trusted with her care, since he was just barely out of his apprenticeship.

Honor is the Ascendant, that much she is sure of. What she doesn't know is just what he has done to her.

Chapter

8

Why? Is the first thought that fights its way through the confusion, the shock, the hurt. *He is a Black-Wing,* the part of her mind that sounds like Father says. *He doesn't need any more reason to deceive you than that. You were foolish to ever think that he would be anything but an enemy.*

Even more for him to be angry about when she returned.

If.

If she returned. Who knows what Honor will do to her now that he no longer has to pretend to be her friend?

Grace clenches her fists tightly and grinds her teeth together. She lets the rage flow through her. It is better than the fear. It is better than the quiet, persistent hurt that bites at her heart.

Honor has probably spent every night laughing to himself about the poor, gullible White-Wing he had almost convinced to…To what? What was the point of all of this? Why did Charity allow him anywhere near her? She must have known that there was a chance of Grace figuring out the truth.

It doesn't matter if you know the truth, her mind whispers. *You're in his city, in his cell. You have no chance of escaping and telling Father. And attacking him? For all that he's put on the guise of a healer, he's probably killed more people than you've ever met.*

But *why?*

Why bother? To get her to cooperate? For his amusement?

This is simply the way of the Black-Wings. They get close, convince you that they are your friend, and then reveal their treachery. She knows how the war began, but she still fell for the same trick that Justice had uncovered.

Honor is a Black-Wing, her mind says. *He cannot help but be evil. It is his birthright.*

Her heart refuses to accept it.

She growls and paces the short distance allowed by the chains. They have kept her as a prisoner, she reminds herself.

Honor hadn't felt like a jailer, though; he had seemed like a friend.

Grace shakes her head furiously, feathers bristling at the thought. *He. Is. A. Black-Wing. That is all he has ever been, and that is all he will ever be. They don't cry over the death of an enemy, and neither do you. That is war, and that is the way it is.*

She stops pacing and takes a deep breath. She cannot let emotions take over, not when she is surrounded by danger. Once Charity gets control of her emotions and gets Honor as far away as possible, she will have to do something about Grace. Kill her, perhaps. Or maybe she'll just hand her over to Honor.

Grace feels the rage creeping up from the corner of her mind, and she forces it back. She has to think rationally about this.

Charity had devoted a good portion of their discussion to telling her about the White-Wing they had "adopted"—kidnapped, more likely. Do they intend to do the same thing with her? Keep her isolated, give her a friend, hide the facts of the war, until she forgets that they are enemies and becomes Honor's perfect weapon against the Citadel?

She cannot allow that to happen. She has to escape, to get back to Father, tell him Honor's identity, and gain his forgiveness, and then this can all be behind her. She can go back to training and do what she was meant to do. She sits on the bed and runs a hand through her hair.

Now all she has to do is find some way to escape from the heart of the Black-Wings' hidden city. She wants to laugh at the hopelessness of it. The Black-Wings take no chances; they won't give her any opportunity to escape. Likely they will drug her and move her to another cell, if Charity doesn't decide to kill her outright.

She takes a deep breath and leans back against the pillow. Her eyes slip closed, and just for a moment, she allows herself to feel hurt, to feel shocked that Honor would betray her. Then she forces herself to accept that he did and move on. It doesn't work, but she grits her teeth and shoves the emotions back down to the base of her skull so she doesn't have to think about them.

The silence gathers around her, and her feathers prickle. Even though it is warm in the cell, she almost feels a chill sweeping up her body. A tiny sound, the echo of an echo, whispers past her ears, a voice, high and frightened, thick with tears: *I'm sorry, I'll do better. Please, just let me out. I can do it better.*

She pushes the memory away. Now is not the time to think of old failures, old punishments. Still, the part of her that will always fear the cold and lonely dark cannot help but cower in the Black-Wing cell.

This isn't the same though. In the Citadel it was only a punishment. Only temporary. Father only wanted to teach her a lesson; he did it because he loved her. The Black-Wings certainly

126

don't. Unless she escapes, she will be locked in this cell for the rest of her life, however short that may be.

She is left alone for the rest of the day. The guards don't even open the door to bring her meals; instead they shove them through a gap in the door. Grace doesn't touch them, not when Honor has undoubtedly drugged them. The smell is tempting though. She barely ate anything that morning, and when the evening meal comes, the scent of the hot food makes her stomach groan.

She ignores it and sits calmly on the bed, legs folded under her, hands on her thighs. She loosens the muscles of her shoulders and closes her eyes, lets the temptation drift by her without acting on it. She breathes through her mouth so she doesn't have to smell the food. She is used to going without; this will be no worse than the times before.

Grace only manages a light doze that night. In the twilight of sleep, her mind keeps dredging up old scraps of dream-memories. A cold, long-fingered hand on the back of her neck. Father's cool, calm voice in her ear. Darkness, cold, Father's voice tight with rage.

Her jaw clenches, and her fingers twitch into a fist. She wants to pace, but she restrains herself—she will need to keep her energy up for the days to come. She breathes deeply and tries to go back to sleep.

She is woken by the scrape of wood over stone. The scent of porridge fills the room, and her mouth waters. Such a meal was a special treat. The farmlands along the river that the Black-Wings hadn't taken over were mostly used to grow food for the herds on the other side of the White Mountain. Wasting such precious space on grain wasn't often done.

Despite herself, she breathes deeply through her nose and detects a faint sweetness to the scent. *It is drugged,* she tells herself firmly. *Or poisoned.*

127

ASCENDANT

It would be worth it, part of her thinks. She shoves the thought away.

It would not be worth it, no matter how good it smells. Her eyes dart to the small gathering of plates and bowls by the door. There is a little pile of fruit on top of the porridge. Her stomach groans longingly.

She ignores it and closes her eyes. She knows the Black-Wings' plan now, and it will not work. They may try to put her off her guard by being kind and gentle, but she won't fall for it, and then she'll escape and get back to Father.

And what will he do? asks a shadowy corner of her mind. *Do you think he'll be gentle and kind when he learns how much of a fool you were? You let yourself get captured, you let yourself believe that you could be friends with a Black-Wing, with the Ascendant of the Black-Wings.*

She ignores the voice. Father will understand. Perhaps her training will intensify, but that will be good. She doesn't ever want to face being captured again. He will be proud of her for discovering the identity of the Black-Wing Ascendant. A smile crosses her lips. If she can just escape, then everything will work itself out. All she has to do is get back to the Citadel, back to Father.

***

That evening, the door opens, and the creaking hinges jerk Grace out of her half-formed plan of escape. Glory stands there, looking down at the abandoned food with his customary blank expression.

"You are not eating," he says.

Grace doesn't answer. She closes her eyes and turns away again, but her wind feathers stay up, in case he comes closer.

128

"Why?" Glory asks after a few moments.

"I'm not letting you drug me," Grace says.

"It isn't drugged."

She gives him a flat look. His wind feathers twitch backward, an annoyed gesture, then he resettles his coverts dismissively.

"You will have to eat eventually." The door locks behind him with a click.

Grace sneers after him, but she knows he is right. Eventually, she will have to eat, or she will be too weak to fight them when the time comes. She looks over her wings, at the nearly sprouted primary feathers. If she can just hold out long enough for them to grow in, she can fly.

It won't be pretty. With the other gaps only half-filled, she'll fly worse than a fledgling. But her escape doesn't have to be pretty, it just needs to happen.

Dinner slides in through the gap, pushing the other meals further in. Fresh fish and fruit. She ignores it and tries to sleep.

"You are being needlessly stubborn," Glory says in the morning. Grace doesn't bother to respond. "You will eat," he says, voice low, "even if I have to force you."

She whips around to glare at him. He is still standing in the doorway, another bowl of porridge in his hand. "I'd like to see you try," she says in the same tone.

He leaves again.

She pays more attention to the footsteps in the hallway after that, because Glory could very easily follow through on his threat. There is nothing to stop him from bursting in with guards to hold her down.

Grace shakes her head and tries to think of a way to escape. She cannot get out until someone unchains her from the wall. They will eventually move her to a more secure cell—she is certain of that—and it will be hard to fight her way through the guards, but if she can get out into the hallways and find some way out of the Refuge, she has a chance.

***

"What are you writing?" Haven asks, perching on the corner of his desk.

Endurance shifts a wing to block the page. "Nothing."

"If it's nothing, then why are you hiding it?" she asks, feeling playful for what feels like the first time in weeks. She tries to pull his wing away, but he closes the journal and slides it to the opposite side of the desk.

"Nothing important to you," he says, a hint of laughter in his voice too.

She gasps, mock offended. "I am your wife. Everything you do is important to me."

"You said something very different when it was your turn to cook," he retorts, dodging her attempt to lunge across the table. They overbalance the chair and both end up toppling to the floor with shrieks and laughter.

"Give it!" she commands, lunging for the book again. He scrambles to his feet, holding it over his head.

"I am your Ascendant!" he squawks as she trips him with a sweep of her wing.

"Two days and you're already using your title against me," she mourns. He snorts and is distracted enough that she manages to

130

snatch the book from him. She spins as he tries to grab it, then holds him at bay with arched wings and tries to read at the same time.

I have known this day would come since the queen's untimely death. There are few other options for Ascendant besides myself. Still, even I almost have a hard time believing that the court has chosen me to be king.

I have decided to keep a personal record of my reign to pass on to my own Ascendant when the time comes.

The mention of Clarity nearly sobers her, but this is the first time she has felt truly lighthearted since her death, and it doesn't fade easily. Endurance snatches the journal back, grumbling as though she has greatly insulted him.

Haven laughs and follows him back to his desk, where he rights the chair and resumes his entry. "You're being arrogant, you know," she says, laughter still in her voice, as she watches his quill move across the page.

Haven says that I am being arrogant, but she is also laughing, so I'm not sure that I believe her.

"Don't write that!" she laughs, shoving his shoulder. She can see him smiling as he continues writing.

She is telling me not to write this. She—

She snatches the journal from him again, and the quill. She only has the chance to write half a frantic sentence before he steals it back from her

Endurance is a liar of the highest degree. You must not believe anything he writes

in this book. It is all terrible lies—

Endurance snatches the book away, laughing. She lets him keep his prize and crosses the room to lounge in a chair of her own. Endurance smiles faintly as he writes, and she commits the expression to her fondest memories. The curve of his mouth, the arch of his wrist, the way the light glitters against the black feathers of his wings.

***

She nearly shoots out of bed. The faces and features of the people in the dream-memories usually faded quickly, but the image of Endurance's black feathers burns in her mind as though it is permanently branded to her memory.

Her mind spins, trying to put the pieces together.

If the dreams are real, then is Endurance the one who murdered Haven? Was that the purpose of the dreams? To warn her away from trusting any Black-Wing, no matter how friendly or kind they seem?

It's far too late for that warning now.

Something scuffs in the hallway outside of her room. Grace sits up, wind feathers searching the darkness for any hint of motion. Nothing. The lock clicks, and the door swings open, flooding the room with light. She expects Glory, come to make good on his threat, but it isn't him.

It's Honor.

Grace blinks at him for a moment, almost convinced that the light is playing tricks on her. She glares at him when she realizes that Honor really is in her cell. "I thought your *mother* would have carted you off by now," she says, her wind feathers folding back.

Don't let him know you're afraid. He would probably like that. She summons up the cloak of rage. She can be angry, but she will not be afraid.

"She would agree with you," Honor says. His voice is quiet, almost apologetic. Grace almost rolls her eyes at the obvious play: *I'm breaking the rules for you, you owe it to me to listen.* Her lip curls.

Honor sighs. "I know that you feel betrayed. I would too. This isn't how I wanted you to find out."

"Yes," Grace agrees, "it would be far more convenient if I never caught on to your lies, wouldn't it?" She shouldn't be talking to him, shouldn't give him the satisfaction.

"I didn't want to lie to you in the first place," Honor says. "It was the only way Mother would allow me to see you."

"Why?" she asks. "Why would you want to see me at all? Are you really so eager to see your enemy helpless before you? I should have expected as much from a Black-Wing."

A muscle in his jaw twitches, and she pushes further because she wants to see him rage, wants to see the evil that lurks beneath the kind, bookish healer who she thought was her friend. She cannot hate that man, but she can hate a Black-Wing who screams hatred back at her. "Is that why you're a healer? So you can watch people *suffer*?"

"No!" he snaps. "Why would you think that?"

"I know what you do!" Grace shouts back. "You...experiment on people. You twist them. Make them evil. Like *you*."

Honor actually takes a step back. "Is that what they say about me in the Citadel? That I'm some sort of monster?"

"It's what you are," Grace says. "And whatever you did to me to make me think I was your friend isn't going to work anymore."

"What I *did*," Honor says, his tone is wavering like he is trying very hard to control it, "was be *kind*. If you wish to find monsters, perhaps you should look closer at yourself."

"What does that even mean?" Grace snaps. She turns away from him. She cannot bear to look into his eyes as he lies right to her face. Whatever he did will wear off, but for now it still affects her. It makes her heart ache. "They were right. You are mad."

"You talk in your sleep, you know," Honor says, his voice quiet, but not calm. "Or at least, you did when you first came. You were calling for Concord. Begging him to forgive you. You were screaming, Grace." She hears him take a step closer, and she turns without really intending to. "You say he's your father, but when you call for him in the middle of a nightmare, it is to beg him not to hurt you. And you sit here and call *me* a monster."

Grace swallows hard. "He saved me," she says, voice low.

"Did he?" Honor asks. "are you really better off with him than where you were before? What about your parents?"

"My sire is dead," Grace says, "and my dame didn't want to raise me. Father took care of me."

"He turned you into a soldier," Honor argues. "Even though you are a child."

"There is no room for children in war," Grace snaps.

"Do you even know what you're fighting for?" Honor demands.

"Peace," Grace says, "an end to this war. We are fighting to live in a world without you and yours in it." Her chin lifts.

"But why? What have we done to deserve death in your eyes?"

She sputters for a moment. "You're *Fallen!*" she says when her thoughts finally get back in order. "You're evil. What other reason could there be?"

"Are we?" Honor's voice is low and quiet. "You have spent more time in my presence than any other White-Wing in all of Caelam, so you of all people should have the evidence. Am I evil?"

His eyes are fixed on hers with the same intense look that Father sometimes got, the one that made her think that he could see through to her heart and read all of the secrets written upon it. She wants to look away, but she is trapped by his gaze as surely as the chains upon her wrists.

"You've been acting," she says. "Pretending to be my friend so I'll join you."

"And Glory? He certainly hasn't tried to be your friend. Is he evil?"

"You ordered him to behave," Grace counters.

"My mother? Or do you think I can command her as well? She didn't even want me to see you, much less talk to you or befriend you. If you're right, and all of this has been an act to sway you to our side, do you not think that she would have sent in someone else? Someone besides her heir?"

Grace clenches her jaw, but he is right. It would have been logical for Charity to send in a normal soldier, or even a different healer, to gain her trust. And if, for whatever reason, it was absolutely necessary for Honor to be the one to befriend her, then why risk their relationship by hiding his true identity? Somewhere down the line, she would have figured it out, and that would have destroyed any trust between them, just as it has now.

"Then why?" She winces at the naked desperation in her voice. "Why risk yourself like this?"

"Because sometimes all a person needs is a chance," Honor says. "And I don't think you have been given many."

Grace isn't sure what she would have said, but she never gets the chance. Just as she opens her mouth, the door bursts open. Glory gives her a glare harsh enough to make her shrink back on pure instinct.

"Honor," Glory says, "I believe your mother wishes to see you."

ASCENDANT

"I imagine she does," Honor replies. He makes no move for the door.

"Right now."

"I am having a conversation."

"I believe that is the problem." Glory grabs Honor by the arm and tries to tug him away. Honor braces himself and pulls back.

"Tell my mother I will be there shortly," Honor orders.

"I'm not going to leave you here with—"

"Yes," Honor says curtly, "you are."

They have a conversation in harsh whispers too low for Grace to understand, no matter how she strains her ears. She is determined not to let this display weaken her resolve. This is no doubt more play-acting from both Glory and Honor, and she won't allow it to move her.

She grits her teeth and glares at the both of them.

Glory whirls around and stalks out of the cell, the door slams behind him, and Honor sighs. "I'm sorry about that," he says.

"Why did you come here?" Grace asks him.

"To explain things. And I was hoping that you would eat." He glances down, but the guards have started taking away uneaten meals, and there is only one dish on the floor. A cold plate of meat and bread.

Grace folds her wind feathers back and glares at him.

"Will you at least tell me why you aren't eating?"

"I'm not letting you poison me," she says.

"It isn't poisoned."

She raises an eyebrow. "Then you eat it."

Honor stoops down, picks up the bread, and takes a large bite without any hesitation. Grace leans forward, carefully scanning his face for any hint of something going wrong. She is suddenly aware that if the food *is* poisoned and Glory comes back to find Honor dead on the floor, what the queen might do isn't going to be a problem.

She knows that she is supposed to think that her death would be worth it to kill the Black-Wing Ascendant. Or that she is supposed to be afraid of dying at Glory's hand. Neither of those thoughts are what make her chest lurch uncomfortably. Instead it is the thought of Honor choking and dying just out of reach that makes her want to flinch.

She shakes her head, trying to get rid of the feeling. She shouldn't feel this way. Honor is her enemy. He isn't her friend.

"I am a healer, Grace," Honor says. There is something almost hurt in his tone. "Just like the ones in the Citadel. I have taken an oath not to hurt those who need me."

Sometimes all a person needs is a chance.

"Why do you fight?" Grace asks, before she has even processed the thought. "The Black-Wings."

Honor's eyebrows make for his hairline, he regards her for a long, silent moment. "To survive," he says quietly. "We are tired of war, but we cannot simply lie down and let Justice slaughter us all. There are children here. We fight for them, for their futures, however bleak they may be."

Children. Somehow, she had never considered that there were Black-Wing children. When Father finally found the Refuge, what would happen to them?

They will die, before they grow up to avenge their parents.

She recoils from the thought. Father wouldn't kill children, would he? What other choice would there be though? For peace to return, the Black-Wings had to be eliminated.

But to kill children...

"How do you think the war began?" Honor asks. He is still talking in that calm, gentle tone. She wishes he would stop. She wants him to be quiet, to stop challenging everything Father has taught her.

"The Black-Wings are Fallen, but they convinced everyone that they weren't. Justice learned the truth when they—you—killed his sister."

"How?" Honor asks. "How did we convince everyone that we weren't Fallen? I think that people would notice."

"You have powers," Grace says. It sounds weak even to her own ears. She has never questioned it before, how the war began. Father didn't encourage tales; they distracted from reality, and the reality was that the Black-Wings needed to be defeated.

"So how did Justice see through it?" Honor asks.

"He...the Trinity granted him the clarity to see through your lies."

"Why only him? Why thousands of years after these lies supposedly took place?"

"It isn't my place to question the ways of the Trinity."

"The Trinity, or your king?"

"What are you trying to prove?" she snaps. She wants to get up, pace around the room. She wants to scream and make Honor leave, but he sits on the bed beside her. She can feel the warmth radiating from his skin.

"I want to show you something," Honor says. There is something hesitant in his face, but it is overshadowed by determination. "It is a journal, written by the king before Justice. You may not believe me, but I swear to you on my wings that it is real."

Grace's eyes widen. To swear on your wings was not an oath taken lightly. She had only heard it sworn a few times in her life. The last time had been a man accused of treason, and the oath had made even Justice reexamine the evidence.

"I'll read it," she says quietly. There is a feeling in the air, a tension hovering around her shoulders, like the air before a storm. The book Honor hands her is old. The cover is singed, as though it were in the Great Library and only just escaped from the fire.

Her hands brush over the cover, and her heartbeat roars in her ears. She knows this book. Knows the feel of it in her hands.

She has held it before.

No, not me, Haven.

She opens the front cover and squints at the slanted script on the half-burnt page.

Chronicles of the Reign of Endurance

Ascendant to Clarity

She knows that handwriting, saw it in her dreams. Her breath comes faster at the thought.

This isn't possible.

A pit of dread grows in her stomach, but she still turns the page. She has to know.

I have known this day would come since the queen's untimely death. There are few other options for Ascendant

139

besides myself. Still, even I almost have a hard time believing that the court has chosen me to be king.

I have decided to keep a personal record of my reign to pass on to my own Ascendant when the time comes. Haven says that I am being arrogant, but she is also laughing, so I'm not sure that I believe her. She is telling me not to write this. She—

There is a long streak of ink, and then there is writing in a different hand. Neater and smaller than Endurance's.

Endurance is a liar of the highest degree. You must not believe anything he writes

in this book. It is all terrible lies—

The ink smears again and Endurance's handwriting returns.

She remembers them writing those words. Remembers Haven play-fighting with Endurance over the journal, remembers their laughter.

Tell me this isn't real. Tell me there's something wrong, something different.

Haven has surrendered my journal, and we have come to an accord. I will not write down any of her mistakes, and she will not take the journal again. I have not asked her how she intends to make sure I do not if she isn't allowed to take it from me.

That is a good first lesson, I think. To my future Ascendant: Your spouse is your greatest ally. Haven is calling me away now, I shall have to continue this later.

There is another entry in Endurance's writing on the next page. Her hands shake as she flips the fragile paper.

To my Ascendant:

Today is my third day as Ascendant. I regret that I have missed a day. You will have to excuse the oversight, for the day was so busy that I feel I was pulled in sixteen different directions.

There are so many things to keep track of now. To be honest, most of them don't seem entirely necessary for me to keep track of personally. Why should I care about disease among the livestock? I can hardly go out and heal each and every sick animal.

Thankfully, Lady Valor agrees with me. She has agreed to have her staff handle some of the smaller issues. I will have enough to keep track of without having to watch out for every tiny detail of my kingdom.

I fear being king will be more tiresome than I was anticipating. Still, for the good of my people, I will shoulder that burden.

Another page, another entry. She doesn't think she's breathing anymore. Honor says something, but she can't hear him over the jumble of her thoughts.

To my Ascendant:

Another day come and gone. There were fewer pointless things for me to deal with today, thankfully. Lady Valor is truly the best ally I could ask for. With her support and through it, the backing of the rest of the court, my Trials shall be a simple affair.

I imagine that I should be worried about presenting myself to the people, but they have supported me since before I was named Ascendant. They will hardly stop now. They know that I am their best choice. Haven says that I am being arrogant again, but it is simply fact. How can that be arrogant?

She says that I'm not supposed to *agree* with everyone when they say it.

She could just stop reading over my shoulder if she doesn't want me to write down everything she says.

I must leave this entry as it is for now. Haven insists that I invite her brother for dinner. Another lesson for you, future Ascendant: Ensure that you can live with your spouse's family.

Haven, of course, is perfect in every way (though I will admit that I am biased). Her twin brother, however, is a sullen sort. Determined to disagree with me on every available front. I am tempted to point out a sheep and call it white to see if he will declare it black just to disagree with me.

I think he is jealous that he no longer has sole claim to Haven's heart. No one can claim to truly like Justice; Haven has always been the twin that people have liked the best. She is kind and gentle, beautiful and patient. Justice is more likely to spit on a person than he is to help them up.

He is near inseparable from Reverence's student. Why the court would let the student of any Fallen, much less one responsible for the death of the queen, live is beyond me. Lady Valor has made no secret that she resents being charged with Concord's education. They say that Concord was as much a victim of Reverence as Clarity was, but one of them is alive and the other is dead, so I find it hard to believe.

142

I must go. Justice has arrived.

Father. She knows in her heart that it is him. She remembers Valor's apprentice from another vision. A man with pale hair and blue eyes. Father was there, Father was Lady Valor's apprentice. And before her, he'd been apprenticed to a Fallen.

Her stomach churns, and she feels she will be sick, but she has to finish this first.

To my Ascendant:

As I expected, my Trials have gone smoothly. The people are glad to have me as their king. There were a few who spoke against me, but they are simply holdouts from Clarity's reign, unwilling to move on and accept that she is dead and so is the past.

They will see soon that I am just as good a king as she was queen. Better perhaps. I certainly won't let myself be ambushed and killed in my own throne room. Our people do not need a poet to lead them; they need a warrior. I will lead us to greatness.

I hope your Trials go as smoothly as mine, future Ascendant. It is good to have the court on your side. It is even better to have someone like Lady Valor supporting you. Who could speak out against the word of someone wise enough to see Reverence's treachery before everyone else had even an inkling?

That is my advice to you. Make your friends carefully, and look for them in high places.

It won't be long until I am to Ascend. Mere days now that the Trials are over and the court firm in their decision.

She barely reads the words, seeking something to deny the growing certainty in the back of her mind.

To my Ascendant:

ASCENDANT

The day has finally come. In a few hours I will give my oath before the people and before the Trinity, and I shall become a Herald. I wonder if it will feel any different. Some say that Heralds can see the fabric of the universe itself.

At times like these, I find myself wishing that Clarity had not been killed. I suppose I shall find out soon, however. Lady Valor is calling me now. I shall return to finish this entry after the ceremony.

***

I do not understand. I followed all of the steps. I delivered my oath, and the people accepted it. I don't know why I didn't Ascend. I should have. I am king, the court chose me, and Lady Valor herself assured me that I was the best choice. The people declared me their king.

Why was I not made a Herald?

I did everything right. I am the best chance our people have going forward. With the state of our own city and the state of earth, they need a strong king to lead them forward. I cannot focus enough to write. I will return to this later.

She turns another page, sure that there would be some proof that Honor was lying. That the Black-Wings were evil. That the visions aren't real, only dreams.

To my Ascendant:

This is your next lesson: Our people, no matter how much they claim to love you, are fickle. Already there are those among them who have turned against me. As though it is being a Herald that makes me king. Lady Valor and the court are still behind me, at least. And Haven stands beside me as always.

Though there are calls for me to surrender the throne, I will not. I am their king, Herald or not. I am sure that soon this will resolve itself. Then they will see that they were wrong, and everything will be the way it is meant to be.

She turns another page.

To my Ascendant:

It has been several weeks since my last entry. The people continue to whine about me not being a proper king. Lady Valor stands beside me as ever, even though some of her brothers and sisters among the court have been muttering to the people about my unworthiness.

They even turn against Haven now. They say that Reverence was not the great disaster that the twins were born to foretell, that I am the true monster. I have no doubt that Justice and his pet, Concord, are behind at least part of those rumors. I don't believe that Justice would ever speak against his sister, but Concord is a cold sort.

How many times did Father tell her about how easily people could be manipulated by rumors? How many times did he tell her not to believe the soldiers' tales?

To my Ascendant:

It is not only my people who betray me. Now my own guard have raised their weapons against me. Three of them attempted to strike me down in my own rooms just this morning. Thankfully Haven was there with me, along with the few loyal guards who were able to stop them.

ASCENDANT

Lady Valor herself came to collect them. Her reassurance that I am doing the right thing is always a comfort, though I hardly need it. Soon the people will come to see that I am their rightful king, and I will be made Herald as I was meant to be.

They have always harbored resentment for me in their hearts. They might have spoken my praises, but they were not the truth written on their hearts—that much is clear. The best I can do is be patient and wait for them to realize that they are wrong.

She skips several pages ahead. The proof must be further in. There must be something.

Justice and Concord are getting bolder with their rumors. I want to send them both away, but Lady Valor has advised me against it. It is better to have your enemies close, where you can keep an eye on them.

Concord, at least, has made absolutely no attempt to disguise his resentment toward me. I wish now, more than ever, that he had been put down like the mad dog he is when his teacher was killed.

More pages flutter past her fingers.

It has been months since my last entry. I find it impossible to find the will to put quill to paper. It is impossible to write my emotions in ink when I feel as though I have none. My wife is dead. Ripped from me in the very garden where I met her.

Lady Valor insists that I remain on the throne, and I shall, in Haven's memory. They may have taken her from me, but they cannot take the throne.

146

***

Justice has returned to court. He has been in the healing houses for months. They say that he simply stopped responding. That he fell as a puppet with its strings cut the very moment Haven was killed.

He is mad now, I think. He blames me for her death. As though I don't feel the same pain that he does.

Endurance's wife. Justice's sister. Dead.

Just as Father told her.

Just as she had seen in the vision. The arrow piercing through her stomach as she was about to share some good news with Endurance. The pain, the darkness. Justice screaming in her mind.

Justice left mad in the wake of it.

Just like Father said.

She, perhaps better than anyone aside from Justice himself, knows just how connected their minds were.

She skips more pages.

He comes to court every day to rant at me. I cannot bring myself to care. None of the guards seem inclined to stop him. Perhaps they think this is a fitting punishment for me. Perhaps it is.

More.

Justice came to court again. He is even more mad than before. He spent nearly an hour ranting about how my feathers were a reflection of my soul.

A reflection of the soul beneath. How many times had she heard those words? Said them? Thought them? A sob catches in her chest.

This can't be the truth. There has to be something to prove that this is fake. That her life, her purpose, hasn't all been a lie.

There was a murder today. There has not been a murder since Haven. A black-feathered man, found dead in an alleyway. Rumors say Concord is responsible, but of course he has a perfect alibi.

The rest of the pages are blank. "Where's the rest of it?" she asks. She can barely recognize her own voice. "That can't be it."

Honor reaches out, gently pulls the book from her hands, and sets it on her pillow. "That was his last entry. After that…you've heard the stories."

Yes, she has. She had lingered in shadowed corners to listen to them, despite Father's orders. The Burning. A tale of victory. Of White-Wings finally ridding their city of the Black-Wings.

A story of a rebellion, noble and righteous.

A lie.

She doesn't want this to be real. She wants this to be a dream, a nightmare. She wants to wake up in the Citadel with Father just down the hall.

But when has what she wants mattered?

"Endurance survived the Burning though," Honor says, quietly, hesitantly. As though he isn't sure she wants to hear it. She isn't sure, either, but she can't bring herself to stop him.

"He led everyone who was against Justice and Concord out of the Citadel and helped establish the Refuge. After that was done, though, he left. He gave my grandfather his journal and took those who couldn't or wouldn't fight Justice to search for a place of safety. That was the last anyone saw or heard of him." He glances to her uncertainly. "Unless the White-Wings—"

Grace shakes her head. "I'd only heard his name a few times before. If he was found, it was kept quiet."

That's unlikely though. If Father and Justice had tracked down the one they thought was responsible, then they would have crowed it from the rooftops, not hidden him away.

Father lied. Pain lances through her skull.

The mere thought is almost enough to make her flinch. Even thinking such a thing feels wrong in a way that makes her gut clench and her heart race. Her ears are ringing.

Father wouldn't lie to her though—he couldn't. She is his daughter. He wouldn't lie. The pain subsides.

No, it is Justice, with the dark madness in his eyes. Justice who sent her on this mission in the first place because of his paranoia. Justice lied to Father, that was all. He had been taken in just as Grace had. Justice has lied to them all—to her, to Father, to Hope and Faith, and Amity. Even to Liberty, though she knew it.

The thought is like a punch to the chest. Liberty had known. She must have been one of the white-feathered Guardians who didn't believe Justice. Her parents must have escaped the Citadel during the Burning, and at some point they or Liberty returned as spies.

Grace had killed her.

Her and the Black-Wing soldier.

The thoughts threaten to overwhelm her, but she forces herself to keep thinking. She cannot get lost in her grief, not now. She has a mission to complete. She can almost imagine Father's voice: *Make this right, Dear One.*

I will, she promises.

Honor's arm rests hesitantly on her shoulder, as though he is unsure of his welcome. "I'm sorry," he says, as though that is enough to change anything.

"I needed to know."

"Yes, but it isn't an easy thing to learn. Do you want me to go?"

She shakes her head. She doesn't know what she's supposed to do now. She wishes Father were really here to give her this mission, to give her a plan to carry out. She'll just have to manage on her own until she can get to him and tell him the truth.

What if he already knows? part of her asks. *He was student to a Fallen. A real Fallen. What if he knows, and he just doesn't care?*

No. He isn't evil. He's her father, and he loves her. He's done his best to do what is right for her and for everyone else. Maybe he was just confused.

Maybe he's mad too. Like Justice. Seeing evil where it isn't. She can show him the journal though. Show him where the real evil is. He'll believe her—he has to.

"Grace?" Honor asks hesitantly. She realizes that she has been silent for too long. He catches her eye, and she feels something in her crumble.

"I'm sorry." She can barely understand the words herself with how ragged and cracked her voice is, but Honor seems to make them out alright. Her vision is too blurry from tears to see him, and she is glad for it. She can't bear to see his face. Not now that she knows the truth.

"It isn't your fault," he says. His hand pushes gently against her shoulder, and she suddenly throws her arms around him. She freezes, hardly daring to breathe. Honor tenses, and for a second she thinks that he might push her away, but instead he gently wraps his arms around her in turn.

Hesitantly she relaxes. Before, they had spent time together, but they'd never done more than occasionally brush hands. Now things have changed—now she knows the truth, all of the truth. She doesn't fear him, and he has no reason to be wary of her.

"It isn't your fault, Grace," he says, quiet but firm. "You were lied to by people you love, by people who were supposed to take care of you. You had no reason not to believe them."

Father has hugged her before, but they are always quick, over before she's realized that it's happening. He has whispered absolution into her hair, but she has always been to blame, has always been the one to pay the price for the wrongdoing.

Honor is gentle and warm. He isn't standing over her as a superior officer, as a father. He is beside her, an equal. Is this what it feels like to have a flight? A wing-mate to fight and fly beside you. Is this what it's like to have a brother?

She thinks she likes it.

Chapter
9

"What happens now?" Her voice is rough, and her head aches, but the tears are gone for the most part. A dull sort of numbness descends upon her. She can't make herself pull away and sit up like she thinks she probably should. Honor doesn't seem inclined to make her move either, so she stays.

"I imagine that my mother will want to talk to you again," Honor says. "After that...I suppose it is up to you."

There is really only one choice though, isn't there? She can't just ignore everything revealed by the journal and the visions and go back to the way things were before. She can't go on hating the Black-Wings and obeying Justice's every order.

Honor must pick up on her thoughts because he holds her tighter for a moment. "It'll be alright. I'll be right there with you."

"I lied to you," Grace says, because she cannot bear the guilt of that along with everything else. "About those things I said to Glory. I tried to manipulate you by acting scared."

"It isn't as though I was entirely honest with you," Honor replies softly.

"That was for your safety though."

"So was what you did. Even if we never would have harmed you, you had no reason to believe that. We both did what was necessary, and we both feel poorly for it. Perhaps it is best to agree to leave it all behind us."

She looks up to meets his eye. "Alright."

He nods firmly. "Alright."

And just like that, they are on even footing. No lies or guilt between them. No hatred and wariness.

The door of the cell bursts open. Grace flinches hard, but she doesn't move, though Honor raises his arm briefly to let her up if she wants. Glory and his customary pair of guards take up the same positions they had the first day she woke in the Refuge. After them, Charity steps into the cell.

Her eyes sweep over them and a muscle in her jaw twitches. "Honor," she says, an entire book's worth of lecture in that one word.

"Hello, Mother," Honor says pleasantly.

"Please do not *hug* the prisoner that wants to kill you." Charity sighs.

"I'm not hugging the prisoner that wants to kill me," Honor says, as though they aren't sitting close enough that Grace can feel the warmth radiating from his skin.

Charity closes her eyes for a long moment, and Grace can almost hear her praying for patience before she looks back to them. She looks even more tired than she did at the table where she accidentally revealed Honor's identity. "I see." She looks at Honor, as though waiting for him to declare the whole thing a joke. When he fails to do so, she turns to Grace.

She studies her for a long moment, eyes taking in the tear tracks that Grace itches to wipe away and lingering on the journal in her hands. Charity's face is nearly unreadable, but there is a flicker of something like relief, or maybe hope, in her eyes, quickly hidden.

"So. You no longer wish to serve the mad king, then?"

Grace doesn't allow herself to twitch at the title. Even that is a test, the first of many that she expects to be placed before her. A White-Wing soldier would never tolerate the king being spoken of in such a way.

A few hours ago, *she* wouldn't have tolerated it. Now it is simple fact.

"No. I will not serve him. His goals are evil. *He* is evil." Her hands tighten on the frail cover of Endurance's journal.

There is a calculating gleam in Charity's eyes. "Why should I believe your words? You have lied to me before."

"That was before I knew the truth. I have already had more than enough opportunity to kill your son if I wanted to. What goal could I have that would be worth setting that aside?"

Charity concedes this point with a regal nod of her head. "The journal convinced you then."

"Yes." Grace finds herself wondering just how much of Charity's "accidental" slip was really accidental. Had she really gambled her son's life on Grace believing a half-burnt journal?

Charity's face reveals nothing. "Still, I can hardly accept your defection just like that." She pauses, as though considering, but perhaps she has had this planned all along. "A trial period, then. To prove your loyalty."

To give Grace time to make a slip if she really is a spy.

"How long?"

Charity considers her. "Three months, I think."

"Mother, you can't expect her to spend three months in a cell," Honor argues. "She's already been here for nearly six."

"She may earn her way to a better room, if she behaves," Charity says dismissively. "Since you're so keen on being her ally, she will continue to be your responsibility."

"Very well."

Charity turns back to Grace. "Don't disappoint me."

"I won't," Grace promises.

"Unchain her," Charity commands.

Glory steps forward to obey, and he looks Grace in the eye the whole time while he releases her, as though he is promising her that if she betrays them, she will have him to deal with.

When Grace is freed, Charity sweeps from the room without fanfare.

Glory's guards go with her, but Glory hesitates at the door. "You're an idiot," he tells Honor.

"I know."

Glory snorts and follows Charity out of the cell, muttering to himself.

They sit silently for a moment, listening to the footsteps in the hall growing fainter. "That went well, I think," Honor says.

"As well as it could have."

Grace sighs and allows herself to slump against him. Father would never let her do something like that; at most, she could get away with holding his hand. If she were smart, she'd get herself under control before it becomes a habit, but she has always felt starved for contact. If Honor doesn't have a problem with it, she's going to take advantage of as much as he's willing to give. Perhaps it will tide her over after she returns to the Citadel to tell Father the truth.

"You should get some sleep," Honor says quietly. "I can't imagine that you've gotten much since all of this started."

Grace nods and makes herself sit up again. "You should take this back. Put it somewhere safe." She hands him the journal. She can't help being relieved to have it out of her hands. As much as it showed her the truth, she still hates it. Hates that it represents the shattering of a lie she was told her entire life.

Because of this one book, she has turned her back on her king. Abandoned the duty she thought was her birthright. She is no longer a White-Wing. In three months, she will be what she was raised to hate. She doesn't regret it, but it still brings a bitter taste to her mouth and opens a hollow place in her chest.

Honor takes Endurance's journal from her gently and stands. "I'll be back when you wake up," he promises. "Light on?"

"Yes."

When he opens the door, Solace slips into her cell, tail waving in an agitated way. Honor picks him up and scratches him behind the ears. Solace presses up into his hand with a soft meow. "Were you worried too?" Honor asks, a hint of laughter in his voice. "How many mothers do I have?"

As if offended by the comparison, Solace leaps out of his arms and crosses the room to hop up on the bed. He claims Grace's pillow as though it is his due and closes his eyes.

"If you'd like to be alone—" Honor begins, making a motion to retrieve him.

"He's fine," Grace says quickly.

Honor nods and shuts the door quietly behind himself. Grace allows herself to fall back against the free space on the pillow with a gusty sigh. Solace makes a low sound of complaint but doesn't seem to think it is worth moving. Her hands absently rub at her wrists, unchained at last. She gets up and paces the cell. It feels bigger now that she isn't chained to the wall.

She pauses, staring down at her hands and her unchained wrists. For just a moment, she allows herself to feel lost, to feel scared that everything she has ever known was a lie and now her whole life is going to change.

Nothing has really changed. She was raised and trained to rid the world of evil. All that is different now is that she has learned where the true evil lies. It still feels overwhelming though.

She takes a deep breath. Everything will be alright if she just has faith that Father will listen to her. He will fix all of this. He can set it all right. She just has to get to him and show him the proof.

She can't tell Charity, though, or Honor. They won't want to trust Father; they've spent too long as his enemies. They won't believe that he is only being lied to by Justice, as Grace was. Once she shows him the journal, though, he'll realize that Justice is wrong.

She paces back to the bed and falls asleep before her head touches the pillow.

There are no dreams.

***

The beginning of her trial period is nearly indistinguishable from her imprisonment. Aside from being unchained, her day passes in much the same way. The guard comes in and lights the lantern. A few hours later, Honor arrives with breakfast, and they spend the time until lunch reading or playing a card game. At lunch, Honor

157

slips away to attend to his duties as Ascendant and healer. He leaves her with a book or a puzzle to pass the time, and she doesn't see him until dinner. Solace keeps her company though, usually he sleeps but sometimes he can be enticed to play with a piece of loose string.

After the first week, though, things begin to change. It begins with Honor arriving at her cell—or is it her room now that she isn't a prisoner?—and offering to take her for a walk.

"Is that allowed?" Grace asks dubiously. She can't believe that Honor would try to get her in trouble, but it still seems odd. She never went for walks in the Citadel—she had no time for anything as useless as that.

"I asked Mother this morning," Honor assures her. "We won't go anywhere exciting, but I bet you could do with a change of scenery."

"I wouldn't mind it."

Honor smiles and offers her a medallion. "I don't think anyone would attack you in the Refuge, but just to be safe."

Grace takes it and loops the string over her head. Engraved on the surface is a pair of crossed wings, made silvery gray by the metal, but she imagines that they're meant to be black and white.

Honor opens the door and lets her precede him into the hall. She falls into step with him, but she soon has to loop her arm into his to keep herself from getting ahead of him. Medallion or not, she doesn't want to wander around alone in the Black-Wing city.

They don't go anywhere particularly interesting. They certainly don't go above ground. They do eat their breakfast at an actual table for once. After breakfast, Honor doesn't take her back to the cell though.

KIMBERLY GREY

"Where are we going?" she asks when it becomes clear that he isn't just taking the long way back.

"The library," Honor says. "I thought I'd let you pick out your own book for once."

"The library is underground?" In the Citadel, only the dungeons and the storerooms were underground.

"Sunlight can damage the books," Honor says with an oddly apologetic look in his eyes. Grace raises an eyebrow at him but he doesn't explain.

"Right," Grace says and drops the subject.

The strangeness of the exchange isn't enough to dampen the wonderful sight of the library. There are at least ten shelves with nothing but books on them. She has been to the burnt-out shell of the library in the Citadel. Once she thought that the Black-Wings had been the ones to destroy the books, but now she suspects that it was Justice.

The empty shelves of the library in the Citadel stretch from the floor to the ceiling, and there are ladders and stairways to get to the higher shelves. She knows that this is only a fraction of the knowledge that they once had, but it is still more books than she has ever seen in one place.

She dares to reach out and touch one of the spines. From the title, it is the journal of an explorer from the Age of Unity on exploring the forest. The one beside it is a field guide of plants and animals on the plains.

The next shelf is full of histories from earth. A thin volume containing a poem about the reign of the Great Dragon on earth. A history of the Fae Empire, mythologies and theories copied over from the humans.

159

ASCENDANT

"I want to read them all," she whispers.

"Let's start with three." Honor laughs.

"Four."

"Three."

"Five."

"Two." He gives her a challenging look.

"Three," she agrees begrudgingly.

"They aren't going anywhere," Honor assures her.

In the end, she chooses the explorer's journal, the book of the human's legends, and the poem of the Great Dragon's reign. They take a wandering route back to her cell, even though she's excited to read something new, she is tired of being caged there and not eager to return.

They pass a few Black-Wings on their way, and at first Grace is nervous. They don't seem to mind her presence, though; most barely take the time to look at the medallion hung around her neck. They offer polite dips of their heads to Honor and, at most, a small wave or smile to her before they continue on their way.

"Do you want me to stay?" Honor asks, lingering in front of the door to her cell.

"You have your duties," Grace says, but she can't quite make herself tell him to go. The silence of the cell still unnerves her, and she would rather not be in it alone.

"I have time," Honor says. "Besides, you're my responsibility, remember? You are my duties."

"Do you think you could bring Solace too?"

"Of course."

They spend a long time in her cell pushing back the looming quite with discussions and laughter. Honor attempts to show her a few of the tricks he's taught Solace and Solace watches him with undisguised boredom and makes no move to obey the commands.

After a few hours, though, Honor does have to go attend to his other duties, and she is left in the cell alone. She tries reading, but the confines of the cell seem so much smaller now that she has been allowed out of them.

Without him, Solace is quiet company and while Grace manages to distract herself by petting him while she reads, the quiet seems to creep closer and closer until it looms over her.

She paces along the far wall and hums to keep the silence out, but the memories of past mistakes still hover close around her. *This isn't punishment,* she tells herself firmly.

What if it is though? What if Charity was alright with her going on a walk but not with her visiting the library? What if she confines Grace to the cell for even longer? What if she stops letting Honor visit? What if she takes away the lamp and the candle and leaves her alone in the darkness and the cold?

What if she leaves her there forever? Father had usually only left her in the cell for a few days, and then she had been allowed to make up for her mistake. What if Charity thinks that Grace will betray them and never lets her out?

That won't happen, she tells herself. *Honor wouldn't have taken me to the library without permission.*

Would he? He hasn't really been obedient when it came to her. What if this was just one more in a long line of rules broken? What if it's the last one Charity will tolerate?

Even though it's too late to fix it, Grace sets the books aside. As though it will help that she hasn't read them. Her stomach churns dangerously with nerves, and she makes herself stop pacing to sit on the bed. It is a long day.

Honor returns in the evening and Solace paces around his feet meowing loudly. He has been agitated all afternoon as well. "My mother wishes for you to join us for dinner," Honor says, picking up Solace and giving him a concerned look.

"Is she angry?" Grace blurts out the moment she processes the words.

"Angry?" Honor looks taken aback. "What would she be angry about?"

It seems stupid to say it out loud. "Nothing." Grace looks away.

"Grace," Honor says softly. "Why do you think my mother would be angry with you?"

She almost expects there to be suspicion in his eyes, but there is only confusion and sympathy. Still she hesitates a moment longer before she makes herself say, "We went to the library. You said she was okay with you taking me on a walk, but you never said anything about the library."

Honor's eyes flick over to the books, stacked neatly by the door. "I wouldn't get you in trouble," he says gently. "If I took you somewhere that I wasn't supposed to, *I* would be the one in trouble, not you." He lets Solace drop to the floor and steps across the room to her.

When he puts it like that, it sounds perfectly logical, and it makes her feel foolish for being worried about it all day. She can't bring herself to voice the feeling, though, so she simply shrugs.

Honor sighs and puts a hand on her shoulder. "Do you want to wait to do this until tomorrow?"

"No," Grace answers immediately. Even if she isn't in trouble, it seems too dangerous to refuse Charity's request. She would never deny Father something if she was already on thin ice with him.

"It's alright if you're tired," Honor says.

"I'm fine."

He looks at her for a long moment, and she forces herself to meet his gaze and tries to make her expression confident and unbothered. She doesn't think it's all that successful, but he still sighs and says, "Alright." He motions a guard in and takes a small cloth bundle from him. In it is a simple shirt and pants and a comb and tie to brush her hair with. "I'll let you get dressed," Honor says, and he and the guard duck out of the room.

Grace dresses quickly and runs the comb through her hair. It's nice to have her hair back in her customary braid instead of hanging around her face. She straightens her shirt and takes a deep breath, willing the nerves to go away. Then she crosses the room and knocks on the door to let Honor know that she's ready.

"It'll be fine," he assures her as Solace winds around their feet. Grace nods quietly, but she can't find it in her to share his enthusiasm. He's just going to dinner with his mother. She's eating with the queen.

Chapter

10

They don't follow the same route, but Grace thinks that the room where Charity is waiting for them is the same one where she and Grace had breakfast together. It feels like that meal was a lifetime ago. Grace can barely remember what she ate. She does remember the sheer amount of food though.

There is just as much this time. The only difference is that there is a third chair for Honor to sit in. Charity is already waiting for them at the head of the table, and Honor leaves Grace's side to greet her with a kiss on the cheek. "Evening, Mother."

She smiles at him, and Grace stares.

"Good evening to you as well, my son," Charity says with warmth in her voice.

Grace wonders if there are actually two queens running around. The most emotion she has ever seen from Charity was the day she revealed Honor's identity. And Grace still isn't certain that wasn't an act.

The dignified mask of queen is only half on when Charity turns to Grace. "Good evening, little one," she says as though Grace were simply an acquaintance.

Grace dips her head mutely, too surprised to make herself speak. Charity inclines her head in reply and motions to the free chairs. "Do sit down, the both of you."

Honor pulls out the chair at the side of the table, placing himself between Grace and Charity. Grace sits at the other end of the table, and even though she and Charity are supposed to be on the same side now, she can't help being nervous.

It's stupid. She knows that objectively. Even when they were enemies, Charity had never harmed her, never even really threatened her with harm. There is little reason to believe that she will change that now.

Logic matters little to her mind, it seems.

The table is small enough that Honor can catch her hand beneath it and give her a reassuring squeeze. *You're fine,* he mouths. She nods and takes a deep breath, trying to quiet her mind. Charity has no reason to be angry with her.

"I should congratulate you," Charity says, pulling Grace from her thoughts. "You are doing very well so far in your probation."

Grace isn't sure that she's done anything particularly worthy of praise. She has mostly been doing the same thing she has done since she became prisoner. Still, she wasn't about to argue with Charity. "Thank you," she says quietly.

Charity motions for Grace to begin eating, and Grace blinks at her in surprise for a moment. Then she realizes that it is no small wonder that the Black-Wings have the same customs as the White-Wings. They are all the same people.

As the lowest-ranking person at the table, she serves herself first and passes the plate to Honor.

ASCENDANT

Father was not much of one for the tradition, and they rarely took their meals together. She has never had to share a meal with Justice, but she can't imagine him following the custom either. It was an old one, from a time well before the Burning. Grace once overheard a father explaining it to his fledglings. According to him, it was meant to ensure that a ruler remembered that they were a servant of the people, not the other way around.

She is almost surprised that Charity has applied it to her, but she supposes that if all goes well she will be one of Charity's people before the year is out. That thought makes her stomach lurch with the uncertainty of it all, so she shoves it away.

"Did you enjoy your walk today?"

A thrill of fear races down her spine, but Grace makes herself remember that Honor wouldn't get her into trouble. "I did."

Charity nods. "So long as you have Honor with you, you may leave your cell to walk with him. If you continue to do this well, you may be leaving that cell in another week's time."

Grace stares at her for a second, unsure of what to say. In the end, she simply dips her head again and murmurs, "Thank you."

"Continue to behave, and you shall continue to earn my trust," Charity says simply.

The rest of the meal is quiet and uneventful, and Grace finds herself relaxing. Honor gives her an encouraging smile when she finally starts to eat and engages his mother in a conversation about something Solace had done that day.

After that, she and Honor go for walks daily. Sometimes multiple times in a day if the cell starts feeling too small. Honor never asks about those days, the days when she walks a little bit too quickly out of the door with her eyes just a little bit too wide, but she knows that he notices. Those are the days that he loops her arm through his and takes the long way back to her cell.

True to Charity's word, after another week she is invited to dine again with the queen. Charity congratulates her for continuing to remain out of trouble and gives Grace her own room.

It's not really all that different from the cell, in all honesty. She still cannot leave without Honor at her side, and there is no window, so it must still be underground. The door isn't locked behind her, though, and she can turn the lantern on and off at will, and that makes more of a difference than she thinks it really should.

Moving from a cell to a room also opens up more of the city to her. Honor brings her to public areas. They're mostly filled with soldiers, but there are a few civilians among them.

Oddly enough, none of these areas have windows either. Her new room is up several flights of stairs from her old cell, and the marketplace Honor brings her to is up several more, but there is still no way to the outside world.

She could understand not giving her a room with a window, or moving a table down to the dungeons for the meals with Charity. She cannot, however, believe that Honor managed to relocate an entire marketplace just so that they could visit it.

"Why is this underground?" she asks Honor as they leave the market.

"Everything is underground," Honor answers. "All of the Refuge. That's how we've remained hidden for so long."

Grace stops dead in her tracks. "You what?"

"Built the city underground."

"How far below the surface are we?" Grace asks, eyes darting around as though the entire thing will collapse on her simply because she is now aware that it is a possibility.

"It's very stable," Honor says reassuringly. "We've not had a collapse in centuries."

"But there *were* collapses."

"Centuries ago. When we were first learning." Honor puts a hand on her shoulder. "The whole structure is reinforced, I promise you."

Grace casts one last mistrustful look to the ceiling. "Alright," she says, but her voice is dubious.

The city manages to stay standing for the next three weeks. At the end of each one, Grace is invited to dine with Charity and another restriction is taken away. Before long, she is hardly a prisoner at all. The only limit still in place is the one about going to the surface.

"We try to limit how many people go in and out at once anyway," Honor tells her. "Big crowds attract attention."

She is even allowed into Honor's office when he forgets something after one of their walks. There are papers scattered all over his desk that could contain enough sensitive information to give the White-Wings more of an advantage than they've had in centuries. Honor barely bats an eye at letting her through the door though.

Determined to prove worthy of this show of trust and not so much as glance at his desk, Grace distracts herself with Solace. He leaps onto her shoulders as though he's been invited and drapes himself around her neck. His tail wraps around her wrist, and she strokes the soft fur. He presses the top of his skull under her chin, purring loudly.

There is a thump and a grunt from Honor's desk, and she turns around to find him glaring at an open cabinet drawer and gingerly

168

touching a spot on his head. "If you would organize things so that you could close the drawer, that probably wouldn't happen," she tells him.

"It is organized," Honor says, as though his office doesn't look like three separate storms passed through it. Grace raises her eyebrows at him. "I know where everything is."

"You're the only one," she whispers just loud enough for him to hear. He rolls his eyes at her and goes back to looking through the lower drawer. Solace leaps from her shoulders to bat at a loose page on Honor's desk.

"Don't make things worse," she scolds him. The paper flutters to the ground, revealing the book underneath. Out of habit, her eyes skim over the words, and she pauses in the middle of reaching to put the page back on the desk.

The pages aren't burnt by fire or bent by water, but it is undeniably Endurance's journal. The original is sitting beside it, open to the same page.

"You're rewriting it?"

It makes sense—the information within the journal is too important and the journal itself too fragile. In fact, making multiple copies would not go amiss. Still, it makes her stomach lurch to see the journal again. It seems impossible that her entire life could have been overthrown by something so small and damaged.

"It seemed prudent," Honor says quietly. "If it could convince you, then…"

Then it might convince others too, Grace finishes mentally. It might even convince Father. She wouldn't just have her word; she could show him physical proof. The thought stays with her long after they leave his office.

ASCENDANT

It is the first thing she thinks of when, a few weeks later, Charity sets her fork aside and looks Grace in the eye, her face blank. "Well, little one, your three months are up."

"They are," Grace agrees quietly.

A small smile breaks through the mask. "You have already earned my trust," Charity says. "This is simply the end of your probation."

Grace feels her heart race. Her probation is over; she no longer has to stay in the Refuge. Now she will return to the Citadel. Now she will have the chance to tell Father the truth. Now the war can end.

She will miss Honor, but surely with Father at her side the war will come to an end quickly. Especially if she has the journal to show Father and others. It won't be too long before she can see Honor again, and then they will be at peace.

"When will I return to the Citadel?"

Charity looks up from her cup. "You won't."

Grace blinks. "But—"

"I have more than enough spies," Charity says. "There is no need to risk you in the Citadel."

"I am trained for—"

Charity raises a hand. "You are not going within a hundred miles of the Spymaster if I can prevent it," she says. There is something strange in her eyes. Almost like fear, almost like anger, but closer to sadness. "And I can prevent it."

Grace opens her mouth and shuts it again. She knew that Charity wouldn't trust Father at first, but to not even allow Grace back to the Citadel...

The rest of the meal is quiet and tense. Even Honor is unwilling to attempt a conversation. After Charity leaves, he puts a hand on Grace's shoulder. "It isn't personal," he says quietly.

170

"I could tell people in the Citadel. If I could show them the copy of Endurance's journal, we could end the war!"

Honor closes his eyes. "I know, but it will have to be someone else who does it."

But it *couldn't* be anyone else. Father would trust Grace; he would believe her—she is his daughter. He won't trust it if someone else tells him.

"It isn't because she doesn't trust you, Grace. She's lost enough people to Concord in the past."

"Your grandfather?" Grace asks quietly, remembering whispered stories of the former Black-Wing king.

His hand squeezes her shoulder. "Among others." There is something careful in his voice. "How much do you know about your sire?"

Grace narrows her eyes at him. "He was named Noble. He was a soldier who served with Allegiance. He died before I was born." *Killed by the Black-Wings.* She doesn't say it, though they both know. Some said that the Ascendant had taken him. The pale-haired, red-eyed Ascendant that stalked the nightmares of White-Wing soldiers. The one who haunted battlefields and stole dying soldiers.

Honor sighs. "Did my mother tell you about the White-Wing boy that her father adopted?"

"You're not saying—"

Honor nods. "My grandfather found him wandering in the forest. He didn't remember where he came from or who his parents were. Like Mother told you, they adopted him, so he was her brother. They grew up beside each other, and when he was old enough he went undercover in the Citadel."

Honor sighs, looking down at his hands.

171

ASCENDANT

"Mother didn't want him to go, but my grandfather allowed it. At first, things were going well. Then his reports started mentioning Allegiance—he loved her, and he thought that he could convince her to switch sides. He was exposed before he had the chance. Another operative gave his name to Concord's interrogators. Once Concord knew that he was my grandfather's adopted son..." Honor looks away. "He didn't have a quick death."

"I—" She doesn't know what to say. She never knew her sire. She had only seen the aftermath of his passing: Allegiance's bitterness, as though all the love in her heart had died with Noble. She had rarely acknowledged Grace's existence.

Until she had met Father, Grace had thought she was a ghost that didn't realize it was dead. Only there to haunt her dame with the memory of her sire.

Was it all Father's fault?

No. Father didn't know that the Black-Wings weren't evil. He was still confused by Justice's lies. He still *is* confused. No matter her sire's fate, he will believe Grace when she tells him. It isn't his fault.

Charity would have been her aunt by adoption if Grace had grown up in the Refuge, and Honor her cousin. For a moment, Grace wishes for that life. It seems like a lifetime ago that she had wondered if she inherited anything besides her talons from her sire. A family would have been far better than any weapon.

"I won't be like Noble though," Grace says. "I can do it. With the journal, I could prove what I'm saying is true." *And Father will believe me.*

"Maybe," Honor says quietly. "But even with proof, there will be those who don't want to believe the truth. It would be dangerous, Grace. Incredibly so. You're so close to Concord, one slip and..."

Grace sighs, but she knows he won't believe her if she tells him that Father wouldn't hurt her.

Honor pats her shoulder. "Your probation is over at least, so you can visit the surface tomorrow if you want."

She nods. It will be good to get back to the sky. Have a chance to stretch her muscles and fly for real. There are rooms and hallways in the Refuge large enough for flight, and in the soldier's barracks the sparring field is large enough to practice flight combat. It isn't the same as flying in the sky though.

Honor walks her to her room, and she can't resist wrapping her arms around him. "Goodnight."

"Goodnight, Grace." He leaves with a hopeful smile. Grace feels sick to her stomach.

He won't be smiling tomorrow. She hopes Honor will understand

She waits for an hour after he leaves and slips out of her room. She has memorized the way to Honor's office by now. There are no guard patrols out of the dungeons, though there the occasional person wanders about. None of them see her; the shadows in the Refuge are thick and plentiful.

The copy of Endurance's journal sitting on Honor's desk is complete now. The trip back to her room is just as simple. A tiny part of her wishes that someone would notice her. That they would make her take the journal back and give up on her plan.

ASCENDANT

Part of her knows that Father is still going to be angry with her before she tells him the truth. After, of course, he will be angry at Justice, but first he will be angry with her.

Honor will be, too, probably. That thought makes her stomach lurch even more than the thought of Father's anger. Father, at least, will have Justice to blame. She hopes that Honor will forgive her.

She doesn't sleep well that night.

***

The morning comes too soon. Honor knocks softly on her door as he hasn't since she was in the cells. "Grace?" he calls through. "Are you alright?"

Grace scrambles out of bed and tosses a pillow over the journal. Her stomach is churning again, but she ignores it. She nearly trips over her blanket and has to brace herself against the door.

She forces herself to take a deep breath before opening it. Honor is standing in the hall, his hand raised to knock again. "Grace?" he asks, his brow furrowed with concern.

"Good morning," she says, her voice sounds calmer than she feels.

"You're usually up before me," he says, head tilted.

"I didn't sleep well last night." That, at least, is the truth.

Honor smiles. "Too excited?"

"Definitely." She smiles, and somehow it doesn't come out as a grimace.

Not even seeing the sky again can calm the fluttering of her heart. The forest is loud with animals waking and going about their business. Sunlight falls through the leaves in golden patches. Tucked beneath her shirt, close to her body, the journal feels like it weighs a million pounds.

174

"Glad to be out?" Honor asks, laying a hand on her shoulder.

"Yeah," Grace says softly, and she is. Now all she has to do is get to Father, tell him the truth, and help him end the war. Then she can come back. On impulse, she whirls around and wraps her arms around Honor.

He embraces her in return almost immediately. "Excited?"

She looks up at him and smiles. All she has to do is get to Father. Everything else will fall into place after that. She takes a deep breath. "I am." She nearly pulls away, but she can't quite make herself. "I never said thank you. For everything you've done for me."

"You don't need to. I was happy to help you."

She tightens her arms around him. "I wish I'd grown up here. With you."

Honor laughs quietly. "You would have been a pretty nice cousin." He hesitates a split second, as though he isn't sure how she will take his next words. "You're a great little sister though."

The guilty churning of her stomach clashes with the explosion of warmth in her chest.

"You're not a bad brother yourself," she manages to say. Her voice is thick. She pulls away from him. If this goes on any longer, she'll never leave. Then the war will never end. She has to do this.

"I'll come back," Grace promises.

"What do you—" The smile slips off of Honor's face, but she's already leaping into the air.

She can't quite bring herself to simply leave without giving him an explanation, and she stops on an ancient bridge. "I'm going to make this right."

"Grace, come back down here." With his wingspan, Honor has no way to reach her.

ASCENDANT

"I have to do this," she calls back. She should go now; she's given him her reason. She needs to go. She needs to find Father and set things right. "I'll come back, I promise."

"Grace, you're going to get killed!" She grits her teeth against the pain in his tone. If he knew Father like she did, he wouldn't worry. He would know that Father will believe her and that he will help her set things right.

"I'll be back," she says, and she launches into the air once more. She rises above the treetops only for a moment, to get her bearings. The White Mountain looms far overhead, perhaps three days' journey from where she is. At the top of it is the Citadel. She only has to get to White-Wing territory and flag down a patrol. They will take her to Father.

She turns her wings to the mountain and dips back beneath the trees.

Chapter

11

Get to Father. Get to Father. Get to Father. It reverberates in her mind, echoes the pounding of her feet against the ancient wood as she runs across the forest. It is in the rhythm of her heart and the staggering beats of her wings when she has to leap across gaps to get to the next bridge.

When night falls over the forest, she forces herself to carry on. She won't get lost in the dark with the river to guide her. She doesn't stop for food or water, only pausing occasionally to catch her breath. She feels like she has gone both a thousand miles and only a few steps when her eyes catch on white feathers in the air.

One of Father's Observants, it must be! She tries to call out to them, but her voice only rasps out of her parched throat. Now that she has stopped, she becomes aware of the shaking in her limbs, the way her wings drag against the ground. Grace falls, without the strength to even try and catch herself. The moss is cool and dotted with dew, and she wishes for a moment to stay there forever.

Then there is a surprised shout above her, and Grace lets herself close her eyes for only a moment. Hands gently shake her shoulders, and she opens them again. From the number of people now gathered around her, it is possible that she had her eyes closed for longer than she thought.

ASCENDANT

But that doesn't matter. She forces her arms to lift her, and hands guide her to lean against the trunk of a tree. Someone offers her their waterskin, and she drains it without a thought. Voices speak around her, but she can't make out what they are saying, though she almost recognizes her name a few times, and then one of them says something about Father.

Father. She needs to speak to him. Where is he? Grace tosses aside the empty waterskin and finally takes notice of her surroundings. An entire patrol seems to be gathered around her. Their healer is kneeling before her, retrieving his waterskin and offering her a piece of dried meat.

Grace ignores it. She can eat later, now there are far more important things to take care of. "Where is my father?" she rasps. Her voice feels like a barbed arrow, pulled slowly from her throat.

"He is on his way," the healer says soothingly, then offers her the jerky again. "You need to eat." He turns to the woman to his left. "Loyalty, give me your waterskin." The Desert Clan woman hands it over without a word.

Grace eats and drinks her fill, ignoring the patrol as they mill around her. The majority of them pretend to be keeping watch, giving her the illusion of privacy. Grace can feel their eyes on her when they think she isn't looking, but she ignores them.

A shadow passes in front of the sun, and her head snaps up. Father lands in the clearing a few feet away, and her eyes follow him as he comes toward her. His customary pair of guards flank him.

Grace struggles to her feet, leaning heavily on the trunk, and manages a sort of bow to her father. He takes no notice; instead, he strides forward and wraps his arms around her. For a second, Grace is frozen with sheer surprise as he gently holds her against his chest, one hand stroking her hair.

Before she can take advantage and melt into the embrace, it is over, and Father steps back and looks at her with his usual assessing gaze. His eyes sweep over her, taking in everything. She used to hate that look, how she could never seem to hide from it, but now it is familiar and comforting. She missed him while she was prisoner.

"Father," she croaks, and winces at the sound of her voice. "I have important information."

His eyebrows raise, and his eyes flick over to the guards and then back to her. Grace shakes her head minutely—this information is not for them to hear, not when any of them could be one of Justice's spies. Father nods and barks to the guards, "Be gone."

Wordlessly, they obey, climbing into the branches of the trees, too high to hear what is said but low enough to keep watch on the ground. Father turns back to her, warmth in his eyes. "What have you brought me, Dear One? Is Liberty dead?"

She was right. Hope did get back to him to deliver her report.

Grace's mouth opens, but no words come out. In all of her desperation to get to him, she had forgotten that he would want a report on her actual mission. "Yes," she says quietly, and a part of her wants to weep for the truth of it. Liberty had not needed to die; she had known the truth before Grace did, she had tried to tell them, but they hadn't listened. Amity and countless others had all died in the name of a lie.

"There is something I need to tell you. More important than Liberty. Something I discovered while I was held prisoner."

He looks at her with pride, but Grace doesn't let herself bask in the glow of it. There are more important things to take care of

179

first. He will be plenty proud of her when she reveals the truth to him. After he is done being angry, and oh will he be angry. Justice won't know what hit him and then the war will be over.

Grace takes a deep breath and begins, "While I was captive, I managed to befriend a Black-Wing healer by the name of Honor." She doesn't say that he is the Ascendant—something holds her back—and perhaps it is best to relate the story in the way that she herself discovered it.

Father nods approvingly. She cannot help smiling at him. The warm glow of his pride is like the sun itself; she cannot live without it.

She takes a deep breath and continues, "After some time, he showed me a book." Grace can feel tension running through her body, vibrating through her wings and hands.

This is it, where everything goes back to normal, she and her father fighting against evil. Side by side, his steady presence at her back, even if the evil they are fighting is no longer the Black-Wings, but Justice himself. "It was the journal of an old king, whose name was Endurance."

Father's face changes. He looks as emotionless as Glory, no pride, no anger, just blank. Grace hurries to continue, tripping over her words. "Honor—they—*I* know it is real. If you'll just read it, then you'll understand!"

Father doesn't react. She stares at him, then rushes to pull the copy of Endurance's journal gently from where she kept it while running and offers it to him. He makes no sound, only takes the book from her hands. He looks at it silently for what seems to be an eternity, then looks back up to her. His face still doesn't change.

Grace swallows down the rising dread. He will believe her; he will do what is right. "It tells about how the war started. Justice has been lying to us this whole time. We don't have to fight anymore." Her voice is a mere whisper by the end of the sentence, and he is still watching her with that blank look. She doesn't like it. She licks her lips and tries to keep from looking away, from apologizing and taking the book back and never talking about it again.

Finally he looks back to Endurance's journal and opens the cover, flips through the pages, skimming over them quickly. Then he sighs. "Oh, Dear One, the Black-Wings have fooled you. This isn't real." He pulls her close with one arm, tucking her against his side. "It is nothing more than lies crafted by the Black-Wing queen to lure naive fledglings to her side. I want you to forget about this. Put it out of your mind, and I will forgive you."

Grace's mouth opens of its own accord, and words spring to her lips, she wants to agree, to promise never to fall for such a trick again, but something deep in her mind shifts and groans. A quiet voice says, *No.* And that is what comes out of her mouth.

Father looks sharply down at her, and Grace rushes to correct herself. She tries to pull away from his side, but his arm only tightens around her, near bruising. She stops, but his grip doesn't lighten. "Father, please, I know it is real. I had these dreams, and—"

When his arm tightens again, she can hardly breathe around his grip. "Grace." His voice is low with warning. "I want you to let this go."

"I can't," she says quietly. "Please, I know it is real. This is the truth, and Justice has been lying to you. I didn't want to believe it either." His arm tightens further, and now she can't breathe. She wiggles a little bit, trying to get free. She looks up into his face and

181

quails when she sees the anger in his eyes as he stares down at her. She swallows again and stills.

He will believe her; he has to—she is his daughter.

His grip relaxes, and as he steps away, she falls to the ground without his support. "I had hoped you were better than this," he says, and the disappointment in his voice is like a knife against her very soul. "I suppose it is my fault, for not better teaching you about the lies of the Black-Wings. Maybe you just aren't ready for missions of this magnitude." He walks away from her, and Grace stumbles to her feet, trying to follow.

"Father, please. Just listen to me!" He stops and turns back to her, and now there is real anger in his eyes. Grace covers her mouth with her hands—did she just *shout* at him? But this is important; she can ask his forgiveness later, when he has fixed everything.

"I—" But she doesn't get a chance to continue. Father's hand flashes out and strikes her across the face. The ground rushes up to meet her, and she just barely catches herself on her hands before her face is smashed against it. Her cheek stings, and Father stands above her, his hand raised to strike again.

"*Never* raise your voice to me," he growls. She cowers against the ground, not daring to speak. "I have told you that this is nonsense. Abandon this, now."

There is something in his eyes, not anger but something buried deep beneath it.

Fear, a voice whispers. *He is afraid. Why?*

It is not just any fear. She knows this kind intimately, lived with it for weeks before Honor showed her the journal.

It is the fear of a liar about to be caught.

And suddenly it all clicks.

There is no anchor in this new world she has been shoved into. Father is a liar, and the Black-Wings tell the truth. He has always known the truth, and he has done nothing about it. He has helped hide it. She feels like she is about to float away, unattached to the world, lost and alone in a great void.

"You knew." The words pass her lips without her permission as she stares at the man she thought of as her father. The great liar revealed before her, a play, performed all around her for her entire life, put on by a cast of betrayers for their naive audience. Father doesn't need to speak for her to know she is right. His eyes confirm what his words have hidden.

How foolish she had been. How naive, to think that he could fix everything. Like he could snap his fingers and right all the wrongs of the world.

How childish. Her mouth wants to curve into a bitter smile. There is no room for children in war.

Father's mouth moves, forms words, and makes sound, but all she can see is the truth in his eyes. It is the last thing she sees before the world disappears

Chapter 12

She wakes alone in a cell, and for one glorious moment, she thinks that none of it happened. She hadn't escaped, hadn't made it back to Father only for him to become the very thing she thought she was fighting.

Then she realizes that there is no bed here. No stool and no book. The chill in the air isn't imaginary any longer. She isn't chained, here. She doesn't need to be.

There is no chance of her escaping from Father.

Staring at her hands, she can almost see the blood dripping from them, still warm and fresh, as though she had just torn her way through an entire patrol of Black-Wings. It is innocent blood, and she had allowed Father to put it there, had let him turn her into…what? What is she?

Not a Guardian, part of her thinks with a bitter laugh. *You don't protect people, you kill them. You're a monster, a weapon, and you always have been.*

She doesn't know how long she is left alone with her thoughts, maybe days, maybe months.

It feels like years before there is a dull thunk from across the room. Grace turns immediately to the sound. A small waterskin and ration pouch sit by the door; other than that, there is no indication that the rest of the world exists. Perhaps this cell, this darkness, is all that there has ever been. Maybe she imagined everything else.

She pulls out the dried meat in the ration and tears into it. It is even blander than she remembers, and there isn't enough water in the skin to wash away the taste.

She watches the door, but nothing else comes. Father doesn't enter. There aren't even footsteps in the hallway. She shivers against the constant cold in the air and wraps her wings around herself. The room is silent. Even her breathing seems far too quiet.

The silence was bad enough in the Black-Wing cells. There, it had only teased at the darker edges of her memory. Similarities, not reality.

She knows what this is though. This is punishment. She shudders.

She begins losing stretches of time. She has no idea how long. Sometimes she looks up and finds that there is another ration pack and refilled waterskin waiting for her, and the other has disappeared. Other times she wakes up in the corner of the cell, breathing hard and terrified of dreams she can't remember.

She tells herself the story of Sanctum again and again. Of the wandering of her ancestors before the city was founded. They had a place to call home, and then it was ripped away from them by war. It was torn away, and there is no getting it back. An entire city lost. For what?

ASCENDANT

Greed? Arrogance?

Grief?

One day there will be no one left to tell that story, she thinks. Justice will kill the Black-Wings, and then he will turn upon his own people. He will see the shadow of his enemy forever.

She stops telling herself the tales after that. There is no point to them; they only inspire fools and get people killed.

The silence is always there, sometimes ominous, other times oppressive, but always present. She begins hearing voices that she knows aren't real—hopes aren't real.

Sometimes it is Honor's calm voice in the steady cadence he adopted when they read together. More often, it is Father's voice, gentle, reassuring. *I am forgiving,* it whispers. *Have I not loved you? Have I not taken care of you? Come back to me, Dear One. I will forgive you.*

She hates the sound of his voice. It stalks her like a nameless, formless monster and lovingly trails needle-thin claws down her spine.

As more time goes on—or perhaps it doesn't, maybe time has stopped, maybe there is nothing but this room and the rest of the world has fallen away—the voices stop repeating things from her memory and begin to take on a life of their own.

"Wouldn't it be easier to just forget this?" Father croons, gently, lovingly. Grace shudders and looks up to find that her ration has arrived. She doesn't know how long it has been there.

Eventually, she doesn't just hear things; she begins seeing them too. Sometimes Liberty stares at her with dead eyes, her throat ripped open and blood cascading down her chest, soaking her shirt and dripping on the floor. She never says or does anything, only stands there staring with her skin pale and cold.

Other times, it is Father before her. "Do you remember when we went to see the herds?" he asks, a gentle smile playing about his lips. "It was just after the calving season, and you had all of the newborns following you about. We could go again if you wanted. If you let this go, I'll take you, just the two of us. I miss you, Dear One."

"Why are you doing this?" she asks.

"Because I love you," he replies. "I have always loved you, and when you put this foolishness behind you, you will see that."

She snarls at the words. *Love?* She wants to scream, *You think this is love?* She wants to rage and wail and a thousand other things. Something, anything to make this end, to make him leave her alone. The next time she sees the vision of him, she lunges, fingers aching to bury in his flesh.

She wakes and finds a bruise on her forehead and blood underneath her nails.

Grace stares at the blood, trying to make sense of it. She has no cuts on her skin, so there is only one possibility: the vision of Father is real. At least, sometimes it is. A shudder crawls up her spine at the thought of him being right in front of her without her realizing it.

The thought is enough to clear her mind, to give her focus. The only way she is getting out of this cell is if Father lets her out, and he has been periodically visiting her, trying to get her back to his side.

He believes that she is broken, helpless and waiting for him to pick her back up and soothe all her hurts. She has to let him think that he is convincing her slowly—he will be suspicious if she does it too suddenly.

The next time Father comes, she snarls and glares at him. "I hate you," she hisses.

His wind feathers twitch, but he doesn't explode into rage the way she expects him to. Instead he sighs and looks sad. "I am sorry that you feel that way," he says, quietly, calmly. "I only wish to bring you back into the light, Dear One. I only want to clear your mind of Charity's lies. I know it doesn't seem like it, but I do this because I love you. I brought you food. Please eat." He sets the waterskin and ration down and leaves the cell.

She has to bite her tongue to keep from calling out after him, begging him to return so that she can apologize. Guilt worms into her heart, nearly painful, and a ringing sound echoes in her ears. He is manipulating her. It is painfully obvious now that she knows to look for it, but that does not mean it is ineffective.

He may return a few hours later, or even a few days—she has no way of knowing. Hunger claws at her belly again, but that is the only way she knows time has passed.

"Hello, Dear One," he says as he enters. Grace cannot keep herself from shuddering. "I am sorry I was gone for so long. The Black-Wings attacked one of our patrols, and I had to see to them."

Bile rises up in her throat—more Black-Wings dead. "They're innocent," she says. She wants to shout, but she cannot make herself shout at him. "You killed innocent people who were only defending themselves."

His wind feathers flick backward, but he still doesn't get angry with her. "I know that Charity has tricked you into believing that, but they attacked us. We were the ones defending ourselves. Should we simply allow the Black-Wings to kill us without offering any sort of resistance?"

"The White-Wings started the war," Grace says. Quiet and insistent. "You know that, you know that this is wrong."

His eyes narrow, and she braces herself for a blow, for his anger unleashed upon her at full force. "I am sorry that you still refuse to see the truth." His voice is quiet and calm, coaxing, almost. "I wish that you would return to me, Dear One. We need you. People are dying without you."

Another shudder runs down her spine. *He is manipulating you,* she reminds herself. *He only wants to make you his weapon again.* She refuses to speak or acknowledge him for the rest of his visit.

When he leaves, the visions rise up around her once again. Honor's voice reading one of the legends. Charity staring down at her, accusing. *They died because of you,* her eyes seem to say. *For the things you did not see, for the things you were unwilling to see.* Liberty stands and watches her with glazed eyes and blood drying on her skin.

"I've brought you a treat," Father says the next time he comes. "I know it is cold, so I brought you something warm." The scent of fresh fish rises to her nose, and Grace cannot help but breathe deeply. Father smiles and places the plate onto the floor. There is a fork and knife on it, but she cannot make herself even consider attacking him. *It would be foolish to try,* she tells herself. He would surely win. She could never hope to match him in battle, and then what? She would still be trapped beneath the Citadel.

ASCENDANT

"Thank you," she murmurs, hesitant. *See what I want you to see: You're getting through to me. I'm beginning to regret what I said, what I did. I'm ashamed of myself.*

"Of course, Dear One," he replies.

This is a turning point. His visits are more frequent, he stays for longer, and he always brings her a gift or a treat. A blanket, a pillow, warm tea, better food. In turn, Grace acts grateful but shamed, as though she cannot believe that he would treat her so well after what she did.

Finally, she hunches her shoulders and looks down at her feet and whispers, "I'm sorry, Father."

He smiles and pulls her close. Somehow, his skin is even colder than the air of her cell. Still, she makes herself relax into the embrace. "I forgive you," he whispers into her hair. She calls up tears and buries her face in his chest. He lets her stay there for what must be nearly three minutes.

"You have done so well, Dear One," he says. "Now tell me, where were you held?"

She doesn't allow herself even a flash of victory, though this is the moment she has been waiting for. She swallows hard and speaks. "It was in the desert, at the base of the Merciless Mountains. They called it Sanctum. The queen was there. I saw her once."

There is every chance that he won't believe her. That he will see straight through this lie and she will lose all of the trust she spent so long trying to regain. If he does believe her though...If he believes her, he will tell Justice, and Justice will command Allegiance to send their forces out to the desert. Those who aren't killed by the forest will spend who knows how long seeking a city that doesn't exist.

She thinks it's the closest thing she can do to actually sending them to hell.

190

By some miracle, he does believe her. Father hugs her once again and whispers praises into her hair, tells her how proud he is and how brave she was to face the queen alone. Grace accepts it with a tiny nod and doesn't let him see the victory in her eyes.

***

The cell door opening wakes her up, and anxiety prickles down her spine. This has never happened before—Father always comes when she is already awake—and then she sees that it isn't Father at the door. Glory's red hair seems to be made from fire in the flickering light of the lamp, and for a moment, Grace wonders if she is seeing things again.

"Glory?" she whispers just to be sure.

"Come on." He waves her forward with his hand, glancing up and down the hallway.

Grace doesn't hesitate. She slips out beside him and studies her surroundings. She knows where she is. She motions to Glory, and they slink through the hall, wind feathers flared, seeking any sign of movement. Silently, she takes the lead, guiding them through the labyrinth of the White-Wing dungeon.

They don't speak, but Grace's mind is spinning with questions. How did Glory find her? Why did he come? She cannot ask them, though, not until they are out of the Citadel at the very least.

Finally, finally, she can feel the brush of wind against her feathers and their face, even though they are at the base of the mountain. The air has the cold bite of winter. *How long have I been prisoner?* Grace tries not to think about it, tries to just appreciate the feel of fresh air across her wings.

She stands for a moment with her feathers flared wide to the wind, her eyes closed. Glory rests his hand on her shoulder, and she

191

looks over to him. There is a hint of sympathy in his gaze, but he motions to take off without a word. Grace swallows and nods, and they launch themselves into the air.

Her wing muscles ache, and Grace nearly drops back out of the sky. Glory silently takes a place in front of her, as close to a long-distance formation as they can get with just the two of them. "Just glide," he calls back to her, and Grace shoots him a confused look. She isn't Desert Clan—she can't soar the whole way out of White-Wing territory. But she does as he says anyway, locking her wings and settling in for a long flight.

The wind *moves* in a way entirely unnatural and all too familiar. Grace gasps and nearly rolls away out of instinct, but at the last moment she holds when she remembers Glory is a Wind Weaver. She stares at him with wide eyes, and even though she is sure that he can feel the weight of her gaze, he doesn't look back. If anything, he speeds up a little bit.

They fly for what Grace thinks is ten minutes, and then Glory shifts his wings for a gradual descent. She follows gratefully, her own wings shaking with exertion. Glory lands gently on the bank of the river while Grace falls from the sky, but she does manage to land on her feet instead of her face. She is breathing hard and pauses to take a long drink from the river while they are there. Then she turns to her rescuer.

"I know you have questions," Glory says before she can get a word out, "but now is not the time for me to answer them. We aren't safe yet."

He steps over to a tree marked with three horizontal cuts and climbs up to an abandoned forest cat nest relatively, low to the ground, from which he pulls out a small box. He tosses it down to her, and Grace opens it to find her gauntlets and the rings that unfold into her talons.

She cannot help trailing appreciative fingers over the polished surface before she puts the gauntlets on. Someone even took the time to buff out the numerous scratches. She slips on the rings next and then flicks her wrist to unfold the deadly claws. They have been sharpened and polished as well.

Glory nods approvingly and crouches to take off, his wings flared and muscles coiled. A flash of silver appears over Grace's shoulder and a knife buries itself in Glory's wing with a fleshy thud. Glory makes an awkward half leap before the pain in his wing forces him back to the ground with a hoarse cry.

Grace flares her wings and turns to face the direction the knife came from, keeping herself between Glory and the danger. Father steps from between the trees, his face impassive and another dagger in his right hand. "Dear One," he says, in that same disappointed tone that always makes her want to cringe and apologize, "I thought we talked about this. You were doing so well." He holds out his empty hand. "Come back to the Citadel with me."

Grace swallows hard and looks away from him. Her mouth opens, but the words won't come out. Behind her, she can sense Glory rising to his feet, and she glances at him over her shoulder. His face is set in the emotionless mask more firmly than she has ever seen. There isn't even a crease around his eyes to give away the pain he is surely in. He folds one wing, but the one with the dagger embedded only twitches feebly and drags on the ground. Father must have hit the joint.

Father's right hand lifts, dagger held ready to throw. Grace flares her wings, blocking Father's throw. Pain lances through her skull, but she ignores it. "Father, stop!"

His icy blue eyes glare into hers. His anger is cold and foreboding in the air between them, like stepping into the middle of a frozen lake and hearing the ice groan. She freezes in place, hardly daring to breathe.

"Move," he says quietly. Her feet shift, but she makes them stop. Her head is pounding with the sound of his voice echoing through her mind, *Move, move, move.* She steps to the side without meaning to.

"Father," she manages to say. It is barely audible, but she still says it. "Please stop. This isn't right, you know it isn't. I don't know what Justice told you, but he was lying."

"Enough!" Father snaps and takes a step toward her.

She cannot help taking two steps back, but now that the words have started coming, she can't stop them. "You don't want to do this, it's wrong." She dares to look up at him, begging him with her eyes to just *listen.*

"Dear One, come here," he says levelly. "We are leaving."

She knows he will take her back to the cold, lonely cell in the dungeons. She knows that he will leave her alone for even longer this time. She takes another step away from him.

"Now!" Father snaps.

"Stop!" she shouts back, and then stares at Father with horror. He crosses the distance between them in a blink and grabs her by the chin, forcing her to look into his eyes.

"I want you to think very carefully about what you just said to me." His voice is quiet and sharp, like the first cracks appearing in

194

ice. "You do not order me. You obey my orders, and I am ordering you to *stop this*."

The pain in her head is growing unbearable; she closes her eyes and grits her teeth against it. "I won't," she manages to say and rips away from him. She stumbles and nearly falls, but Glory catches her arm and pulls her back to her feet.

"We are leaving," Glory says, voice just as hard as Father's, though how he intends to leave is a mystery to Grace. She can see that he has pulled the dagger from his wing, but flying on it will be far too painful to maintain for long.

"You are in no position to give orders, boy," Father says with a sneer. "Leave now, and I will let you live."

"No."

Father's eyes narrow, and for a moment, everything is perfectly still. Then he lunges, the dagger in his hand glinting in the sun. Glory shoves Grace to the side and leaps back in one smooth motion. The dagger he pulled from his wing is in his hand, and he uses it to block Father's blow.

Grace watches them. She knows that she must get up, must help Glory. She can't allow Father to kill him, can't allow herself to go back to the Citadel. She will have to fight him. She flicks her wrists and extends her talons.

A wave of pain washes over her skull, nearly driving her to her knees. She barely has the presence of mind to not cradle her head in her hands. Father's voice booms through her mind, *Never attack me. Do you understand, Dear One? You are* never *to raise your weapon against me.*

She can't seem to make herself move.

ASCENDANT

The air buzzes as Glory flares his working wing and a breeze rattles the bare branches. Nowhere near as powerful as it was the last time she had felt him use his power for combat, against Faith. With only one wing, he won't be able to summon up a strong wind to blow Father back.

Get up.

Father kicks Glory's knees out from under him, and Glory goes down with a choked scream. "Grace," he gasps. His dagger has fallen out of his hand, and Father is approaching him. He will kill Glory, and then he will take her back to the dungeons of the Citadel. Glory risked everything to get her out—she has to help him.

She climbs to her feet, but her legs refuse to cooperate. They want to collapse beneath her. Her hands shake and her head pounds to the beat of her heart. The ringing goes even higher.

Glory tries to rise, but Father kicks again, catching him under the chin. Glory falls back, his mouth stained with blood. Father advances on him with another dagger, and he drives it into Glory's leg.

Glory screams, trying to drag himself backward with his hands. There is nowhere he could go to escape Father though. No one could escape him. Father is absolute, unstoppable, unbeatable. No one could hope to defeat him.

But she must.

She takes a step, but her legs lock. Her hands are trembling, and the world lists and spins around her.

You are never *to raise your weapon against me.*

She shakes her head. She has to help Glory. She has to fight Father.

Father's wings flare wide. Even Glory seems to cower in the shadow they cast. The dagger in his palm glitters with malice. His eyes are like chips of ice, cold, uncaring.

Her knees give out. Her breath is coming in great, heaving gasps. She can't make herself get up. She can't make herself attack Father. She couldn't beat him even if she could. He outclasses her in every feasible category.

He is everything.

And she is nothing.

She has always been nothing without him. She cannot stop him, cannot defy him. She is a blade of grass, and he is the sun. He could scorch her into nothing if he wished. She lives by his mercy. Trying to survive without him would be her death. She cannot exist without him.

"Grace," Glory says again. Their eyes meet, and she tries to convey her apology. He will die for her, because of her.

Father sends the dagger into his throat with a casual flick of his wrist. Grace watches as he chokes, gasping around the blade. His hands flail. One catches on the pommel of the dagger, and he pulls it from his flesh without hesitation.

A fountain of blood springs up in its wake. It goes on for a hundred thousand years. His choking, rattling gasps are deafening. The glaze that creeps over Glory's eyes moves as slowly as a glacier.

Three, she thinks. *I have killed three innocent people.*

"We are leaving." Father says.

Grace turns away from Glory's body.

Glory is dead. Because of her. It is her fault.

"Come, Dear One," Father says. He is across the clearing from her. So close, but so far away. Too far away to reach her. Too far away to stop her. She stands, and he smiles, satisfied with her obedience. "It's time to go home," Father says.

Home.

ASCENDANT

Where is home? Not with Father, not in the Citadel. Not in cold halls and dark dungeons. The ringing sounds faintly in her ears, but Grace grits her teeth. She is going home. She is following orders.

She turns away from Father and springs into the air. He isn't capable of following her any more than Honor was. This time, she makes no promise to return. She will never come back to him, not if she can help it. That doesn't stop him from shouting after her.

She shuts out his voice and focuses on the strain of her muscles.

Chapter

13

Father's voice fades swiftly behind her. Lost in the roar of the wind. She flies for nearly an hour before she lets herself stop. It won't be for long—Father will be back to the Citadel by now, handing out orders to find her.

Her heart is pounding too loudly in her ears, her breath coming too quickly. Her mind races with one thought after another, a hundred thousand worries and the looming mountain of guilt and anger and despair. Glory is dead. Father killed him right in front of her, while she stood there and watched.

Glory is dead, and it is her fault.

Her current path would have taken her right to the heart of Black-Wing territory, but Grace realizes that she can't go there. Even if she could be forgiven for Glory's death, even if she could ever look Honor in the eyes knowing that she had stood by while his friend was killed, she cannot return to the Refuge. Father will be hunting her, and if she returns, she will bring him right to their doorstep.

She grits her teeth and steels her heart. *I have no home.*

The ringing fades, as does the pain in her head.

The pain in her heart only intensifies.

She told Father about the Black-Wings' secret city in the desert. The one she had made up entirely. She will bring them there. If she survives that long.

It is the beginning of winter, and she has no supplies but the thin prisoner clothes on her back and her talons and gauntlets that Glory brought for her. That she could have used to defend him. She grits her teeth again and pushes the thought away. She cannot get caught up in her guilt. Not if she is going to lead Father and whatever Observants he brings with him out into the desert.

She remembers Hope's foraging lesson, though it seems like it happened in another lifetime by now. Grace knows how to hunt and how to fish. She can do this.

As long as the plants last. As long as the ponds don't ice over. As long as the animals don't all hide away from the winter snows. As long as Father doesn't catch up to you.

She will have to survive and outrun him. There is no other option. She refuses to die now, when she finally knows the full truth. She will lead Father through the forest and leave him to die in the desert. That is her mission, and failing is not acceptable.

Her limbs ache, and her wings feel as though someone is trying to tear them off of her back, but Grace dives off of the branch and keeps moving. She only has so much lead on the White-Wings— she needs to make the best of it.

***

As the days go by and winter looms closer, her fingers and toes freeze. Her muscles ache constantly, and her stomach feels like a gaping hole in her abdomen. Some days she only travels a mile at most, desperately searching for food. Other days she makes good time, but when she stops she collapses and her stomach cramps with hunger.

Always, Father is at her heels. She smells smoke not from her fire; she hears the whistles of a flight communicating to each other. Sometimes she even catches a glimpse of white feathers from the corner of her eye.

She doesn't know why Father hasn't come to claim her already. She is barely keeping ahead of him, and she wouldn't be able to fight off an entire flight. At this point, she might not even be able to fight off a single soldier.

Hunger makes it hard to think, but eventually she comes to the conclusion that Father is allowing her to lead them to the Black-Wings. She is all the more grateful for her decision to avoid the Refuge. Her path has taken her in a wide arc around the heart of Black-Wing territory.

She avoids Black-Wing patrols just as much as she avoids White-Wing ones. They would only want to bring her back to the city. In the darkest, hungriest nights, she wonders if they would return her to her cell. Honor wouldn't be there to read and offer distractions this time. Not after what she allowed to happen.

She sits with her back against the reassuring strength of a tree trunk and allows herself to rest. The sun is starting to set, and it is far too dangerous to fly at night. She will get back up and walk along the ancient Forest Clan bridges in a little while, but for now she pulls out a shriveled piece of fruit and eats slowly.

I'll rest for just a little bit longer, Grace tells herself. Despite the cold and the hunger, her eyes slip closed. She sleeps.

ASCENDANT

Heavy hands roughly grab her arms. Her eyes fly open. The sounds are too loud, the light of the moon too bright. The haze of sleep is ripped away, and she is dumped into reality.

She is under attack. There is familiar armor on all sides. Walls of white feathers that once meant safety. There is no safety now.

Fight!

She digs her heels into the tree bark and flares her wings wide. The two holding her arms are unprepared, and she knocks them aside. She leaps from the branch, diving to the forest floor, and hears shouts behind her. Pursuit. From the sound, there are at least three of them.

She lands softly and darts into the deepest shadows she can see. They are not far behind her, and she cannot take on three Observants in this state. Not half-frozen and half-starved. She runs, disappearing into the shadows without a sound.

At first, she thinks that Father has changed his mind and sent out orders to capture her. As time goes by, however, she realizes that it is more likely that these soldiers are simply disobeying orders. They're all of lower rank, trying to prove themselves invaluable, and they think they can do it by catching her.

Orders or not, they follow her for days, hunting her. They don't give her time to stop and sleep. By the second day of their pursuit, she is weaving drunkenly in the air, trying to fly straight when the entire forest is spinning around her uncontrollably.

She will not lose this hunt to them. She will not go back.

A noble statement, part of her says, *but not exactly practical at this point.*

And it isn't. Something has to give, and it will not be her.

Sleeping the whole night is too risky, and wasteful. She can move with impunity at night, none of Father's soldiers are better than her at stealth, but if she sleeps the day away, then they will find her while she is vulnerable. She catches sleep whenever she can, day or night. Tiny snatches, just enough to keep her going.

No matter how far she flies, how little she sleeps, they find her once again. She is exhausted, and it is far too easy for them to overpower her. One forces her arms behind her back and pins her wings against his chest. They turn her hands so her palms are against her own back. She can't unsheathe her talons without slicing into her own wings and spine. She grits her teeth against the pain as the position nearly dislocates her shoulder.

It is daylight now, and she can see them clearly for the first time. These aren't Observants. They aren't wearing the familiar hoods and dark colors of Father's forces. They are wearing full armor—these are Allegiance's men.

Questions flood her mind: Why are Allegiance's men all the way out here? Why have they been hunting her? What are they going to do now that they have her?

Their leader stands over her as the man holding her arms forces her to her knees.

"My father didn't send you," she says. It isn't quite a question, but the soldier answers anyway.

"No. Concord is too soft to do what needs to be done. The Air Commander isn't."

Grace nearly laughs. She doesn't think that anyone has ever referred to Father as *soft*. It's much less funny when the rest of his words sink in and she realizes that they're going to kill her.

ASCENDANT

It's better than going back to Father, part of her thinks. The rest of her is caught up in trying to find some way out of this. Some way to escape.

"Why did my father allow this?" she asks, a little desperately—anything to buy more time. Her eyes dart around. They're high on a branch with no impromptu weapons in reach even if she had her hands free. As though he senses her thoughts, the soldier holding her arms tightens his grip. Her shoulder edges closer to dislocating, and she can't restrain a pained gasp.

"Temperance!" the third soldier barks protest. Grace had almost forgotten that he was there. He's standing rather distant from his companions, lingering in the shadows so that they hide his face. He toys with the ax on his belt.

Never lose sight of your enemy, Father's voice murmurs in her ear.

She feels the one holding her—Temperance, apparently—draw breath to argue, but the lead soldier cuts him off with a gesture. "You betrayed us. The Spymaster may have the king's ear with most things, but even he knows that Concord is too close to you. Allegiance is the rightful second-in-command. Concord can't order her to do anything."

Unless one of Father's Observants finds them right now, there is no way she is going to get out of this alive. Her heart pounds in her ears. For a fleeting moment, she wonders if going back to him would really be worse than death.

Unbidden, the memory-vision of Haven's death rises up behind her eyes. The pain, the creeping cold, the looming darkness. Her breath is coming too fast, and her thoughts swirl in useless circles of *Get away! Get away!*

The soldier draws his sword. "For crimes of conspiracy and high treason, you have been sentenced to death. Do you have any final words?"

She is going to be killed. For Justice's lie.

No. No. She can convince them. Can show them the truth.

"Justice is lying to you!" she says, too quickly, so desperate even she can barely understand herself. "Please, if you'd just *listen* to me! I can prove it."

The soldier's eyes narrow with disdain. "A poor choice, Black-Wing," he hisses, looming closer to her. Their noses are nearly touching. She can see herself reflected in his eyes.

She is going to die.

The creeping cold, the looming darkness. Death hovers at her back, waiting to claim her.

She doesn't want to die.

She *can't* die. Not here. Not like this.

Fear and desperation crystallize into action. She lunges without conscious thought. This is not a calculated strike; this is nothing more than animal impulse to escape, to fight. She embraces it. It engulfs her, is within her and around her in the very air.

Her lips pull back from her teeth, and she sinks them into the flesh of the White-Wing's nose and gives a savage twist. Coppery blood floods her mouth, and there is a deep crunch from beneath his skin. He screams and scrambles back, a hand rising to his face.

The lunge costs her though. Even as the White-Wing holding her arms loosens his grip in shock, she pushes her strained shoulder too far. With a deep crack that reverberates through her rib cage, it slides out of socket.

Her scream mingles with the White-Wing's, but she can't linger on the pain. She has to move, has to get up, get away. No, this has to end here. Now. She can't allow them to catch her a second time.

She cradles her right arm to her chest, hunching around it even as she flicks her wrist to unsheathe the talons on her left hand. The leader is still staggering back, hand to his face as though that will staunch the flow of blood. The bigger threat is the one that was restraining her.

He lunges for her, trying to crush her skull with his mace. She dips beneath the blow and slides forward to one knee. Her wing flashes out and slams against his knee.

He staggers with a scream as the joint snaps and begins to fall forward. She lunges for his throat, bared in his distraction. He falls off the branch without another sound.

She spins and regains her feet, wings flaring. The motion jars her shoulder, and she bites her lip to keep from crying out. She tastes blood.

There is only one more soldier standing before her. *There were three. Where's the third one?* It takes a moment for her eyes to find the limp body of the soldier, crumpled on the branch. The leader. Utterly still in death.

The third soldier, the one who had protested when his companion had handled her roughly, lets his bloodied ax fall from his hands. It clatters against the wood, a dull sound, but all too loud. She flinches from it as the ax slips off the side and into the forest below.

There is only one scenario that ends with this, but it doesn't make sense. She stares at the soldier.

One of Charity's agents?

One of Father's?

He raises his hands in surrender. "I'm sorry," he says, voice quiet, ashamed. "I should have stopped them sooner."

She stares at him. "Why?"

"There have always been those of us who had…doubts about Justice and his war on the Black-Wings." He looks away from her. "The Spymaster makes a point of hunting down anyone who says anything, but we do exist. Most of us get ourselves assigned to forest patrols and just…leave, but I was never brave enough." He straightens and looks into her eyes. "I had my doubts, but these orders"—he shakes his head—"they go too far. Some might consider me a coward for not standing up before now, but coward or not, I'm not letting anyone kill a fledgling in front of me." A desperate light enters his eyes. "You said you had proof? That Justice is wrong?"

"While I was with the Black-Wings, they showed me the journal of the king before Justice. Before I ever left the Citadel, I had dreams—visions—of those same events through Haven's eyes." She takes a breath and admits to him what she couldn't admit to herself: "I think they were sent by the Trinity. To show me the truth."

He nods, relieved.

"Tell them," Grace says, surprising even herself. "Spread the word as quietly as you can."

"I will," he promises, dipping his head as though he is receiving orders. "Do you want me to set your shoulder?"

She nods hesitantly and allows him to gently grasp her arm.

"On three."

Resetting her shoulder is nearly as painful as getting it out of joint in the first place, but it does lessen the pain afterward. She is going to have some spectacular bruising, but she isn't dead, and she has gained an ally.

Of course, they can't stay together for too long. He has to return to Allegiance and make his report, and she needs to put more distance between herself and those hunting her.

She doesn't return to a normal sleeping schedule. Now that she knows Allegiance's men are hunting her as well as Father's, she can't bring herself to sleep for very long. She can't count on there being a soldier of conflicted loyalties in the next group that catches up with her.

***

Days blur into weeks, weeks into months. Winter slowly loosens its grip on the forest and storms rage in the skies. It makes traveling hard, the wind is strong enough on some days to rock even the massive trees of the deep forest, and flying would be suicidal.

There are days when even walking along the branches is dangerous and she has to hole up in whatever shelter she can find and do what she can to pass the time. She is trying to remember exactly how the tale of Sanctum goes as the storm settles down when something cracks and shifts outside of her shelter.

She freezes, ears perked. Rain patters down the leaves, and she feels a soft breeze on her wind feathers.

From outside, a low voice inquires, *"Mrrr?"* Faster than thought, she is crouching on the branch, talons unsheathed, staring into the semidarkness of evening, wind feathers flared as wide as possible, ears perked. A forest cat slinks carelessly out of the shadows, tail waving in a lazy fashion. She tilts her head, allowing her muscles to relax. She has been plagued by cats all through her journey—they seem to have a sense for when she has scraps available.

"Go away," she hisses to it, settling back onto her branch. She will have to leave soon. The clouds are darkening again, and soon there will be another storm. The cat ignores her, stopping just before the toe of her boot and imperiously holding out one paw.

She stares for a moment, wondering just what it wants from her, and then she realizes. A small leather cuff around the cat's leg holds a little roll of parchment. Hesitantly, she tugs the parchment free, and the cat purrs and rubs against her hand in a familiar manner. She squints at it in the low light. The spot by its ear is a blobby sort of sword shape. "Solace? How did you get all the way out here?" His fur is longer than she remembers, but perhaps it is a winter coat, not yet shed?

Grace shifts to sit cross-legged on the branch. Solace takes it as an invitation and happily curls up in her lap. Her hand falls thoughtlessly to stroke his silky side. He is a welcome warmth against her skin. A quiet falls over her mind; it is simple, sitting like this, with nothing to do but run her fingers through Solace's fur. She spends far longer than she should lost in the texture of his coat.

Eventually, she unrolls the parchment and squints at the dark ink against the page, but the sun has fallen too far for her to read it. There is only one person it could be from, but Grace isn't sure what Honor could be contacting her for. He has to know by now that Glory is dead, that she stood by while Father killed him. Like a coward.

As afraid as she is of condemnation and anger, there is another part of her, the part that wandered the empty rooms of Allegiance's apartment and felt like a ghost in the years before Father, that insists she open the letter. She tries to silence it, but she is starved for more than food—she is hungry for another person to speak to her, to acknowledge that she exists. This is likely as close as she will get to that unless she wants to return to Father.

Honor's handwriting is a messy, slanted scrawl, barely legible. His letters are spaced widely, but the words are crushed together so they are nearly impossible to pick out.

Grace,

Our spies told us what happened with Glory, and I was worried when you didn't come back· Mother says it might be because you feel guilty for not standing up to your father, but you must know that Concord holds the only blame·

I know you have little reason to trust me, or anyone, right now, but I promise that if you come to the Refuge, you will be safe· Solace will guide you back if you tell him to find me· I hope that you will come, but even if you don't, any Black-Wing you meet will help you if you show them this note·

I hope you decide to come back·

~Honor·

Grace reads the note three times, trying to commit the words to memory. She aches to return to the Refuge, even knowing that doing so would only get everyone there killed. She is so tired, she wants to lay down and sleep for eternity, wants to eat her fill and be able to move without looking over her shoulder constantly.

She carefully folds the note back into her belt. Wishes and dreams do not change reality. She has to keep going, has to see through this mission that she has set for herself.

Thunder rumbles above her, distant now. She has been here too long. It is time to get moving.

Solace is still curled happily in her lap, eyes closed, purring loud enough to match the storm. She shifts her leg. He curls tighter. She shifts it again. The purring comes to a stop and needle-sharp claws dig into her calf. Wincing, Grace carefully lifts his paw away from her body and shifts her leg again. He still doesn't open his eyes.

With a sigh, Grace burrows her hands underneath his body and lifts him out of her lap. He goes with a petulant sound, yellow eyes glaring at her in the dark. "I have to go," she tells him, trying in vain to dust fur from her legs. He's definitely shedding. She stands before he can sneak back into her lap and gives up on her pants.

As though he has been invited, Solace leaps smoothly to her shoulder, curling around the back of her neck with his tail trailing over her chest. Grace cranes her neck to look at him. "Are you coming with me?" She cannot honestly say that she has the heart to make him stay behind.

Experimentally, she steps off the branch and flutters over to one across from it. Solace digs his claws through her shirt, but otherwise stays firmly in place. A few pinpricks at her shoulders are a small price to pay for company through the night. Grace launches herself back into the air and spreads her wings for a long flight. She will have to travel far to make up for lost time.

Solace relaxes after she takes off, apparently used to being transported in such a way. She has to stop again when the moon is high in the sky, limbs shaking with cold and exhaustion. The ache in her muscles has become so constant that she hardly notices it. Solace leaps easily off her shoulders and sits on the branch beside her, looking up expectantly.

Unsure of what he wants, Grace sits beside him and offers a bit of precious dried meat. Her store is getting low, but she hasn't found anything to hunt or gather. If she runs out, it won't be the first time she has gone hungry. She allows herself to rest for a few minutes. *Just a moment, just to eat and regain some energy. Not for long, never for too long, or he will find you. And he will take you back. You can't stop him—you can only avoid him.*

She leaves before she is truly rested, but she cannot stand to stay still for a moment longer.

She pulls out Honor's note when daylight comes, unrolls it, rolls it again. She puts it back and takes it out over and over. Eventually she leaves it in her belt—She has to keep moving; she can't take the time to stop and read. Grace allows herself to forget the note is even there and only remembers it when her fingers brush against the worn parchment.

Days go by, empty of anything but the constant motion of her muscles and Solace's weight against the back of her neck as she flies. He seems content to stay with her rather than return to Honor. The days slowly grow warmer, and the storms calm. Whether this is from the season changing or her getting closer to the desert, Grace isn't sure.

She is holding her waterskin under a stream of water falling from a leaf when she hears it: a familiar voice over the pounding of the rain. It is close, far too close.

"Report," Father commands, glaring at the Observant standing before him.

"There is no sign of her," the Observant says hesitantly. "We have searched miles ahead, but we cannot find signs of her passing."

"Then look again."

The Observant dips his head and darts away.

The sound of Father's voice falls over her softly, like threads of spider's silk. Soft and gentle, touching lightly against her skin, against her mind. She wonders if insects feel the same way when caught in a web, until they, like her, see the spider sitting in the middle, until the gentle strings become harsh and binding, holding them helpless as the spider pumps poison into their veins.

Run.

The thought flashes through her mind, pounds with the too-fast beating of her heart, but her feet won't move. Her wings weigh her down like heavy stones, and her eyes are trapped staring at the back of Father's head. All she can hear is the harsh rasping of her breath. Can he? Does he know she is there, watching, trapped by his mere presence?

The world grows muted and dark around the edges. It is tempting to let the darkness consume her entirely, to let the world fade away into nothing. To not have to worry about the cold or the hunger that hunts her just as surely as the White-Wings do.

Please don't let him see me, she begs in her mind. Perhaps it is a prayer, or perhaps it is only a feeble hope.

Pain bites into her shoulders, and she nearly screams. At the last moment, she bites down on her tongue hard enough to draw blood. Solace rubs his cheek against the side of her head, a low purr rumbling up from his chest. She pulls him off her shoulders and hugs him tightly, burying her face in his fur and trying to shut out the world, just for a moment. Even though she is probably suffocating him, Solace doesn't stop purring until her breathing begins to deepen and her heartbeat slows.

213

She looks back up, and her heart skips what must be three beats—Father is staring directly at her. Their eyes meet, but he looks away, his eyes searching the leaves above her. No, he didn't see her; he can't have, or he would have sent the Observants after her. Maybe even come himself.

No, she realizes. Even if he does see her right now, he isn't trying to take her back just yet. He is counting on her to lead him to the Black-Wings.

She forces herself to look at him again instead of running. He looks the same as he always has, with pale skin and icy blue eyes, his hair so light it is nearly white, like all the color and warmth has been leached from him. She wonders how she ever found comfort in his arms.

He had been the one to soothe away the hurts that he caused. Always with that gentle voice in her ear, *I do this because I love you.*

The thought fills her with a senseless rage, the same anger that lurks beneath her mind at all times, burning beneath her chest, blackening her rib cage until her brittle bones cannot hope to hold it any longer.

Love, he had called it when he locked her in the cold dungeons. It was *love* that made him drive her in training until she was ready to drop. *Love* that made him strike her for disobeying him.

Was that love?

She doesn't think that he is capable of love. There is something withered and twisted up inside him. Something stunted and *wrong* that grows into his heart, filling it with thorns and poison. If he *does* love her, he doesn't love her for who she is. He loves her for who—for *what*—he made her.

And she hates him for the same reason.

A dark curl of anger twists in her gut. She will see him blackened and bloody. She will burn this forest to the ground if it means he will die with it. She will see fear in his eyes as the final darkness closes in and he realizes that he has *lost* and she has won.

She will whisper in his ear as he dies, "I hate you. I hate you so much."

She is so caught up in this thought, she almost misses Solace wiggling out of her arms. At first, she is flooded with guilt, thinking that she has squeezed him too tightly. She lets him go immediately, but he doesn't seem all that bothered.

He rubs his head against her knee, and before she has realized what he is doing, he has leaped down from her branch and is heading toward the White-Wing camp with single-minded determination.

"Solace!" she dares to hiss. He ignores her, making his way down through the branches to the edge of the camp. Once there, he leaps onto the shoulder of one of the guards, as happy there as he had been on her own shoulder a moment before.

The guard doesn't seem disturbed, either. He reaches up with one hand to stroke Solace's tail and check the pouch on his leg. It is empty, of course, because Honor's note is with her.

The man reaches into his belt and gives Solace something from it—a treat of some sort, Grace thinks, from the way Solace gobbles it down. Once he has licked the guard's fingers clean, Solace leaps off his shoulder and saunters back toward Grace.

Horrified, Grace lifts her eyes to see that the guard is staring right at her hiding spot. She holds her breath, waiting for him to sound the alarm. Only he doesn't. Instead, he nods to her and then turns away, as though nothing had happened.

She sits frozen on the branch, heart and thoughts racing until Solace returns. He buts against her limp hand, asking to have his ears scratched, and she glares at him.

"What was that?" she says as loud as she dares. As near as she can figure, Solace just sold her out for treats. Solace purrs and nibbles at her hand until she scratches him.

How had he known the guard even *had* treats?

The pieces slot into place. Honor had mentioned that he was teaching Solace to carry messages, and the best way to do that would be to reward him when he found the right person.

The guard is a traitor, one who has worked closely with Honor and perhaps even Charity before. That was why he hadn't sounded the alarm. Solace must have recognized him from when he was being trained.

Still, Grace should leave. Now. She has lingered here for far too long, and she doesn't know if anyone else saw Solace's little stunt. Another thought makes her pause. This might be something she could use to her advantage.

She has been leading Father and his Observants through the forest with the intention of letting them get lost in the desert. But if Father is here, then it means that the Citadel is down a good portion of its security. Maybe enough that Charity could take it.

Her mind mostly made up, Grace falls back to watch the camp from a safer distance. It is nearly midnight by the time the guard slips out of camp and wanders casually away until the camp is nothing more than a speck of light in the distance.

He whistles softly, and Solace leaps down from her shoulder to dart to his side, already sniffing his hands for food. "Greedy thing." The guard laughs softly, but he surrenders the treats.

Grace follows more cautiously. He could always be a triple agent, setting her up for an ambush. She casts the thought aside—this is her only chance, and she cannot ruin it by letting fear get to her. If it is an ambush, she will fight her way out, and if she can't…If she can't fight her way out, then she isn't going back to the Citadel again. No matter the cost.

"Our mutual friend has been hoping you would make contact," the guard says to the air.

Honor. The note in her belt seems to weigh even more at the mention of him. She hesitates for a moment, a reply half-formed on her lips, but in the end, she keeps silent.

The guard doesn't seem bothered. "Your father is quite determined to get you back."

"He isn't my father," Grace snaps before she can stop herself. Tension floods her muscles—was that too loud? Had the guards in the camp heard her? Is this guard just waiting for her to reveal her location to spring the trap?

"I am glad to hear that," the guard says. "Many of us were concerned when you were not found after you escaped the Citadel. We expected you to return to the Refuge."

"I would have led Father there," she says. "He would have found your city."

"We have remained hidden for centuries," the guard says.

"He would have found you."

ASCENDANT

The guard shrugs, leaving the disagreement as it stands. "I don't think you risked exposing us both to speak about what could have been. Concord will not capture you yet. He intends to follow you to the desert—you have not disguised your destination. Allegiance is said to be on the move as well."

"I know," Grace says. "I've seen a few of her flights around."

The guard shakes his head. "No, Allegiance herself is on the move, and not just with a few patrols. Justice sent his whole army out after you."

Grace's heart leaps. This is even better than she had thought. If Allegiance is coming, she will be bringing an army. Grace thinks that there haven't been this many soldiers on the move since the beginning of the war. The Citadel won't just be unguarded—it will be all but empty.

"Do our mutual friends know about this?" Grace asks, trying to restrain her excitement.

"I haven't had a way to get a message to them," the guard replies, "but now I do."

The smile slips off of her face. Right. Of course the only way he could get a note back to Charity is if he sent it with Solace. He can't exactly duck out and go himself, can he?

Even in the dark, she can see the sympathy in the guard's face. "You could go with him, you know."

For a second, Grace allows herself to think about it. Seeing Honor again, returning to the Refuge while Father hunts for her a thousand miles away. Being *safe*. Then she tosses the dream aside. "No, if they lose my trail, they may go back to the Citadel, or worse, they won't lose me and I'll lead them to the Refuge."

218

The guard sighs, but nods. "I won't be able to do much, but I can try to keep the others from getting too close."

Grace nods firmly and waits as the guard writes the letter by the light of the moon. Solace extends his front leg and allows him to tuck it into the leather cuff. "Take it right to Charity, alright? Charity."

Solace leaps gracefully from his shoulders and winds around Grace's feet. She feels tears burn at the corners of her eyes, but she forces them back and bends down to scratch him behind the ears. He gives her hand a rough lick, and then he disappears into the dark forest.

"I can't stay away from camp much longer," the guard says. "I wish you luck."

"And I you," Grace replies, and then he too is gone, and she is once again left entirely alone.

She hadn't realized just how much she missed talking with someone, or even just having another person there beside her. Solace could only do so much, and he was no conversationalist. Grace had drawn the line at having one-sided conversations with a cat. Most days.

Though, from the way Solace responded to such conversations, she isn't sure Honor hasn't had his own talks with him.

She doesn't let herself linger for long. She still has a long way to go before she reaches the desert. Grace travels hard for the first day, trying to regain the lead that she had somehow lost. By evening of the second day, she feels as though her wings weigh a thousand pounds and her feet have simply fallen off.

She can't go further, no matter how much she wants to—needs to—not until she's rested. She sleeps for a little while, tucked up in the highest branches of the canopy, covered by leaves and shadows.

When she wakes, she eats a solid meal of fresh berries and dried meat and looks out over the forest. There is no sign that Father and his forces have caught up to her while she slept, so she thinks she can afford to linger just a little bit longer.

She idly traces the patterns of the bark with one finger, staring without really seeing. She misses Solace, misses having another being to interact with, even if they couldn't speak. Even more than that, she misses intelligent company. She misses being able to talk with Honor, to debate their different ideas and laugh with each other.

Without her telling it to, her hand dips into her belt and finds the worn edge of Honor's letter.

She had promised him that she would come back.

That was before you got Glory killed, before Father started hunting you.

Does that change the fact that she made a promise? Broke that promise?

It isn't broken yet. There is still time.

If this all succeeds, then the war will end and she can fulfill her promise without putting him in danger. It seems impossible now, but impossible things have happened before.

One day, if I'm not dead, I'll go home. The thought brings a faint smile to her face. She has a home, she has a brother and perhaps even an aunt, if Charity is willing to forgive her escape.

First, though, she has to survive.

Chapter

14

She sleeps even less now without the comforting presence of Solace at her side, ready to stir her if a nightmare takes hold. She eats occasionally with disinterest, telling herself that she will need to save food for the desert. Alone, she keeps from speaking too much. There is no reason to speak, and it will only draw attention from the White-Wings. Though she isn't sure any will attack her now that she is so close to the desert, where they believe she is leading them to the Black-Wing city. Still, best to be cautious.

Days pass, she isn't sure how many.

Reality wavers and drips around her, sliding past her consciousness without her knowledge. It grows hot and dry. She has to fill her water more often than she used to, she thinks.

It is quiet in the forest. Her very thoughts seem to echo against ancient tree trunks, repeating endlessly until they are unintelligible. She is only aware that she needs to keep moving, that she needs to get to the desert. There is nothing beyond that.

And then she is there.

The trees thin out, growing younger and smaller, weaker, until they give way to grassland. Grace stares, her palm pressing up against the trunk of the very last tree before the great openness.

ASCENDANT

She had…not forgotten, but not considered that there could be this much space. She hasn't ventured above the treetops in far too long.

The Merciless Mountains are a hazy line of bumps on the horizon. Her eyes are drawn to them, and she can't make herself look away. Her pilfered waterskins are full, she has as much food as she could get, and her talons are sharpened. She is as ready as she ever will be.

The very air seems to hum with tension. There will be fewer places to hide out in the open, so she will have to be constantly vigilant. The forest has been her home for only a short time, but it is a truer home than the Citadel ever was. Grace takes a deep breath and lets her hand fall away from the tree trunk. She lifts her chin and walks away from the edge of the forest. She will not be swayed by sentiment.

She leaps into the sky and beats her wings. An updraft buoys her higher and higher, and she locks her wings and glides back down to the ground, only to find another updraft before she hits.

Outside of the forest, she is at a disadvantage. She is not built for flying long distances; her wings are made for close quarters and tight maneuvers. If Father spots her out here, there will be no escaping him. He could overtake her in a heartbeat. She clings to the reassurance that he is waiting until she leads him to the Black-Wings' imaginary city before he tries to take her back. If it is one of Allegiance's men, at least she won't have to worry about Father anymore.

Solace will have made it back to the Refuge by now, and hopefully the Black-Wings are on their way to the Citadel. Perhaps they have already taken it. Now all that is left is her part.

She just needs to lead the White-Wings out into the desert, away from sources of water, and let the desert wear them down. She will lead them to the Merciless Mountains—it seems fitting enough, as long as the desert doesn't kill her first.

Below her, great herds of animals race across the plains. They almost look like deer, but they are far more sturdily built, and they have no antlers. When she stops to rest near a small group of them, there are wobbly-legged newborns testing their speed against one another. She stays and watches them for a while, and even finds herself laughing when one takes too tight a turn and tumbles gracelessly onto the grass.

Their mothers watch her with a wary eye, grazing in a path that keeps their bodies between her and their children. Grace takes off again before they decide that subtlety isn't working. There are other creatures about, but they move like predators, and Grace is less willing to risk setting down near them, in case they prove more hostile.

As idyllic as the plains seem, it is still impossible to forget that she is being hunted. One evening when she sets down for a break, her eyes drift over the land, looking back toward the forest. A curl of smoke stands out against the setting sun. The White-Wings have followed her out onto the plains.

First there is only one fire against the setting sun, but a few days later the evening sky becomes hazy with smoke. Allegiance must have caught up, then, and brought her army with her. Grace wonders if Justice came as well. She cannot recall him leaving the Citadel during her time there, but never before have so many White-Wings been on the move at once.

She keeps going.

ASCENDANT

The grass grows shorter and sparser, slowly being pushed back by sand. Flying over the desert is a trial in and of itself. There are constant updrafts during the day, but her wings are not built to take advantage of them. At night the temperatures drop steeply, until it is so cold that she thinks she is back in the Citadel. She hadn't thought it could *get* so cold in the desert.

Grace shivers her way through the nights and tries to save water during the day. She has heard that there are oases in the desert, but they were few and far between, and she doesn't know if there are any along her route.

The Merciless Mountains loom larger as she gets closer to their base. She can see the foothills now. Hopefully there will be water there, or she will die in this desert. Or worse, be recaptured.

She watches the smoke from the White-Wing camps rising into the sky. She hopes that the Black-Wings have taken the Citadel by now and that when Allegiance and Father get tired of chasing her— or when she is no longer alive to chase—they will return with a small enough force that the Black-Wings can crush them easily.

The sun is relentless. It shines down upon her from a cloudless sky, and the heat is reflected back up from the sand. Grace is sure it is slowly baking her alive. Her skin grows red and tender, and then it begins to blister. She moves stiffly, trying to keep from aggravating the burns, but for the most part she fails.

She tries to ration her water, only allowing herself a small sip once every hour, but all too soon she is halfway through her last waterskin. In the dips between dunes, the air shimmers and ripples, and sometimes she dives from the sky, convinced she has found an oasis, only to find nothing but sand. She grows sluggish, and the twilight hours between the blazing heat and freezing cold become her only salvation.

She swallows as best she can around her dry throat. Breathing heavily, she sets down, stumbling to a stop in a humorless parody of her once-graceful landings. Father had worked her for hours until her landings were perfect, she dimly recalls, but she cannot summon up the anger and betrayal that might motivate her to keep going.

The heat of the desert seems to have burnt every emotion out of her until all she is aware of is the need to keep moving, to find water and shelter from the unforgiving sun. Her head pounds in time with her heartbeat, and she licks her cracked lips with a dry tongue. The very air burns in her throat.

When twilight comes, she collapses gratefully beside a boulder and can't make herself move for hours. As the moon rises, her sweat freezes against her skin, and her teeth chatter. She thoughtlessly rubs her hands against her arms, and a harsh cry creaks its way out of her throat as she pops the blisters from her shoulders to her elbows.

Holding back reflex tears, she forces herself to get up and keep moving. Her wings hang limp from her shoulders, primaries dragging in the sand, making little furrows after her. She doesn't even try to take off; instead she stumbles forward on foot, struggling against the sand shifting beneath her feet.

The ground slopes upward, and she has to crawl to the top of the dune. She doesn't have the energy to get back to her feet and allows herself to roll to the bottom. This proves a mistake when the sand burns against her skin and the blisters on her legs and the few intact ones on her arms pop. She stays there in a heap at the bottom of the dune trying to breathe through the pain until the cold numbs her fingers and toes, then she forces herself to get back up and keep moving. She watches her feet, listens to the shifting sand in her wake, and goes on.

The ground slopes up again, and she closes her eyes and forces herself to keep going. At the top of the dune, she takes the cap off of her waterskin with shaking fingers and raises it to her mouth. It is so tempting to guzzle what little remains down, to let the cool water flood down her throat and into her belly. But she can't. She forces herself to stop after only a sip and put the cap back on.

She gets up and stumbles down the dune, crawls up the next one. She keeps crawling. Her calves burn as the dune gets steeper and steeper. The ground feels solid beneath her feet. Grace looks up—this is no dune. She has made it to the foothills of the Merciless Mountains.

A smile opens the cracks on her lips, and she tastes blood when she runs her tongue over them, but she doesn't care. With renewed vigor, she keeps climbing until she reaches the top of the hill and then looks out over the desert below. It is perhaps another mile to an even taller hill, with sand in the small valley between them. But more importantly, there is a shimmer in the heart of the valley, surrounded by green smudges.

Grace slowly spreads her wings, ignoring the protests of her muscles, and leaps from the top of the hill. Gliding down the other side of the hill saves her perhaps half an hour of walking before she is forced to flap a few times to keep her altitude. After about an hour of short bursts of flight broken by periods of walking, she reaches the outskirts of the oasis.

Her palm rests against the solid reassurance of a tree trunk, and she stumbles to the edge of the water. She only pauses a moment to check her surroundings; the horizon is clear, and there is no motion but the leaves swaying in the wind. She falls to her knees beside the water and brushes her fingers against its surface. It is deliciously cool against her palm, soothing the burns on the back of her hand.

She reluctantly pulls her hands out of the water. She doesn't dare drink it directly from the pool—she isn't quite that desperate. Instead she opens her waterskin and finally allows herself to drain it.

She gives herself ten minutes to rest and then begins pulling whatever wood is on the ground into a pile. She breaks branches off of low bushes, and before too long she has a small fire surrounded by stones. She fills every waterskin she has and hangs them from a stick propped over the fire until they boil. She drinks her fill and then does it again. By morning she is asleep underneath one of the bushes, with full waterskins tucked close to her body.

Surviving in the foothills is far easier than in the open desert. Water gathers in the small valleys between the hills, and there is plentiful prey for when she has to hunt. Grace doesn't dare eat any of the fruits hanging from the trees; though it is tempting, she has no idea if they are poisonous or not.

On the third morning, there is a smudge on the horizon to the west. Grace doesn't think it is the White-Wings; from the smoke she saw last night, they should still be miles away. Still, she pushes herself back into the air and puts on as much speed as she dares. She can't afford to exhaust herself if it is White-Wings. Not if they are looking to capture her.

She dips one wing into a gentle turn and flaps to gain altitude. From above, she can see that this is not caused by any Guardian. There is a great cloud of sand rising over the desert. It must stretch at least a mile wide, crawling toward the Merciless Mountains. Grace rises higher and turns away from it. It seems to be moving slow enough that she can keep ahead of it for now.

By midday, when she has to stop and shelter in the semicool shadow of a large boulder, the cloud has moved closer. She would guess it is perhaps half a mile away. If it catches up to her before the heat has died down, she will need to come up with a plan.

The air before the cloud is blowing hard, picking up grains of sand and pelting them against her cheeks. Perhaps the entire cloud is like the blizzards that sometimes spring up in the Citadel, only with sand instead of snow.

She will need better shelter than this small boulder. Even though the sun is beating down on the back of her neck, Grace takes off and shoots upward, looking for the shadows of rocks that may shelter her. Her eyes dart back to the storm, and she misses a beat of her wings. It has gotten closer, much closer. It is nearly on top of her now, the upper edges of it buffeting against her. She blinks away sand as it finds its way into her eyes. Her wings miss another beat as stinging tears blur her vision, and then she is falling.

The wind bowls her over, spinning her until she has no idea which way is up and which way leads to the ground. If she opens her eyes even a tiny slit, sand blinds her again. It is everywhere, stinging against her skin, in her ears, in her nose and mouth, down her throat and into her lungs. She coughs, choking against the onslaught. The wind jerks her around again, roaring in her ears like a towering beast. She beats her wings frantically, but there is nowhere to go—the storm is endless.

She falls, and then is pushed back upward, to the side, and then shoved down again. She manages to pull her shirt up over her face, even though it leaves more skin exposed to the harsh blast of the sand, she can at least breathe again, and just barely see. The world is dim and tinged orange for the few feet she can see, and it is colder than it was outside the storm.

The wind jerks her to the side, wrenching her right wing back until the muscles scream protest and Grace nearly joins them. She needs to land; she needs to land and get to shelter.

With a deep breath, she half folds her wings and lets herself glide for a few feet, just until she is sure of which way is down. Then she tentatively spreads her wings wider, trying to glide gently to the ground. The storm doesn't allow for gentle. It catches her wings and spins her again, and she is lost once more. Her shirt slips down from around her face, and she breathes more sand.

Her wings fold as she chokes, and she loses more altitude, then she flares them wide with desperate downbeats. She doesn't know how high she is. She could go too fast and crash, and if she crashes she might break a wing, or a leg, and then she would be stranded. The storm catches her left wing and blows it upward, sending her into another tailspin. Her foot brushes something solid.

The wind howls in her ears as she kicks wildly, trying to find whatever she hit before. Her hands flail and then brush against gritty rock. The storm rips her away, but she has found her shelter now, Grace beats her wings hard and fast, wingtips nearly touching on each downstroke and upstroke.

Her fingers wrap around the stone, and she folds her wings tight against her back, keeping her wind feathers plastered against her wings. She wraps her legs around the pillar of stone and shimmies her way down to the ground. She keeps herself curled around the stone, wings folded and head down between her knees, and tries to focus on breathing. The world disappears into the roaring of the wind and the sting of sand against her skin.

ASCENDANT

What must be hours later, the roaring stops, and the sand is still around her. Grace cautiously lifts her head and blinks out at the peaceful sands. The world is still dim, and when she looks up, she sees that the storm still rages above her. In fact, she appears to be in a tiny bubble of clear space, surrounded by the raging storm. There is no way this is natural—there has to be a reason, but Grace cannot bring herself to think of it. She is too grateful that the storm has stopped, at least for now.

She stands slowly. Her muscles ache from being locked in one position for so long, and she carefully works the stiffness out of them. She shakes the sand off of a waterskin and takes a sip. Her wings are a gritty, itchy mess. The storm seems to have driven an entire desert's worth of sand beneath her feathers. Despite the pain in her right wing, she fluffs her wings and shakes them vigorously, stirring up a miniature sandstorm, trying to get every grain out.

Grace freezes and then flaps her wings again, watching as the sand swirls up into the air and then falls back to the earth. *Impossible,* she thinks, but the longer the thought is in her head, the more it makes sense. If she can stir up a tiny storm by beating her wings, what could a Wind Weaver manage? Or entire flights of Wind Weavers, working in concert? She imagines they could conceal an entire army beneath the storm and keep a pocket of clear space to move through, if they did it right.

It must be the White-Wings, hoping to sneak up on Sanctum. Her first instinct is to get out of the eye of the storm. She has no idea how close the army is or even what direction they're in. One look at the wall of wind and sand around her makes her hesitate. She isn't eager to jump back into that. Not so soon after she has gotten out of it, and not with her wing injured.

With a wince, Grace stretches and refolds her right wing. The storm wrenched it nearly out of socket, and she is hesitant to put too much strain on it. She looks back to the edge of the clear space. It

is still a good distance from her, and she can walk for a while if she keeps up a fast pace.

She takes a step and grimaces. There is sand in her boots, too, and in her socks; she can feel it between her toes. She looks again to the storm—she has time. Leaning against the stone, she pulls off her boots and dumps them, and then her socks. Her hand slips against the smooth, curved surface of the stone and onto the dunes. Spitting more sand out of her mouth, Grace sits up and glares at the offending rock.

No, not a rock. She can see it is something else now that she is looking at it: a pillar. A few steps away, there is another one beside it. Curious now, she puts her boots back on and stands back to look for more pillars. Was this some ancient Desert Clan building uncovered by the sandstorm?

If it is, it had been a very small building, because there are only the two pillars. Between them is a low rock, mostly buried, but Grace digs it out easily. The stone is flat on one side, and faintly, worn away by countless years of wind and sand, there is writing. Grace blows away the sand that has been caught in the remains of the carved letters and tries to make out what they say. The vast majority are faint shadows in the stone, impossible to read, but toward the bottom she can almost make out a line:

A monument to the lost, the bloody consequence of war.

Whatever it was, she has no way of knowing. Grace stands and makes herself start walking. She has no desire to get caught in the storm again. The inscription on the stone provides something to think about as she walks, at least, but when she lies down to catch a quick nap an hour later, it is still lingering in the back of her mind.

Grace closes her eyes and tells herself to forget about it. Even so, it still takes a few minutes for sleep to claim her.

She doesn't let herself sleep for long. The storm is close at her heels, and her right wing is still sore from the last time. Grace pushes herself to her feet, takes a sip from her waterskin, and starts off once more. She nibbles on a bit of dried meat as she walks, but not too much lest it make her thirsty.

She keeps an eye on the sky above her in case she stumbles into whichever army is controlling the storm, but walking is monotonous and the storm is concealing the Merciless Mountains so she can't even keep an eye on her goal. Briefly she considers that she may have gotten turned around in the storm and is now walking away from her destination, but she throws the thought aside. It doesn't really matter now if she leads them all the way to the mountains.

They would lose any sign of her in the storm anyway; they're searching on their own now. She just has to stay out of their way.

It is cooler in the heart of the storm than it was outside of it, perhaps because she is no longer directly underneath the sun, or maybe because of the constant winds; either way, she is grateful. Her sunburns have almost healed, but she has no desire to add onto them.

It grows cooler, slowly fading into true cold as Grace assumes the sun begins to set. She fluffs up her feathers and curls her wings around herself. If this storm keeps up through the night, it will be too cold for her to risk walking through it. She needs to find a small place to curl up for the night, but she is worried that the edge of the storm will pass over her and bury her alive.

She looks for high places to shelter, eyeing cliffs and caves high in the hills. It grows colder, and she shivers even with the shelter of her wings.

Deserts are a terrible place, she thinks, glaring at the endless sand. *I don't know how anyone survived out here.*

Even if she was lonely and hunted, the forest had been far better than this, with plentiful food and shelter, and *shade.* Grace thinks back to it fondly, trying to convince herself that she is tucked away in the safety of the trees. It doesn't work.

She glances back to gauge how far she is from the edge of the storm, but it is far behind her now. Grace stops dead in her tracks. Has it stopped moving? When did it stop? She scolds herself for getting so caught up in her thoughts that she didn't notice an entire storm halting around her, but she is too relieved that she won't have to worry about getting buried alive to be too harsh.

Grace picks up her pace until she is beneath a hollow in a canyon wall that she has been eyeing. She spreads her wings gingerly, but her right wing only twinges; it will be enough to get her up there, she decides, and leaps into the sky. Pain shoots through her wing with every stroke, but Grace forces herself to move through it until she can dig her talons into the sandstone and pull herself into the hollow. It is cramped, but that will be good if it gets as cold as she thinks it will. Grace curls tightly in her wings and falls asleep to the sound of wind blowing past the entrance to her shelter.

Chapter 15

The shape of the air as it comes through the entrance of her shelter changes. Her wind feathers twitch. Something is blocking the breeze.

Grace snaps to awareness. She cannot see in the dark of the hollow, but there is something there. The only thought her mind seems capable of processing is, *That better not be a snake.* If it is a snake, she is pushing it off the cliff, and she won't feel bad for it. The snake will deserve it; snakes don't belong this high up.

Her eyes adjust, and she shifts her arm, prepared to handle any scaly visitor with swift and concise action. And absolutely no screaming.

None.

But it is not a snake that sits silhouetted against the moon at the entrance to her shelter. It is a visitor of more mammalian nature, and a far more welcome one at that.

"Solace!" She reaches out a hand and scratches the blobby sword-shaped spot on top of his head. He purrs and butts his skull against her hand, but there is something in his mouth.

"What have you got?" she asks. In all likelihood, he's brought her something dead and she's going to have to toss it out, no matter his offended look. Bracing for something disgusting, she holds out her hand for the offering.

It is a black feather, crushed and tattered as though it was used to mark someone's place in a book.

Honor.

How did Solace get all the way out here though? It would have taken him months, if not years to get here on his own. Not to mention the odds of him dying before he reached her.

So he didn't get here on his own.

It isn't the White-Wing army that is creating the storm. It's the Black-Wings.

What are they doing here? They're supposed to be taking the Citadel and waiting for Allegiance's army to return weakened and exhausted.

Grace runs her fingers through Solace's fur. She could go, find their camp and ask them just what they think they're doing. She could see Honor again, fulfill her promise at last.

The more she considers it, the more she warms to the idea. She misses Honor and the particular quiet that seems to linger around him. The smooth, steady cadence of his voice, the steadiness of his healer's hands. She slips back into sleep easily. She will find them in the morning; now is the time for rest.

When the sun rises, it finds her far less confident in this plan. How is she supposed to find them in the middle of this storm? How is she going to get close enough to identify herself without being shot on sight for the color of her wings? It had seemed much simpler in the dark with Solace's warm weight pressed against her; now it seems terrible.

Grace folds her wings and squeezes her way back out of the narrow entrance of the hollow, then clings to the rock as Solace climbs up to her shoulders. She flexes her wings carefully, but she seems to have recovered from yesterday. Her waterskins are about halfway empty—she needs to find more water.

And where there is water, she is willing to bet that she will find the Black-Wings as well, or at least some sign of them. She will deal with the everything else later. For now, she will focus on finding the army.

One problem at a time, she tells herself and kicks off into the sky. She flies a spiral pattern through the eye of the storm, searching for the flash of dim sunlight off of water or armor. There is nothing for most of the day, and when she sets down to rest a few hours before midafternoon, Grace wonders if she will be able to find them at all. Perhaps they have too great a lead on her, or she could be ahead of them and not even know it.

She scans the endless dunes, searching for something out of place, anything different that might tell her where the Black-Wings are. Her eyes catch on something, and she lands before she realizes it is a mirage.

"I don't suppose you know where Honor is?" she asks Solace. She is only joking, but apparently Solace understands at least some part of her question, because he makes an odd purring chirp and digs his claws into the skin of her neck. Wincing, Grace turns to look at him, but he is already launching himself onto the sand and trotting purposefully over the hills.

Grace blinks after him for a moment, and then jogs to catch up. There is only one reason he would abandon his perch. Sure enough, Solace leads her back the way they came, moving at the same mile-

236

eating trot for at least an hour before she hears the faintest sound on the wind.

As they draw nearer, the sounds only grow louder: the murmur of voices, the rustle of feathers, and the clanking of gear and armor. Grace stops at the top of a dune and looks down on the Black-Wing army.

For a moment she stares uncomprehendingly at the sheer amount of bodies before her. There must be hundreds of soldiers moving and talking, their black feathers flaring in the weak light of the setting sun. Their voices overlap, and she is far enough away that she only catches the occasional word without context.

One of the soldiers shouts something to another, and a great roar of laughter washes over her. Another soldier playfully lunges at his comrade, and they wrestle on the sand for a moment before springing apart and going back to their duties. A few steps away, a tight knot of soldiers, a flight probably, huddles close together and stares intently at something. Elsewhere, a pair are working together to unfold tent canvas from its carrying bag, overseen by yet another Black-Wing, who is also discussing something with someone beside him.

There are too many to keep track of, all doing different things, speaking to one another, looking in every possible direction. She can't sneak in among them, and she isn't sure she wants to. It looks far too chaotic from out here, and she doesn't want to think about being trapped in the middle of all of that.

Grace shakes the dust out of her wings and takes a few indecisive steps backward, toward the quiet of the open desert. If Honor is somewhere in that mess, she has no way of finding him in the heart of a Black-Wing camp, not without calling attention to herself.

Another wave of laughter sweeps over the camp, and somewhere someone starts up a song, which is soon taken up by the entire army. Their voices roll over her like a physical weight, heavy with the feeling of lives and thoughts and bodies and *people*. Far too many people. Someone takes off and circles above the camp, another person, another set of eyes.

Grace shakes out her wings again like she can push the weight off of herself and turns away from the camp. She will stick around, keep near them in case she spots Honor, but she can't find the courage to walk willingly into the middle of a camp full of her enemies. Former enemies.

She shoves the thoughts away. Now is not the time. She rubs a hand over her face and takes a sip from her waterskin. When she lowers it, Honor is standing there.

Not the imaginary Honor that her mind conjured up sometimes to torment her, but the real Honor, with dark skin and short, curly hair, watching her with blue-green eyes like she is some sort of wild creature that will bolt if he so much as twitches. Perhaps she is, because she feels like running. She was wrong—she isn't ready to see him again. She isn't ready to see anyone again. She never wants to have to interact with another person for the rest of her days.

Numbly, her hands fumble to put the cap on her waterskin. He doesn't stop staring, and she won't stop staring either. She doesn't know what to do. Smile? Speak? Wave? Collapse into a sobbing heap at his feet and beg for forgiveness?

"Grace?" His voice is quiet, almost level if not for the tiny questioning waver at the end.

She nods, but she can't bring herself to speak.

"You came back."

She can barely hear his voice, and she isn't sure hers is strong enough to reply, but she still opens her mouth and croaks, "I promised."

He seems to realize that he is staring and jolts back to himself. Grace just barely keeps herself from flinching at the motion. He wets his lips and looks away for a second, but he can't seem to stop staring as he says, "I'm glad you came."

She nods again, she can't think of anything else to do, she is trapped here by his gaze, by his presence. She isn't sure if she will ever be able to leave. She isn't sure she wants to.

He sighs and shakes his head, raising a hand to his forehead. He closes his eyes and breathes deeply for a moment. The tension drains out of his frame, feathers lying sleek against his wings again, wind feathers folding into a more relaxed position. She feels the tension drop from her own shoulders in answer.

He opens his eyes and looks at her again, but it is different now, not staring, just assessing. A healer's gaze. A frown creases his brow. "You don't look well."

I don't feel well. Grace thinks, but she still can't make herself speak. She has too many things to say, but at the same time, no words present themselves at her mouth. She wishes that she could just send him her thoughts and feelings, all of the tangled emotions impossible to explain with words: *I missed you. I'm sorry. Forgive me. Everything has changed now. I don't know who I am anymore, I don't know who I will be, I don't know who I was. I wish we could go back.*

He holds out a hand across the distance between them. "Come back to the camp with me?"

ASCENDANT

She takes it and lets him lead her down the hill to the edge of the chaos. She stops there, and he pauses, waiting for her to continue. Grace steels herself. She has survived far worse than walking into a camp of Black-Wings beside their Ascendant. She lifts her chin and glances at Honor. He looks dubious, but he still steps forward.

She should drop his hand, walk into the camp on her own, unaided, unattached. She is not a lost fledgling being led back to have her hurts fussed over by her elders. She is loyal to no one; she depends on no one. She has survived a winter in the deep forest, walked through the desert alone, and came out alive.

As they step into the camp, though, she is glad she kept his hand. The guards at the edge of camp straighten to attention as they catch sight of Honor, but when their eyes rest on her, they widen and stare as she walks past.

Every Black-Wing they pass stops when they catch sight of her and stares. A hush falls over the camp, and a path opens for them through the center column of tents. Grace can feel their eyes on her back, on her face, her hands, her wings, and has to restrain a shudder. Her hand clenches tightly around Honor's, and he gives the slightest squeeze back—an apology, a wish for courage.

Behind them, whispers spring up, half-stifled by neighbors but still audible. Grace's feathers are nearly standing on end now, and it is only Honor's hand in hers that keeps her from flaring her wings. Every instinct is screaming at her, *Run! You have been seen. Back to the shadows, back to safety, never be seen. To be seen is to die, or worse. They will find you here.*

She locks her eyes on the pavilion at the end of the path. That must be where Charity is, so that is her goal. She only has to make it that far. Her breathing is coming harder now and faster, like she is running. She wants to run, to fly away from all of the staring eyes and whispering voices.

She almost wishes they would get it over with and decide to attack her already. She could do something then, defend herself or run back into the desert and never come near people again. But they don't. They just stand and stare and whisper when she has gone past.

Honor squeezes her hand again, and she realizes that they have made it to the pavilion. Charity is standing at a table, discussing something with a pair of soldiers who occasionally make gestures at a map.

Honor clears his throat and says, "Mother."

Charity looks up and catches sight of them. Her eyes widen for a moment, but she catches herself quickly, retreating behind the cool mask that Grace remembers. Honor and his mother stare at each other for a brief moment, eyes flicking meaningfully and eyebrows twitching. Finally, Charity's feathers ripple like she is resettling them, and she looks away.

"If you will excuse me," she says to the two soldiers. They dip their heads and withdraw with murmurs of, "Yes, my queen."

Honor steps farther into the pavilion and lets go of Grace's hand to turn and tug a cord tied to one of the posts, allowing the cloth folded there to fall forward, cutting them off from view. The people are still out there, Grace knows logically, staring and whispering, but it is harder to worry about them when she can't see them.

"Would you like a seat?" Charity asks, motioning to the chairs around the table.

Usually, Grace would decline—it is better to keep her feet, to be ready for trouble the moment it finds her—but her heart is still pounding in her ears and her knees feel weak. She nods and sinks onto the nearest stool. She cannot even summon up the curiosity to glance over the maps spread on the table.

Charity sits as well, but Honor steps to the side and pours them each a glass of water from a jar half-buried in the sand. He hands Grace hers with a stern look. "I want you to drink all of that, but slowly, not all at once."

A smile finds its way onto her lips at his familiar worrying, and she takes a sip to prove that she will listen.

He smiles back and takes his own seat. Solace darts beneath the flap of cloth keeping their meeting private and leaps smoothly onto Honor's shoulders. He must be how Honor knew she was here.

Charity takes a sip from her own glass, and the motion draws Grace's eye. The queen regards her over the rim of her cup. Grace expects to see some lingering suspicion, some hint that Charity doesn't believe Grace's return is genuine. There is only calm confidence in her gaze and, just maybe, a hint of relief.

What must it have been like for her? To know that she had lost her adoptive brother to the same mistake that Grace had made. Had she been certain that she would lose Grace in the same way?

Grace isn't sure where she stands with Charity. She is the daughter of her brother, but they met as enemies and only knew each other as friends for a few months. Would Charity have cared if Grace, too, fell to Noble's doom? The relief in her eyes suggests she would have.

"Grace," Honor says.

She turns to him, and he looks significantly to her water glass. She takes another sip without further prompting.

"Well," Charity says, setting her own glass aside, "we have far too much business to sit around staring at each other." She motions to the map in the center of the table. The edges curl stubbornly upward even though they are weighed down with a few stones, and the ink is faded with age. Grace squints at it, trying to read the names written in tight, curling script.

"We had to dig out quite the old map for this particular occasion," Charity says. "There has not been much call for any Guardian to venture past the forest for centuries."

"Why did you come at all?" Grace asks. "You were supposed to be taking the Citadel."

Charity regards her silently for a moment. "It was a good plan, but it left a great deal up to chance. That you would make it to the desert, that you could avoid Concord long enough to whittle down his army, that the Citadel would be as empty as you hoped. I am not in the habit of trusting luck. We will ambush them here, in the desert. Where they cannot retreat back to their mountain."

Grace wants to argue, wants to say that this was supposed to be *her* mission. But that is stupid. She can't hope to outrun an entire army forever. Not out in the open like this, not when she is barely surviving just fighting against the desert.

Besides, it is not as though she can just *order* Charity to go back to the Refuge and carry out the original plan. So she keeps her mouth shut and turns her attention to the map on the table in front of her.

She thinks that the mountain range nearest to her is the Merciless Mountains, but the mapmaker seems to have added some sort of island behind them, or maybe it's connected to the mainland. She tilts her head slightly. It might be an ocean. Or a smudge. Just how old is this map?

Charity taps a spot halfway down the line of mountains and into open space. "We are around here." Her finder drags back a few inches. "According to the last report from the scouts, Allegiance is here." Now she looks to Grace. "Where did you tell them that our secret city was? Any specific location?"

Grace shakes her head. "I just said the base of the Merciless Mountains."

Charity nods silently, her eyebrows furrowed, eyes flicking over the map. "If this map is accurate, this is where we want to make our stand." She points to a place where the mountain range dips backward, like someone has nudged entire mountains aside, perhaps a day's flight away. "If we can lure Allegiance and her army here and cut them off from the open desert, they will be pinned against the Merciless Mountains."

Honor nods, his face grim. It is an alien look on him, and for a moment, Grace almost doesn't recognize him. "What of Concord?" he asks.

Charity snorts delicately. "He will not take the field, not until after the battle is over."

Grace is suddenly struck by the memory of the rumors of the false Ascendant. The pale-haired ghost of the battlefield, the one who came after the blood was shed, searching for survivors. She knows just how easily rumors are twisted even in the Citadel, but perhaps a story, a tale whispered fearfully in the night, managed to cross the battle lines to be rewritten.

She sets the thought aside for now. Father isn't going to be a problem until after the battle. She will be as safe as anyone can be until then.

"And after?" Honor prods. "If we manage to win, then Concord will still be a problem. He has followed her across the continent—he isn't going to give up easily."

"That's why you're taking Grace back to the Refuge," Charity says calmly.

"Mother—"

"What?!" Grace cuts him off. Even Honor falls silent at the outrage in her tone. "I am not going back to the Refuge like some...child."

Charity regards her flatly. "You are a child."

"There is no room for children in war," Grace snaps. "I'm trained, I'm staying."

Charity lifts a single eyebrow. "No, you aren't." There is no doubt in her tone, no room for arguments or denials. *I am right, and you are wrong,* it seems to say, *but I will wait here patiently until you realize that.*

Grace stares at her, mouth working, but she cannot think of any words to say. The part of her that Father trained, that Father created, insists that she back down. Charity is in charge of her now, and Charity will be the one to hand down punishment. Grace can't bring herself to care.

"You leave tomorrow, when the sun sets," Charity says simply.

"I will not."

Charity's other eyebrow joins the first. "Why would I allow you to risk yourself on the battlefield? Even if I could keep you safe there, Concord will be hunting you afterward. Your only hope of safety is to already be away from him."

Grace glares at her silently. By all logic, Charity is right. Even if Grace were fully grown, she was trained for secrets and shadows.

245

For assassination, not for battle. She would stand little chance on the field in broad daylight against an armored opponent.

She can't bring herself to admit it, though, not out loud. In her heart, she knows that she would end up dead on the battlefield. It would be better than cowering underground and simply *hoping* that things go right.

The thought of doing so makes her hands want to shake. Away from the battle, she has no chance to see if things go wrong, no chance to help.

You wouldn't make a difference even if you were there, part of her argues. *You would only get in the way.*

Charity's face softens a fraction. "I know it can be difficult to put your trust in others, but this time you must cede that control to me. You and Honor will leave tonight, and hopefully you'll be back in the Refuge before the battle has even started."

Honor clears his throat. "Mother."

"Don't you start too. You're going, and that's final."

Honor frowns but dips his head in acknowledgment. "Very well."

She smiles at him gently. "Thank you, my son." Something more than the words seems to pass between them—a wordless conversation, or perhaps a mere understanding from centuries of knowing each other.

Silence hovers around them for a moment, but Charity dispels it by draining the rest of her glass and standing from the table. "Then it is decided. I will call in the flight leaders and give them their orders. Honor, will you see to our guest?"

Honor dips his head and stands as well. Grace moves to follow him, but he sends a pointed look to her glass. Grace sinks back into her seat and empties it in two large gulps. Honor sighs as she stands.

"If you throw that back up, you won't be getting any sympathy from me."

Grace snorts but doesn't say anything because her stomach is rolling just a little bit. She clenches her jaw and breathes deeply for a few breaths. Honor gives her a look out of the corner of his eye that says this has not gone unnoticed. Grace glares at him, wind feathers folded back irritably.

Honor pulls aside the cloth covering the entrance, and Grace hesitates for a half step. The soldiers will still be out there, watching, whispering, judging. Honor offers her his hand, but she forces herself to ignore it. They can stare and whisper all they want; it does her no harm, and if they attack, she can take care of herself. Probably.

Thankfully, there seems to have been some sort of discussion while they were in the pavilion, and all of the soldiers are studiously looking anywhere but at her. If it were not for the way their movements slow as she walks past, she would almost be fooled. One woman methodically polishes the same few inches of her sword, and another man fumbles his fingers around with a bit of rope that is already knotted.

"I'll see about getting you some new clothes," Honor says, "and a pack for traveling."

Grace nods silently. Part of her wants to stay by Honor's side as much as possible. Being surrounded by the stares of the Black-Wing soldiers makes her uneasy, and she has missed his steady calm more than she could have imagined. Her pride, still stung, insists that she doesn't need to accompany him like a *child* and she should find a quiet place to sit on her own.

Grace quietly reminds her pride that pouting at the edge of the camp isn't exactly the picture of maturity either.

"I can get you your own tent if you want," Honor says, drawing her from her thoughts.

"I'd rather stay with you." She doesn't think that she could manage to catch even a brief snatch of sleep in the middle of camp. Not surrounded by Black-Wings who watch her every move. She might be able to sleep with Honor nearby though.

"If you're sure."

"I am."

Honor's tent is just as she expected it to be. It can't have been set up for more than a few hours, but there are papers scattered across the bedroll and no less than three open books beside it.

"It's organized chaos," Honor says to defend himself upon seeing her face. "I know exactly where everything is in relation to the other things."

Grace hums doubtfully, but she is smiling. The argument is as comforting as a well-worn blanket. She knows the ins and outs of it. Of all the things that have changed, Honor is the same, and there is peace in that.

She has only just managed to get her bed set up in a comfortable way when Honor returns with the promised clothes and pack. He sits quietly on his own bedroll as she carefully transfers the meager contents of her belt to the pack. She hesitates briefly over the note, but she doesn't need it when the one who wrote it is sitting beside her. She carefully tucks it into the bag.

"I missed you," Honor says quietly.

"I missed you, too," Grace replies. "I'm sorry that I left."

"I was never angry at you for leaving. I should have—" He breaks off with a sigh. There are too many things that they both should have done.

"I wish I had opened my eyes sooner," Grace says to the pack sitting beside her. "I was blind, willfully blind. I refused to see the proof right in front of my face."

Honor puts a hand on her shoulder. "None of us want to think our parents could do anything bad. If our roles were reversed, I'm sure I would have done the same thing."

"But you didn't," Grace says before she can stop herself. "I *did*. I went back to him, I got Glory killed." Her voice cracks on his name.

"Concord is the one who killed Glory," Honor says firmly. "Not you."

"I was *right there*," Grace argues. "I could have helped him. I could have done something more than stand there."

"Maybe," Honor says. "Maybe you could have saved him. Maybe Concord would have won no matter what you did. Maybe he would have killed you both."

Grace shakes her head at that. "He won't kill me. He'll just take me back." Back to the dungeons, back to the cold and the endless dark. He will leave her there for longer this time, for months, years. Until she forgets her own name, until she forgets Honor's name.

Honor's fingers wrap around hers. "You did what you had to do to survive. You're the only one blaming you for that. I was the one who asked him to go for you. If anything, it's my fault."

"You couldn't have known—"

Honor cuts her off with a quiet look. "I knew it was a possibility," he says heavily. "We both had a hand in Glory's death, but ultimately, Concord is the one who killed him. You have to remember that."

"So do you." Grace meets his eyes at last.

"I'll do my best." Honor's smile is weak, but it is there. She wraps her arms around him, and he rests his chin on top of her head. "I'm glad you're back, little sister," he whispers.

"I'm sorry it took so long, brother," she replies.

"Shall we read something?" he asks. "For old time's sake?"

"Did you bring—"

"The legends? Of course." He laughs. "Sanctum?"

"Of course," she replies.

Chapter

16

That night, she manages to sleep longer than she has for
past month. It is easier to let herself off guard while Honor is still
sitting up beside her, the lamp turned low, muttering to himself as
he works. When she wakes in the middle of the night, jerked out of
sleep by a nightmare, he drowsily asks, "vyrhting okay?" and that
is enough to calm her.

"I'm fine," she whispers to him as her breath slows down.

"Sure?" he murmurs.

"Yes." His hand finds hers in the dark and that makes it easier
to fall asleep.

Morning brings its own problems. They are woken not long
after dawn by a courier with a nervous air about him. "The queen
needs to see both of you," the courier says urgently. "Immediately."

That is enough to shake off even Honor's drowsiness, and they
head for Charity's pavilion as soon as they can. Though the
flap is closed, Honor doesn't hesitate to enter, and Grace slips
in after him.

Inside, Charity stands over the table where the map is spread
out. Honor is already standing slightly behind her to the right,
peering over her shoulder. Two Black-Wings, who Grace assumes
are Charity's generals, are on either side of her.

I am glad you could join us. We have gotten a report back our scouts. Allegiance must have clued in on our ruse, or her ts were following us more closely than we assumed. The hite-Wings didn't stop for the night. Instead they followed almost ur exact path through the foothills."

Charity's finger traces the path over the map. "They must have realized our plan, and now they intend to use it against us. If they keep going at this speed and on this path, we will be the ones pinned against the mountains."

Grace's heart leaps at the words. While she was sleeping the night away, Allegiance was closing in—Father was closing in. She wanted to stay for the battle, and now she has no choice.

"Allegiance will spread her forces thin," one of the generals says. "She doesn't want anyone escaping. She will try to cage us against the mountains and pick us off at will. She doesn't like survivors."

Any survivors will face a fate far worse than death if Father has come with Allegiance. Grace has seen his Observants combing the battlefield for survivors, and she has seen the dungeons beneath the Citadel. She knows what happens to the prisoners that end up in those cells.

Charity nods mutely, looking intently at the map, trying to find some way out of the trap they have unwittingly placed themselves in.

The other general speaks up, tracing her finger through a small canyon right at the base of the mountains. "If we go here, we can use our Wind Weavers to crush her army against the canyon walls."

"It is too close to the mountains," the first general argues. "Even if we could make a stand there, we will be killed by the air currents coming off of the mountains before we get there."

"We may have to take that risk," Charity says. "Allegiance isn't slowing down. If we stay, she will be upon us by midday. We cannot stand here, or we will run into the same problem. We have ventured far too close to the mountains—we won't make it back out to open desert before they catch up."

"Then we have two choices," Honor says. "Stay here where we will certainly be killed, or try and make it to the canyon where we might have a chance."

Charity nods. "Well said. We make for the canyon. Gather your troops." The generals nod and jog from the pavilion, their voices already barking orders to pack up camp before the cloth has fallen closed behind them.

Grace shifts her feathers anxiously. She had been so determined to stay and fight yesterday. Sure that she could somehow control the outcome of the battle if she were only there for it. Now she is going to be in the heart of the chaos, and she knows that there is nothing she can do. She is even more helpless than if she were hiding in the Refuge. Here, Father will hunt for her no matter the outcome of the battle.

Charity glances over to her and a thoughtful expression flits over her face. "You stay with Honor," she orders.

Grace nods silently, glad to have something to do. She can at least help Honor with the wounded, or protect him if it comes to it.

Charity nods briskly and sweeps out of the pavilion without another word.

"It'll be alright," Honor says, picking up on her nerves.

They both know that there is a good chance that it won't be alright, but Grace allows herself to take comfort in the words. They walk out of the pavilion together. There are only a few tents still in the process of being folded down, and all of the fires have been doused and covered with sand.

Soldiers move through the remains of the camp with hands on the hilts of their weapons, wind feathers high and alert. They look to the horizon as much as what they are working on. Within half an hour, the camp has disappeared and the first flights are taking to the sky. The rest follow, falling into formation.

Grace follows Honor into the sky, determined not to let him out of her sight until the battle is over. The dullness of travel is tempered by the knowledge that Allegiance and her army are right on their heels, closing in. Grace glances back frequently, but she doesn't catch sight of them for most of the morning.

At midday, one of the rear guard lets out a sharp warning whistle. Allegiance is in sight. The White-Wings are a great cloud on the horizon. Even at this distance, it is easy to see that the Black-Wing forces are outnumbered. Orders are relayed through the ranks: they will keep moving. The canyon is their only hope now.

The Wind Weavers move back and turn their power to provide speed for the army. After an hour or so, Grace's muscles ache and sweat drips from her forehead. The other Forest Clan Black-Wings she can see are in a similar state. They aren't made to keep up this sort of pace for long. Those of Mountain and Desert Clan seem to be holding up for the most part, but if they do not make it to the canyon soon, they will be too exhausted to fight. The only consolation is that Allegiance's army will be facing the same problems, if they aren't already. Allegiance has already pushed them through the night and all of the previous day; she is banking on numbers to win her this battle. She must not know about the canyon then, or she would be more cautious, and that may be all that saves them.

Honor catches her eye from his place further up in the formation, his brow furrowed with concern. She can almost hear him asking if she is alright. Grace gives him a tight smile even though she feels like her wings are a hundred pounds heavier than they should be. They cannot stop, no matter how exhausted she is.

Honor doesn't look convinced, but he knows they have no choice, and he keeps flying.

Grace follows his example, forcing herself to breathe deeply and glide as much as possible. She lets her mind slip away, losing herself in the ache of her wings as they propel her forward.

She comes back when the Queen's Guard angles into a shallow dive. They've made it to the canyons. Grace casts another look back at the White-Wings; somehow, they have gotten closer. There won't be much time to prepare for them, but hopefully enough to at least rest her wings.

Grace stumbles into a landing, skidding on the loose rocks of the canyon floor. A shallow stream runs through the center. Grace crouches beside it and splashes the cool water onto her face. There are a few others doing the same, though some seem to have gotten stuck at the crouching part and are unable or unwilling to get back up again.

As much as she wishes to join those who have gone the extra mile and are simply lying beside the stream, Grace forces herself to her feet. She will go on, because she has to. There is no other option.

Charity and her generals huddle closely together, surrounded by the soldiers. Grace inches forward, but she is reluctant to get too close to the Black-Wings. She is wearing the ally medallion now, and there are other white-feathered Guardians as well. None of them have a reason to harm her, but that doesn't make her heart stop pounding.

It isn't long before orders are being handed out. Charity's clear voice rings above the murmur of the crowd: "Wind Weavers, to the front lines. Skirmishers, behind them. Healers, dig in around that bend, get water boiling and be ready for wounded."

Grace turns immediately and finds Honor and a small group walking to the bend in the canyon, where hopefully they will be out of the way of most of the fighting. Another group follows behind them, carrying the folded pavilion and bags of supplies. She trails after them, jogging to catch up as they disappear around the corner. She falls into place just behind Honor's right wing as he directs the others to clear a place for the pavilion.

She keeps out of the way as the healers bustle about, organizing stretchers and supplies. Their motions are smooth and confident, practiced. She wishes that she had gotten more than a brief lesson in field medicine from the healers of the Citadel before all of this.

The healers have barely stopped fluttering about when the horn sounds. There is a great roaring, a thousand voices lifted as one, and then wind whips through the canyon. Cries of pain rise from around the corner, and the sound of clashing weapons and bodies.

Honor appears by her shoulder. "Come," he says, "we have much work to do, and it won't be done anytime soon."

Chapter
17

The sounds of the battle echo through the canyon. Screams and the clashing of weapons and armor. The air crackles against her skin as Wind Weavers turn their power against each other.

The healing tent has been erected and organized, but there are no patients yet. A dissonant stillness hangs around them as they wait for the first casualty. Grace ventures away from the tent to watch the path.

Two field medics rush around the corner, a stretcher carried between them with a wounded Black-Wing soldier on it. Honor directs them to a bed and gets to work. Grace hangs back—she knows better than to get in the way of a healer at work, and the soldier is unlikely to appreciate a White-Wing hanging over him while he is wounded. Even if they wear an ally's medallion.

Instead she takes up a position just shy of the bend, watching field medics dart in and out of the chaos, scooping up the wounded from the ground and spiriting them away from the battle. Honor is too occupied to pay attention to what she is doing, thankfully. She thinks that if he did, he would insist on her remaining beside him.

When the medics dart out of sight, Grace has a moment to watch the battle itself. It has mostly left the crowded confines of the canyon and moved to the open sky. Though there are a few Forest Clan skirmishers from both sides trapping their larger-winged enemies where they have the advantage, the main battle is a great churning cloud above her head, steadily rising higher and higher as the combatants compete for greater altitude. Every once in a while, a pair will come spiraling to the ground in a tangle of wings and weapons, only to split apart mere feet from crashing onto the stone.

The field medics come pelting around the corner, hauling a stretcher with two soldiers piled haphazardly on it, both bleeding heavily. On their heels, a White-Wing soldier banks sharply around the corner, cutting them off from the hospital. He dives, naked blade gleaming in the light, entirely focused on the medics and their helpless patients.

This is what she was waiting for.

He never sees Grace. She launches herself into the air and crashes onto his back. Her talons find the gap in his armor between the helmet and the chest plate. He only has the time to make a single hoarse cry before he falls, still and silent.

The medics stare at her for a moment, but one of the soldiers groans in pain, and they snap back to their duties. Grace stares down at the body.

Did this man have a child of his own back in the Citadel? Had he only left them because he was ordered to? Was he, like the soldier from the forest, harboring his own doubts about the White-Wing cause but too afraid to say anything in case word made its way to Father?

"Grace?" Honor's voice pulls her out of her thoughts. "You shouldn't be out here." His eyes catch on the body of the White-

258

Wing. He opens his mouth to say something, but he is interrupted by a piercing whistle: *Reinforcements, urgent.*

Grace's head snaps upward. For a moment, she isn't sure what is happening, but then her eyes catch on a pair of fighters tumbling through the air with at least eight Black-Wings diving after them. It takes precious seconds for her to figure out what this means: only one person on the battlefield would warrant eight guards following them.

When the fighters break apart, the White-Wing swoops low over the canyon, his long wings beating powerfully. A sword gleams in his hand and his silver hair streams behind him. His armor is unfamiliar but brightly polished, and the light catches it as he banks low. Grace knows the face that flashed over her almost too fast to be seen.

It is not Allegiance who has been leading the army. Justice himself is on the field, and he is fighting Charity.

Without a thought, Grace tosses herself into the air after him. Justice is already halfway to his target. He is rising, angling to cut off Charity's ascent, sword gleaming.

Grace beats her wings, pushing herself to the limits of her speed.

Charity's guards fold their wings, dropping altitude to try and reach their queen before Justice does. Charity sees the danger and flares her wings wide, lifting her own sword to block Justice's blow.

They are all just a little bit too slow.

Grace is too far away to hear the sound of Justice's sword striking home, but she can see Charity's blood spouting from the wound, falling like a macabre rain over the thirsty ground. Honor blows past her, watching his mother's limp body slide off of Justice's sword and fall to the ground.

He dives, a wordless cry of grief echoing after him. Grace tries to catch her breath enough to shout after him. He doesn't hear her, or if he does, he ignores her. Justice catches sight of him. Grace is close enough to see the satisfaction in his smile as Honor gives himself away.

Charity's guards are still too far away. Justice is diving. Honor catches Charity's body and sits on the ground, exposed and unwary of his surroundings as he holds pressure over the gaping hole in her chest. Grace thinks she can see Charity's lips moving, and her hand makes a jerky gesture, like she wants to touch Honor's hand.

Grace folds her wings and allows gravity to take hold, falling until she is below Justice, then she unfurls her wings, sharp and fast and holds up a forearm to catch the blow meant for Honor. She kicks Justice away, standing between him and Honor, wings flared.

Justice stares for a second, caught off guard. There is a deep dent in the armor over his chest, and a cut on his forehead is bleeding. Even though he'd won their battle, Charity had managed to leave her mark.

His eyes trace over Grace's features, and then sadness washes over his face. He holds his sword to the side, not attacking, not defending. Grace feels her wings flick with surprise, but she doesn't let it show on her face.

"I'm sorry," Justice says, and there is real regret in his voice. "I'm sorry that I let him take you, turn you into this, but you must understand that I only did what was necessary. The Black-Wings cannot be allowed to continue living. Return with me, and I won't let Concord take you back." He stretches a hand out to her.

"That isn't what this is about," she says. Above them, the battle is still raging, but here on the ground, there is a bubble of quiet. The world seems hushed, waiting. "This is wrong." She gestures to the battle above them, to Honor behind her, still trying to save Charity, even though every last one of them knows she is doomed. "Your sister is dead, and I'm sorry, but that isn't the Black-Wings' fault. It isn't your fault either."

Justice actually recoils, and Grace steps toward him. Her lips form words—she doesn't know where they're coming from, but she doesn't think she could stop them if she tried. "I can't imagine what it's like to lose someone like her, but you can't take that out on everyone else. You have to let her go."

For a second, she thinks that Justice will listen, that he will somehow stop the battle. Thinks that there will be peace, at long last. Then his eyes cloud over with rage and the dark fire of his madness burns brightly in them. His lips curl into a snarl, and the part of her that still remembers the kind, gentle man that guided her out of his study when she was lost is taken aback.

"They've twisted your mind," he says. "Corrupted you. You're just another Fallen."

Justice lunges, and Grace meets him, wings beating furiously. They spin, rising over Honor's head. Justice has Grace's wrists pinned against her chest, but this close, his sword is useless. They shove apart, both taking a parting swipe and both missing.

Grace banks hard, coming around and gaining altitude. Her heartbeat pounds in her ears, her breathing harsh and rasping. She cannot swallow around the dryness in her throat. Her wings catch an updraft, and Grace pushes herself higher.

ASCENDANT

Justice finds the same updraft, and they circle one another as they rise, higher than the rest of the battle, until they are alone in the thin air. She tries to dive back down—she has no chance against him, knows she needs to meet up with the other Black-Wings, someone able to at least help her.

Justice banks and cuts beneath her, rolling to bring his sword to bear. Grace flares her wings and pulls back up. He rises after her, swings his sword in an upward arc.

She uses her greater maneuverability to avoid his sword, but she has no way to fight back. He can keep her at a distance with his sword and outlast her with his endurance. Her eye catches on a large bank of clouds.

She tries to swerve around them, but Justice drives her back. He's faster than her in a dive and in open air; with no obstacles to dodge, his larger wingspan is an advantage. He uses it to herd her closer and closer to the cloud bank.

In the clouds, she'll be blind. Justice will be as well, but he must have a plan if he's so insistent on getting her into them. She can't avoid it, but so far she's tried to go back down. If she gets into the clouds and rises out of them, it might throw him off.

She makes one last effort to dive back down, and when she is rebuffed, she sweeps one wing low, executes a midair half roll, and shoots into the clouds.

It is impossible to see, like being dropped into a piece of paper: blank, featureless white. She can't even hear Justice anymore.

He won't have given up, but he will expect her to try and dive down. She has to go up first.

Grace rises out of the cloud. Somehow, Justice is waiting for her there, sword drawn and eyes gleaming. The blade moves as

262

though it is going through molasses, time stretches to the infinite horizon, one timeless instant, held in perfection a moment from disaster. Grace watches the blade cut down through the air for years, for centuries. And then the blow lands. Blinding pain whites out her vision, blows through her mind, and leaves her gasping for breath that will not come. She cannot think, and she cannot breathe.

She falls.

Dimly, instinct forces her to roll and spread her wings, but agony rips through her, like someone has poured acid over her wing and left it to burn through flesh and bone. Her eyes move of their own accord and catch on her left wing, and bile rises in her throat along with a scream.

Her wing is a broken, bloody mess. Justice's sword is still protruding from the wound. Grace can see where it is embedded in her bone. Her wind feathers are gone, Justice's sword had nearly cut her wing in half. Even as she watches, Justice's fingers curl around the hilt of his sword, and he tugs.

Grace screams. Justice plants a foot on her chest and pushes off, trying to free his weapon. Of their own accord, Grace's hand snaps up and her talons sink deep into his calf muscle.

His scream mingles with Grace's own, and her wings crumple reflexively. They fall together. Justice's brown eyes, narrowed with rage and hatred, meet Grace's gray. Grace cannot think clearly enough to glare back. Agony sweeps through her wing again as Justice pulls his sword free.

"You should never have betrayed us," Justice says.

He starts to pull away, but Grace's hand darts out again, digging into his arm. Breathing is difficult, speaking is impossible. She snarls wordlessly.

ASCENDANT

Her hand rises, and her talons sink into his throat. Through blood and bone. His blood is boiling hot against Grace's skin. Justice chokes a half-aborted sound of pain, and then his sword falls from his limp fingers.

His weight drags him off of her and he falls. He falls as she is falling. One final journey through the sky before they both come crashing to the earth for the very last time.

Faintly, she can hear the horn that directs the White-Wing forces. Father had drilled her on the different calls for hours until she could remember them even in her sleep. *Retreat,* the horn calls. *Retreat.*

The king is dead, and the White-Wings are falling back.

Someone is shouting her name. Grace opens her eyes—*When did they close?*—and sees Honor above her. His wings are folded back, his hands outstretched. She sheathes her talons and reaches back.

Their fingers brush, and she can see the worry in his eyes.

He grabs her wrists and tugs her closer. His wings flare. Pain overwhelms her, and the world disappears for a moment.

When she comes to, they are flying normally, then a voice shouts something—she can't figure out what—and a great wall of air hits them. As they tumble, Grace's eyes catch for a moment on a White-Wing with the distinctive markings of a Wind Weaver on his armor, then he disappears.

Honor clutches her tightly to him as they are forced to follow the air current. She doesn't know how far it carries them. Spinning helplessly through the sky, she blacks out more than once, but then Honor straightens out, and they dive for the ground.

264

The landing is rough, but Honor lays her gently upon grass and snaps his fingers in front of her face. He is speaking, but she can't hear him over the roaring in her ears. She stares at him, uncomprehending. He shakes her gently, and the roaring dulls.

"Grace," he says urgently. "I need you to stay awake. I know it's hard, but please."

Tears run down his face, and she doesn't think they are from the harsh winds. She turns her head and looks to the mangled remains of her left wing. She closes her eyes. Honor taps at her cheek.

"Stay. Awake," he commands. His hands fumble at his belt, and he holds something up to her lips. Grace drinks and nearly recoils at the sharp, bitter taste, but the pain dims, and her mind clears. Honor pulls bandages from somewhere, wads them up, and presses them against the wound.

"Honor," she manages. Her voice seems too loud and too quiet all at once. He doesn't respond. She tries again. "Honor, stop."

"Just keep awake," he mumbles at her.

"Honor."

This time he turns to look at her, and there is desperation in his eyes. His cheeks are stained with blood and dirt, and it makes the tear tracks stand out even more.

"It's useless," she says.

"No." He turns back around.

She reaches out and brushes her fingers against his boot—it is all she can reach. Somehow he feels the touch and drops one hand to pat the back of hers. He leaves blood on her skin and turns back to his work.

"I won't fly again," she tells him.

His shoulders hunch, and he applies more pressure to the wound.

"Honor." Her voice cracks. It sounds small and afraid.

He turns back to her and grabs her hand between his. He doesn't say anything; he doesn't have to.

"I don't want to die as his daughter," Grace says, and suddenly it seems so very important.

Honor is quiet for a moment—not a long moment, she doesn't have many long moments left. She will probably bleed out in the next few minutes. It will be a kindness.

"Alright," he says finally. A surreal calmness surrounds him. As a healer, he has probably seen countless people die, more than her even.

"I would rather die as your sister, if you'd take me."

A shaky smile works its way onto his lips. "I would be grateful."

He takes a deep breath and says in a low voice:

"Though you are not my kin, you are my sister.

Through dark days and the ending of all, I will stand beside you.

To the day you draw your last breath, let the Trinity see this oath and recognize it."

With a wince, he plucks one of his coverts and tucks it into her hair. Grace forces more air into her lungs and whispers back:

"Though you are not my kin, you are my brother.

Through joy and sorrow, I will stand beside you.

To the day you draw your last breath, let the Trinity see this oath and recognize it."

Honor picks up one of her feathers from the ground and tucks it behind his ear wordlessly.

The world is going dark around the edges, and it is getting harder to breathe. "I'm scared," she says quietly.

Honor squeezes her hand. "I am too."

"Don't leave me."

"Never."

"I love you," she whispers.

"I love you too," Honor replies, but she doesn't hear him.

***

Darkness.

Light.

"I am so sorry, little one."

She knows that voice. Has heard it as though it came from her own throat. She turns to the light, letting it wash over her face. There is a sound in the air, like bells, like harps, like singing, but it is far away. She wants it to be closer. It is so beautiful she thinks she could hear it for the rest of eternity and never grow tired of it.

"One day, you will hear it," Haven says. "For now though, you must listen to me."

She has never seen Haven's face before. Her chin is rounder than Justice's, her face narrower and unlined, forever young while Justice grew old.

"You're dead," Grace says.

"Yes," Haven answers.

"Am I?"

"Not yet."

Grace swallows. "I don't want to die."

"You will have to, one day," Haven says, "but not today. I come bearing a message, little one."

"From who?" Grace asks.

"Who do you think?" Haven asks, something like humor sparkling in her eyes.

"Why now?" Grace demands. "After everything that happened, why choose now to speak to me? I asked for him before, and he didn't answer. I needed his help, and I had to do it on my own!"

"He did answer," Haven replies, humor gone now. "He has always answered you. When you were lost, he sent Solace to guide you. When you were in danger, he blinded Concord's eyes so he would not find you. Did you think those were mere coincidences? He has never left your side—know that, little one. And he never will."

Tears sting her eyes, and Grace looks away from Haven's face.

"Will you hear him now?" Haven asks, and Grace nods.

Haven draws herself up. "You will be a messenger of the Father's will, carry with you the knowledge that the war will end."

"How?" Grace asks. "Will he wipe out the Citadel?"

Haven looks sad again. "Do not fall down the same path as my brother, little one. Do you really think that after all this time, more bloodshed is what is needed?"

Grace turns away. "No."

"There will be a sign," Haven says, "to unite them, and you will carry the banner."

"What do I need to do?" Grace asks.

Haven smiles. "Wake up."

Epilogue

Breath moves across her wind feathers.

"You're awake," a woman says, sounding surprised. Her voice is hoarse and creaky in the way Justice's is, aged. Grace's brow furrows—she hasn't met many people who could match Justice for age.

"Your brother has been wearing a groove in my floor," the old woman continues.

Brother? She doesn't have a brother.

Then she remembers the oaths. The battle, the blood. *Her wing*

She throws the blankets aside in her haste to sit up. The old woman watches her from the doorway of an unfamiliar room. Something about her face seems familiar, but Grace doesn't spare it a thought.

Her wing flares and flexes without a twinge of pain as she spreads it, but ice floods her veins nonetheless. The wind feathers on her left wing are gone. Not just gone, there is a divot in her wing where the muscle and bone that supported them has been torn away. As though something came and took a bite out of her wing.

Nausea churns her gut.

She can't think, can't process what she is seeing in relation to herself. It feels as though she is looking at a stranger's wing, not her own. But the feathers ruffle and shift as her mind commands them to.

On her right wing, she can feel her wind feathers flare. There is a faint ache from her left, and she can see something beneath the skin and feathers *shift*. Bile gathers in the back of her throat.

"Breathe," the old woman says, her voice unreadable through the roar of blood in Grace's ears. "Or you're going to pass out again."

Grace reflexively draws a deep breath. It sounds like a shuddering gasp and feels like fire racing into her lungs.

She can't stop staring. She doesn't understand.

From the hallway behind the woman, Honor appears. He pauses for a split second, his face caught between relief and surprise. He pushes past the woman to sit on the bed beside her.

"Grace," Honor says. His hands cup her cheeks and force her to look into his eyes. "It's alright," he says firmly. As though he can make it so simply by being determined.

"My—" Her voice is shaky and barely over a whisper.

"I know. We'll get through it, alright?"

Somehow, logic breaks through the panic. There are hundreds of people who go through life wind-blind. She should be grateful that she survived at all.

"What happened?" She needs to think beyond her wind feathers. She's in a strange room with a strange woman, who, although she has black feathers and seems vaguely familiar, is an unknown.

"A miracle," the woman says, "the first that has been seen in many centuries." She steps closer, and Grace realizes where she recognizes her from. In the same way that she could see Justice's face in Haven's although their ages were vastly different, she recognizes this woman.

The last time she had seen her—the last time Haven had seen her—she was disappearing into what was then the courthouse of the Citadel. Grace has only ever known it as Father's domain.

"You're Valor."

The only indication of surprise is a flick of the woman's wind feathers. "I am, though how you know that is a mystery."

Even Honor is looking at her strangely, and Grace realizes that she never told him of the visions. She isn't really sure how to explain them, now that she is faced with the opportunity.

"It's complicated," she says. It's a clumsy side step at best, but her mind is already spinning with possibilities and implications. "Where are we? This isn't the Refuge," she says, as she realizes that there is light spilling in from a large window overlooking a street lined with bushes and flowers.

It isn't the Citadel either. The air is too warm, and there are no plants that will grow on the mountain aside from a few mosses.

An entirely different city, then, one that had somehow remained hidden despite the war and despite Grace dragging entire armies across the continent. There are no trees, so it isn't in the forest either. It is too lush to be the desert.

"Sanctum," Valor says.

Grace's thoughts screech to a halt. "Pardon?" She looks away from the window, expecting to catch a hint of teasing in Valor's manner. She looks entirely serious.

"We're in Sanctum," Honor echoes. There is a hint of wonder in his eyes, but no humor or laughter.

This isn't a joke.

ASCENDANT

"How?" Grace asks. "Are we the only ones?"

"Yes," Honor says. The wonder leaves his face, replaced by anxiety and dread. "There was a White-Wing Wind Weaver. Somehow she blew us through the air currents above the mountains and into Sanctum. Lady Valor was kind enough to take us into her home." Something in his face makes Grace think that perhaps that isn't the whole story, but she decides that it will have to wait.

Honor shifts beside her and Grace's wind feathers twitch reflexively. The same faint ache comes again from her left side, and she can't stop herself from looking. Distraction could only last so long.

There is an uncomfortable lurch in her gut as she stares at the place where her wind feathers should be and are not. It sits wrongly in her mind, that a physical *part* of her is gone. A shudder runs down her spine, and she makes herself look away.

The rest of her wing is unmarked, and it moves well. She can still fly, so she won't succumb to Sky Hunger. In truth, her wings were more damaged when she woke in the Refuge.

It is only once she forces herself to look past her missing wind feathers that she sees the true miracle that Valor was talking about.

Her feathers, once white, are now silver gray.

There will be a sign, Haven had said. *And you will carry the banner.*

In a world where Black-Wings and White-Wings are at war, there can only be one thing meant by sending a messenger with gray wings: The war must end.